NO MAN'S LAND

THE RESCHEN VALLEY SERIES – PART 1

Chrystyna Lucyk-Berger

Chrystyna Lucyk-Berger / Inktreks

Dornbirn, Austria

www.inktreks.com

All of Chrystyna Lucyk-Berger's books are available for free: Just ask you local library to order them.

Historical notes, backgrounds, list of characters in the series, a glossary and more are available on www.inktreks.com/blog

Sign up to the Inktreks newsletter and receive updates, historical articles, peeks behind the writing scenes and exclusive promotions:

https://www.subscribepage.com/RSV

Publisher's Note: This is a work of fiction. Names, characters, places, and incidents are a product of the author's imagination. Locales and public names are sometimes used for atmospheric purposes. Any resemblance to actual people, living or dead, or to businesses, companies, events, institutions, or locales is completely coincidental.

Book cover design by Ursula Hechenberger-Schwärzler (ursulahechenberger.com))

Cover model: Kathrin Meier

Cover photos by Mario Álvarez on Unsplash and Ursula Hechenberger-Schwärzler

No Man's Land: A Reschen Valley Novel / Chrystyna Lucyk-Berger. – 3rd ed.

ISBN: 978-1-791523-41-1

ASIN: B078WDPDSJ

TO FREDY

*You heard this story take its first breaths
and always believed it would live.*

It must be admitted that the hacking of essentially Tyrolese valley from the rest of the Tyrol was incompatible with the principles of self-determination embodied in the original war aims of Allied statesmanship.

— DAVID LLOYD GEORGE, PRIME MINISTER OF
ENGLAND, 1916–1922

CONTENTS

APRIL 1920, ARLUND

I t seemed a shame to kill on such a fine, spring day. As the
wind rose from the valley, so came the scents released by the
melting snow—of leaves and grass and wood, of new life rising,
resurrected.

Katharina steadied her aim on the hare and held her
breath. *Before the Italians confiscate our rifles again*, her grandfather
had said, *go practice your shooting. Bring us some meat.* The hare
turned its head, haunches tensed, and Katharina squeezed the
trigger. The animal fell but flailed on the ground.

Hund sprang up, but Katharina checked the dog with a hiss.

"Leave it be," she muttered. She leaned the rifle against a
stump before picking up the canvas sack and drawing her father's
knife from her boot.

As she approached, the hare jerked, trying to get on its legs,
panic rolling with the whites of its eyes. Knife in hand, Katharina
grabbed its scruff and drew the blade across the throat. Hund
sniffed the ground where the work left its mark.

The sun reached over Graun's Head, and Katharina rose,
shading her eyes to look up the slope. To the right of the
outcropping, where the summer hut still lay deep under snow,

was the scar from a small avalanche. She slung the bagged hare over her shoulder, Hund panting next to her. Turning her back to the mountain, Katharina had a view of the valley below, revelling in April's lustrous green, a contrast to the alpine path where the snow came over the tops of her boots.

She was glad she'd traded her smock for Papa's britches. The villagers might look sideways when she wore them, but nobody ever said a word. She reckoned her father's good standing in the community had something to do with that. Or because he had died fighting for them.

Only Opa and she were left of the Thaler family—a tragedy, possibly even a disgrace. The whispered predictions about what would happen to the once-prosperous dairy farm when Katharina's grandfather should pass were audible enough. The thought of a future without Opa in it was devastating enough, but for what other purpose did her grandfather work her, teach her, as hard as he had any of his own sons if it weren't to leave the farm in her capable hands?

She looked down at Hund, the bitch pup she'd saved years ago. "It would never cross their minds, would it? A woman running a farm."

A soft wind rose, and she picked up the trail back to the main path, Hund next to her. The sunshine was already softening the snow for the worn soles of her boots.

No. They expected her to marry so that at least a man would be involved when the inheritance was necessary. But whom did they expect her to take as a husband? She was supposed to have studied in Innsbruck, at least that was what her parents had wanted for her. Six years ago she had planned to finish her schooling, travel north to her mother's family in the fall, and become a teacher. Now she was learning to become a farmer.

The Great War, they were calling it; the war that had ended all wars. It had ended their country, in either case, killed many good men, and brought with it a plague of loneliness, an emptiness, a film of sadness that no spring could cleanse.

There were other men in the valley now: Italian guards patrolling the newly attained border. While their job was to keep Tyrol cut in two, they collected bribes from the smugglers. It was the only way for friends and relatives from the north to slip their contraband across, like lovers' notes through prison bars.

On their way back to the main road, Hund, her nose to the ground, loped past and stopped some metres ahead. When Katharina reached her, the dog was scratching at something in the snow.

Katharina crouched to get a better look. Blood. It was blood. She straightened and looked around. Two sets of boot prints. No animal tracks.

Who else? Her heart pounded. *Who else is out here?*

A gust of wind rose from the valley, like the sound of rushing water. Stuck amongst the branches of a sapling, a scrap of paper flapped against the current. She caught one just as it freed itself. When the strip was in her hand, Katharina recognised the symbols and lines of a relief map, similar to her father's before he'd marched off to Galicia. This one, however, showed the ridges and curves of her mountains. More paper summersaulted northwards on the wind. She looked at the kicked-about snow, and the back of her neck crawled.

Katharina returned to the tracks. One pair of footprints was much larger than the other. Up the trail, she found where the smaller person had fallen on all fours. More blood had pooled here. The tracks parted, the smaller footprints east, into the woods. The second pair led north. The border.

No animal but man, Opa had once said, would hunt down another man and leave him to die.

She called for Hund only to realise the dog was still at her side.

After she hitched the rifle over her shoulder, she felt for the handle of her father's knife and looked back towards the valley. It would take too long to get Opa first. With a sharp whistle at Hund, she followed the trail into the woods, remembering the first time Opa had shown her how to track. She'd followed the signs of a fox and a hare, read the fox's final pounce, found a tuft of fur and, finally, the telling red of a successful kill.

This trail came to an end outside Karl Spinner's hut, and the latch to the front door was broken. Katharina's heart tripped up against her chest. She had hardly ever spoken to the hunter, but Opa had never said a bad word about him. When no one answered her knock, she opened the door.

A few shafts of light came through the western window to reveal a dusty floor. There was a wooden table with a smeared oil lamp and four curved-back chairs under the window to the right. Hanging on the wall, and boiled of their skins, was a row of deer antlers and mountain goat skulls. A simple bed was in the far corner, with a red-and-white-checked quilt bunched at the foot of it. And someone lay on the floor in the middle of the room, his back to her, as if he had fallen off the bed and never stood back up. Over the sour, gamey odour of old animal fat, Katharina smelled iron.

"Mr Spinner?" Her voice cracked. "Are you all right?"

No answer. She lowered the canvas sack with the hare and took a step. Another. Katharina stopped just short of the body. The clothes were different. This man wasn't dressed like anyone from the valley. This was not Karl Spinner.

She raised her rifle. "Sir? Are you well?" In her sights, the dark hair was matted with blood.

She knelt beside the body and lay the weapon off to the side. Carefully she rolled the man over, propping his head with her arm. His eyes were closed. Her fingers searched his damp neck until she felt the pulse. Faint. On his side, bloodstains and two cuts in the coat. She pulled at a wide black belt, unbuttoned the coat, and then lifted his shirt. Just below his ribs, two gashes. She leaned in close and listened. The breathing was shallow but clean. Clean was good. His left shirtsleeve was also soaked in blood, and when examining the cuts, she found a deep slash on the arm.

Looking around for something to stop the bleeding, she found only a canteen and a pair of field glasses. Near the edge of the bed, something gleamed, and she reached over the man to pick it up. A cross attached to a blue-and-white-striped ribbon—an Italian war medal—weighed heavily in her hand. She dropped it on the table, turned to the man on the floor again, and pulled out her father's knife.

"There's nothing for it, whoever you are."

She leaned over him, knife poised, and sliced the cloth of his shirt until the upper body was free. The blood from his head and his arm had congealed, but the two slashes near his ribs still pumped thick and red. To bandage the man's head and the arm, she could use his shirt, but she needed something denser for the punctures in his side. The canvas sacks in the corner looked dirty. The sheet on the bed mattress had certainly not seen the washing basin in months either. Her smock, she thought, would have been more practical now. She considered her woollen wrap. No. Jutta had made it for Katharina's mother when nothing else seemed to keep the chill away.

Katharina listened to the stranger's breathing. He was not apt to wake up, so she slipped off her waistcoat, then her flaxen blouse—heavier, thicker than his—put her waistcoat back on, and pressed the cloth against the wounds.

Hund sniffed around the stranger's face.

"Lie down," she ordered.

The dog obeyed.

She examined the man's face. He had a straight nose and a dimpled chin. He was a little older than her. Maybe thirty. And his skin was darker than hers, darker than all of those in the valley. His clothes...definitely not local. So. This was the enemy.

Before she'd gone off to hunt this morning, Opa had called after her. "They can take your land, they can take your weapons, but they can't take the fight out of you." This man's wounds were no accident. Maybe he'd even provoked his attacker.

Though the bleeding slowed with the pressure she was applying, he was likely to die if she did not get help. And if he died, and if he was really Italian, the *carabinieri* might blame her for his death. Or Karl Spinner.

She grabbed a dirty canvas bag, pressed it against the blouse, and took the two ends of the man's belt and fastened it tightly around the bunched fabric. With the Italian covered and secured, she hurried to fetch her grandfather.

Before Katharina could finish explaining what she had found, Opa headed to the front door and released the rope that led to the bell house on their roof. That bell called her family to midday meals, and if signalled correctly, it alerted the valley and the Alpine Rescue Team of any accidents.

"The man's Italian," Katharina called.

Her grandfather halted, both hands staying the rope. "You're sure?"

"He looks it. I mean his clothing. His face."

"Is he police?" He let go of the rope. Above, the bell made a single, muted clang.

She thought of the war medal and went to Opa. "He's not wearing a uniform, but he's not one of our Italian settlers either. If you ring the bell, you'll alert the border patrols."

Opa scratched his beard, then looked hard at her. "Where's your blouse?"

"I had to use it to stop the bleeding," she said.

"Hang up the hare. Bring two blankets."

Her grandfather secured the bell's rope to the hook again and moved towards the woodhouse, and Katharina did as she'd been told. In her room, she put on an old pullover before returning to where Opa now stood in the yard. On the ground before him were two wooden poles. Propped against his right calf was the cone-shaped basket he used to transport the things he needed to carry up the mountains, such as hooks, spikes, and bandages. He was winding a rope around his elbow and between his thumb and forefinger, and Katharina remembered how her uncle Johi would do the same thing when the bells tolled. Was Opa also thinking about the day Johi died up on the mountain?

Their eyes met, and she read mistrust in his.

"I want to know what this is all about," he said. "Before we call the authorities." He looked her up and down.

The temperature was dropping as the last of the afternoon sun hung between the peaks.

"Tie up the dog," Opa said. He jammed the rope and flask of schnapps into the basket, then strapped it onto his back before leading the way.

They quickly reached the path that led to Karl Spinner's hut. Below them, the church bells volleyed off the massifs, calling the villagers to evening mass just like they called them for all matters of importance. The bells for fires. The bells for avalanches. The bells for death. The bells called them together and announced any emergencies. Then came the Great War. Twice. First, the call to the eastern front, and again when their Italian neighbours—their friends—became enemies upon the signatures of strangers. As the valley had emptied, Katharina had thought it odd how those very men, who had been helping hands on their farms, would cross the Italian border to the south, turn around, and take up positions against the Tyroleans.

The bells had continued to toll, a new tone added to announce the arrival of the lists, an inventory of the missing and the dead. Papa's last letter had said his unit was leaving the eastern front to defend Tyrol against Italy. He was coming home, Papa had written. Like so many of the families who'd received similar letters, she and Mama had walked from Arlund to Graun every time the bells had made their disconsolate call. It was the quiet way in which the villagers had opened a space at the wall for them that day that Katharina knew he would never come home. Papa had been reduced to four points in perfect German calligraphy: *Josef Thaler. Of—Arlund. Died—Galicia. 1916.*

"Three boys in two years," someone had whispered behind them.

"What a shame. They were good boys," someone else had said.

"Thaler's boys," they called them, as if the deaths belonged only to Opa and not at all to Josef's wife, the outsider. Not to Josef's daughter, the half-city, half-mountain girl.

Mama had turned to those gathered at the wall, taller than any of them, and fair coloured like none of them, and said, "We have lost them all." To Katharina, she said, "Child, you must find your way home now," as if her mother had known that she, too, would leave them all soon after.

The dying had not stopped with the end of the war. All Katharina wanted was for the fighting and the dying to stop.

When they arrived at the hut, Opa checked the stranger's pulse, then pulled out the schnapps flask, tipped it to the man's lips, and glanced at her. "Gets the blood flowing, but he's not got much left."

Katharina lit the oil lamp, and Opa pointed the flask at her.

"Have some."

She could smell the hint of raspberries, but there was none to have in the taste of it. She swallowed the sharp alcohol down before her grandfather took the flask and tipped his head back, his beard yellow in the lamplight. After wiping his mouth, he gave the wounded man another dose.

"He's Italian, all right." Opa sounded regretful. "Pick up his things. Put them in the basket."

Katharina picked up the canteen, the field glasses, and the belt with the attached gadgets. Then she remembered the war medal and took it from the edge of the table and put it into her pocket.

She stopped at the sight of the bloodstains on Karl Spinner's floor. "I should clean this up," she said.

"Tomorrow."

Opa's ominous behaviour troubled her. She lifted the makeshift gurney at the front with Opa having to manage the weight in the back. After they secured the door as best they could, they picked their way over the freezing path, the light having given way to a dark-blue dusk. It would work to their advantage in going around Arlund, in getting home unnoticed.

As they struggled, she thought of the relief map. The bigger footprints. The blood. Why was the Italian here, on their mountain?

"I wonder what happened," Katharina said loudly.

Her grandfather said nothing. She twisted to look at him, though she sensed his displeasure.

"I wonder what happened to him," she repeated.

"He'll have to make it through the night, girl, before you can find out."

2

A t the Thaler's grave, Jutta knelt before the frosted-over headstone, her knees feeling a creeping heat before the icy chill took over and made them ache. Josef Thaler. Marianna Thaler. One after the other, they'd followed each other in death as they had in life, Marianna shyly behind her husband. She arranged half of the primroses and snowdrops into a glass jar, then stood and pulled her mittens back on before moving to Johi's grave.

Jutta put the remaining flowers in the pewter vase, steeling herself against the chest-tightening sorrow that always followed. When it did not come, Hans Glockner flitted through her mind. She kissed the tips of her fingers and patted the headstone. No matter what happened next, Johi would always take up the most room in her heart.

The grass was still thick with frost. She went to the bench outside the chapel to look down on the familiar layout of the valley below. Reschen Lake to the north and Graun Lake to the south both looked like cracked sapphires under the ice, set on the green-gold of the valley. Her eyes followed the road north from Graun to Reschen, towards the new border—the northern half of

Tyrol closed off to them now—then west around the lake to where Frederick's *Schlößl*, with its rounded tower, the loggia, and three gables, was just a dot on the hill above the water. The road west continued around the lake, rounding off at the hamlets of Gorf and Spinn. From there, the road cut almost a straight line between the two lakes, across the fields back to Graun.

Later, the morning sun would slip down the bell tower of St. Katharina, the town's most recognisable feature. Next to the church, the Post Inn—her inn—still lay in early-morning shadow, but the apple tree in the backyard had taken on the light-green tinge of spring. To her left, the Karlinbach flowed from the glaciers beyond Graun's Head to the east and spilled into Graun Lake. South of Graun Lake were more villages, Lower Lake, and the Ortler Range. Beyond that was the rest of Italy, creeping ever nearer to them.

Jutta watched the three men cutting ice on the south end of Reschen Lake. She had to get back down to the inn. The key to the ice cellar was with her, as were all her keys, at all times. When she rose from the bench, she recognised Father Wilhelm coming up the hill.

"I was just visiting the Thaler graves," she said after they greeted one other.

"And I've come to unlock the chapel. The Widow Winkler wants to decorate the altar."

Jutta eyed his key. "It's hard to believe we can't leave the chapel open anymore."

"Like your pantry," Father Wilhelm said. "Have you found who's been taking things from you?"

Jutta shook her head. "Hans Glockner promised to put on a new lock, but he hasn't got to it yet, which reminds me I need to get back down to the inn. The letters still need to be sorted, and I see the ice cutters are pulling the last blocks out."

Father Wilhelm turned his face to where the sun was just beginning to rise over the mountains, with it a southern breeze, promising warmth. "Yes, spring is finally on its way," he said. "Good to have some warmth."

"It's the foehn. A few gusts of warm wind but they won't last long."

"One more round of snow?"

"Probably tonight."

He sighed. "Hard to believe with this morning."

"Did you hear about the meeting that's been called? From what I've been given to understand, those Italians have got something up their sleeves."

"Is that what Mayor Roeschen says?"

Jutta nodded. Her brother-in-law had never looked more serious when he had come with the notice.

"I'll be there," the priest said. "If you're right, let's hope we can keep those dark clouds at bay."

Jutta sniffed. "The most damaging winds, Father Wilhelm, always come from the south."

Stepping out into the dawn, Katharina could hear the sounds of her hamlet beginning its day. Behind the Thalerhof was the Ritschhof, the multigenerational house filled with life, now that Toni Ritsch was finally married. She could hear someone pouring slop into the pig's trough and someone else sawing away. Farther up the road was Hans Glockner's sheep farm, and she saw Hans heading up the meadow to his corral, probably to fix the posts.

Opa wanted nobody to know about the wounded stranger, yet being this close to one's neighbours would make that a challenge, especially when the doctor arrived. There would be questions.

Hund trotted out from the barn, a stick in her mouth and her tail wagging. "Thanks for the reminder." She ruffled the dog's head before going to fetch wood for the stove.

When she returned, Katharina paused to listen to Opa's coughing. The cattle were stamping their hooves and moaning to one another. The scents of spring made them restless, but Opa's rattling chest concerned Katharina more. The cough had come in fits since March. In just two months, she and their neighbours would lead their animals up to Graun's Head for the summer. Before then, she was certain, there would be at least one more snowfall. Opa had to get better before the work demanded all his strength.

She started the fire in the tiled oven, then heated up the stove for a pot of broth. Opa had promised to dress the hare she'd shot yesterday. When she had everything ready for the midday meal, she climbed the stairs to the top floor. In the hallway mirror above Oma's chest of drawers, she caught sight of her mother in her own reflection. The dark-blond hair, the brown eyes—like the darkest stones on her mother's amber necklace—and Katharina was tall like her too. To see her face in the mirror, she had to crouch a little. She had a streak of ash on her cheek, and she wet a fingertip to wipe it away before fastening the stray braid at the back of her neck.

In Uncle Jonas's old room, the Italian was still lying as he'd been when she checked on him first thing that morning. She went to the bed and took the dried cloth from his forehead. His skin was not blazing anymore, and he was sleeping peacefully. Last night, he had muttered but had never really come to.

The scent of thyme from the mug on the bedside table still lingered. The tea was now cold, but what they'd been able to get into him had helped to lower the fever. She rinsed the fever cloth in the basin on top of the dresser, then traced a finger over the bronze war medal lying next to it. The blue-and-white ribbon was grimy. On the top arm of the cross was a crown with the letters *VE III*. The king. Vittorio Emanuele III. He was supposed to be her king now. In the middle were the Latin letters *MERITO DI CVERRA*. At the bottom of the cross were leaves and whirls.

Katharina turned it over in her palm and saw the five-pointed star on a rayed background.

Whoever this man was, he must have fought bravely if he had earned a medal like this. But not here. Not in Tyrol. She could imagine Opa with Kaspar Ritsch, over their beers, and Opa slamming his fist on the table before demanding, "The Italians never set foot on Tyrolean soil between fourteen and eighteen, so tell me again how they earned the Brenner Frontier!"

She looked at the stranger again. His face now had a blue-black shadow of whiskers that made him look rugged. She liked his thin lips, his strong jaw. He was trim and had graceful fingers, like a pianist. They were clean and soft, an intellectual's hands, such as a maths tutor she once had in Innsbruck. Herr Hefel had also had dark hair.

This Italian was not a threat to them, could not be. The bigger man, the one who had abandoned this one and headed north, was certainly at fault here.

She moved to collect the tea and the fever rag, when the man's eyelids fluttered. She placed everything back onto the dresser before facing him.

As if he had dust in his eyes, he blinked his lids rapidly, but when he opened them, the dark-brown eyes contained a lingering fear.

"There, there now. Everything will be all right."

"*Dove sono?*" His voice was hoarse.

"Do you speak German?"

He muttered a string of questions and tried to sit up.

"No, apparently you don't." Katharina stood over him, trying to remember some of the most basic words. "*Prego*. Don't move. You've been badly hurt. You might begin bleeding."

He winced and fell back onto the pillows.

"*Dove sono?*"

Maybe he was asking her name. "Katharina. I'm Katharina." Her "r" rolled more than usual.

"Katharina?"

"Sì, Katharina Thaler. You're in Arlund. What happened to you?"

The man whispered in Italian again.

"Here, drink this." She held the mug of cold tea to his lips. "I'll bring you something to eat soon," she said too loudly. She moved her hand to her mouth. "Eat. All right? You stay put. Please."

"Please," he whispered, closing his eyes. "Eat."

She smiled a little, took the empty mug, and went downstairs. If they had to be subjects of the Italian king, then she would have to learn the language. That much was certain.

From the top of the stairs, she heard Opa stamping his boots on the mat.

"He doesn't speak German," she said when he came through the door. "Only Italian, and I don't understand what he's asking all the time."

Her grandfather hung up his hat on the hat rack next to the door. "He woke up?"

"He's sleeping again. I need to get some food into him."

"I didn't think he'd be one of our Italian settlers."

"We know most of the migrants around here. Besides, he's not a hawker or a field worker." She bit her lip. "I found a war medal, Opa. A cross."

Her grandfather frowned. "We'll have to report this. First, I want Dr Hanny to check on him. The doctor speaks Italian well enough. Get the story before we go to the authorities."

"What about Karl Spinner's—"

"Don't you worry about that, and don't you go gallivanting on the mountain 'til we've cleared this up." He looked up at the ceiling again. "Did you get a name? Where he's from?"

"No, but he knows mine."

"Well then," Opa muttered. "Some of that soup would be good. And you should eat something too."

Katharina went into the pantry and took down a loaf of bread from the rack and picked up the pot of dumplings she'd made two days before. She cut a wedge of cheese and put the last of the smoked bacon onto the cutting board, then poured Opa a cup of thyme tea.

They stood at the table and bowed their heads while Opa said the Lord's Prayer.

"Amen." He cut the bread, then sat down and slurped his soup.

When they were finished, she cleared away their plates and soup bowls. "I'll wash up later. I'm going to try and get him to eat something."

Opa grunted.

With the bowl of broth, Katharina went back upstairs just as Opa broke into another coughing fit.

He was sleeping, the sheepskins tossed off to the side. Katharina placed the bowl on the table and checked his forehead. His fever had dropped but was still there. Dr Hanny had once told her that the body produced fever so that it could fight off infections. She hoped that this man's was nothing serious.

She covered him with the lambskin again and went to the window to let some fresh air in. The sun was hidden behind piled-up clouds, and the wind carried the smell of rain. The pines mimicked the sound of the rushing water in the Karlinbach so that, if anyone would ask her what spring sounded like, Katharina would say it was the creek carrying the melt to the Etsch River. She smiled, then remembered her ruined blouse in the garden below. Opa had said she could just burn it. She should have soaked it right away, but she'd forgotten it, and now the stains remained. She would have to grab it from the line before it started to rain.

Katharina turned around and was surprised to see the stranger watching her.

"You're awake," she said and closed the windows again.

"*Prego*," he said, and motioned her to open them once more.

When she did, he leaned towards her so that maybe he too could see the pines and meadows. But when he just stared at her, she quickly shut them.

"You have a fever," she said. "The draft isn't good for you."

As if she were not in the room, he shoved the sheepskins off and started for the edge of the bed. Katharina imagined him trying to flee through the hamlet, and she hurried to him and put a hand on his shoulder.

"The wounds. They need to close before you move."

Grimacing, he said something that sounded like, "*Dovehbanyo*."

"Look, I've brought you some soup. You should eat while it's still warm." She moved to the table and took the bowl of broth, then gestured with the spoon.

He shook his head and repeated the word, his voice gravelly and weak.

"You must be hungry," Katharina urged. "Please, eat something."

But his expression was desperate. Slowly, he swung one leg after another to the floor and tried to stand. When she took a step to him with the bowl and spoon, he scowled at her and, with one hand, cupped himself between his legs.

"*Dove è il bagno?*" he insisted.

Katharina's heart fell into her stomach. He looked around the room again, and she discreetly hitched up the waistband of her britches.

What was he looking for? There was only the bed and a simple wooden wardrobe, the chest of drawers, and the side table. She slammed the bowl on the side table, ready to fetch Opa, but then his face lit up, and he said something that sounded like "well."

Bewildered, she raised her voice. "No, it's soup. You understand? Soup."

Pointing to the corner near the window, he gestured at the chamber pot. "*Quella, per favore.*"

"Oh dear God, of course."

She hurried around the bed, smacking her hip on the wooden footboard. With the pot in hand, she returned, rubbing at the sting on her hipbone.

"I'm terribly sorry! All that tea I made you drink, and you've been here for a while..."

He waved her away.

"Let me just...I'll just wait outside. You go ahead." She hurried into the hallway and shut the door behind her, but she could still hear him making water. She should go to her room. Go downstairs. Give him privacy. Just as she moved away, he sighed from behind the door and there was a clunking sound.

"*Finito! Entri pure.*" His voice was stronger and less like sandpaper.

She opened the door. The chamber pot was at his feet, the small washcloth draped over the top. He was examining the bandage on his torso.

She set the waste by the door, then brought him the salve and the bowl of water.

He dabbed at the wound, then sniffed the mixture of pig fat and herbs.

"Thank you," he said in German.

"You rub it on, like this." She made circles over her ribs.

He did so, and when he sucked in his breath, she looked away from the angry skin around his wounds. Beneath the hollow of his neck were tight black curls.

He asked her a question in Italian again, returning the jar to her.

She pointed to herself. "Katharina Thaler."

"Katharina Thaler," he confirmed, and her name sounded like

water rolling over the creek bed in summer. He pointed to himself. "Angelo Grimani." When he grinned, his teeth flashed bright against the shadow of his beard.

"*Signor* Grimani."

"Angelo."

Quietly, she repeated his Christian name. She looked at his wounds again. "I should…you should put new bandages on." She took some from the drawer, but when she tried to hand them to him, he shrugged. She could do nothing but sit on the bed next to him. His eyes moved from her face to her hands. Here, this close, she could smell him, musky, unclean, yet comforting.

"*Tutto bene*, Katharina?" He pointed at her britches.

She glared at him, her cheeks hot.

"Good?" he said again, tapping his hipbone.

"You mean… Oh, yes. *Sì*! It's fine. I'm fine. *Grazie*."

Still embarrassed, she gestured for his arm, and he lifted it with a smile.

"*Mi spiace*, Katharina." He shook his head and glanced furtively down at his legs where he'd grabbed himself before. When he smiled again, Katharina saw none of the callousness from before.

He started to chuckle. First softly, then heartily, and his good arm clung to his torso as if he were hanging on to himself. With his left hand, he opened and closed his fingers as if he were working the mouth of a hand puppet.

"*Blah, blah, blah*." He pointed at the door.

True, she had made a fool of herself by not understanding him earlier. For not understanding him at all. For talking the whole time when he needed his privacy. "I'm sorry too," she said, smiling back, and her relief turned into a laugh.

It felt good, laughing with him, and it went on like that, chuckling and smiling at one another while she bandaged his arm.

When she was finished, he examined her work and nodded.

Katharina felt his closeness and, with relief, remembered the broth.

"You should eat before it gets cold. I'll do the bandage on your head afterwards. I need fresh water."

Mr Grimani, amusement still in his eyes, took the bowl. At his first mouthful, she smiled back.

Against the window, the first drops of rain pelted the glass. The blouse!

She hurried to the bedroom door but stopped and turned back, the room much darker now.

"What happened to you out there?" she asked.

He turned to her, but in the darkness she could not see his face. Something about the way he held his head told her he had understood her question. The way he held the spoon in the air told her he could not—or would not—answer her. She closed the door on the distance that had formed between them.

The last cream scooped off the milk. The last tins set out for pickup. The fresh straw laid out. The water poured into the troughs. Katharina could finally head back to the house. Outside, the rain still came down in soft, steady drops, a spring rain that would melt the old snow around them but fall as new snow above. Katharina hoped that Opa was coming home soon. The sky was already dark. She shivered as she washed in the water trough in the stable yard.

Hund followed her to the front door. Under the light coming from the sitting room, she could see the hope on the dog's face.

"You want to come in," she said to Hund, "but Opa will frown on this."

Hund cocked her head, and her eyes skittered to the door.

"All right. Come in."

In the kitchen, the dog curled up in a corner with a loud sigh, and Katharina stoked the fire before pulling the hare out of the pot. She steeped the tea and heated the soup for the dumplings. The Italian would get a good portion of the meat.

The Italian.

It was not appropriate to call him by his Christian name. They were not familiar enough with one another to do so. Yet calling him "the Italian" was simply rude. She would call him Signor Grimani no matter how much he otherwise insisted.

Her stomach grumbled, so she took down the half-eaten loaf of bread from the rack and cut two slices to dunk into the juices from the hare. In the crock, the butter was low. Her eyes landed on the moon calendar. As she'd guessed, tomorrow was ideal for working the milk. She would churn more butter tomorrow.

When she had stilled her hunger, she prepared a tray for Signor Grimani but heard the sound of people coming up to the house. Opa was home, and someone was with him.

"Evening," he said hoarsely as he hung his hat on its peg.

Behind him, Hans Glockner ducked through the door. He, too, greeted her and hung up his hat. Both men grunted and sighed as they shook off their wet coats and tugged off their boots.

Katharina could smell the outdoors, the snow-rain, on them. "You'll want something to eat."

Hans nodded once, and she saw iced-over drops on his long beard. He limped towards the table. Sometimes the way he walked made her think of a grandfather clock's pendulum swaying back and forth. She guessed the pain in his leg had flared. He and Opa had been out in the mountains half the day and half the night. She checked the remaining portions of hare and covered Signor Grimani's tray with a dishtowel. No need to start a fuss about how much food she was giving the injured man.

Only when Katharina had laid out everything on the table and the men had started eating did she ask her questions. "Is Dr Hanny not coming?"

Opa wiped his whiskers of meat juices and smacked his lips over a thighbone. "Tomorrow. First thing."

"Did you find anything up on the mountain?"

Hans and Opa looked at one another. Hans said, "Yup. Like you said, the tracks went north. Right to the border. We found some chicken feathers and droppings." He jerked his head towards the ceiling. "The Italian must've run into a smuggler."

"Why would a smuggler stab him like that?"

Opa shrugged. "Wrong place, wrong time. Maybe the Italian surprised him. Maybe the Italian tried to steal his chickens. Maybe he thought the chickens were rightfully his, like this valley." Opa chewed a piece of bread and watched her.

Something wasn't right here. They weren't telling her the whole truth. "Did you find Karl Spinner?"

Opa nodded again.

"And?"

He dropped the bone on his plate. "Girl, we are trying to eat. Hans has to hurry and get to his sheep yet. Give us our peace."

Hans slurped his soup as if he'd not heard them.

"I suppose I'll take the tray up to Signor Grimani then," she said.

"Did you hear that, Hans? We have a name now." Opa looked at her. "Did you find out why he's here in the first place?"

His hostility was unsettling. Something had happened. "Just a name," she said.

He jerked his head towards the stairs. "Go on. Mr…"

"Grimani."

"Mr Grimani needs to get his strength and then go back to where he came from."

3

APRIL 1920, ARLUND

E ver since she had moved into her parents' old bedroom, Katharina often looked towards Papa's side of the bed and wondered what he and Mama had talked about between the space of the two mattresses, how they might have kissed and loved one another here, away from the eyes of the others who had once lived in this house, before it had become so empty. Until now.

Behind her bedroom door, at the end of the hall and in Uncle Jonas's bedroom, was a stranger, a man whose dark eyes watched her with interest. She thought of his long, graceful hands and the way he moved them. Sighing, she turned over onto her back. Across the hallway, Opa was moving in his bedroom. His cough had eased up after she'd made him a steam inhalant of pine and rosemary. She still had him, her stoic but loving grandfather. And he expected her to be up already.

The wardrobe near the window was still just a silhouette, but over the down covers, the sky was lightening. At the foot of her bed was her parents' pine chest. Mama had wanted Papa to paint it the same green as the wardrobe so that the two pieces of furniture would match. She'd wanted to paint the chest with the same yellow and pink peonies as on the doors of the wardrobe. Then the two swallows that flew off in opposite directions from the handles of the wardrobe would be painted to land on the sides of the box, in nests tucked into the corners. Mama had sketched out the plans, and after Katharina had coloured them in, Papa took the chest to the workshop with the promise to start the next day. But Oma had died that night, and the chest stayed out there until Katharina's brother came into the world, stillborn. Then a week after that funeral, Katharina found her mother kneeling in front of the box, placed back at the foot of the bed. Mama's lap was full of baby clothes and diapers, and the wooden chest was still plain.

Katharina's loneliness flared up in the pit of her stomach, and she moved to the end of the bed to look at the ruined blouse she'd laid on top of the chest. It was one of the last pieces of clothing she had from her mother.

She slipped off the bed and knelt on the floor, like her mother had all those years before, and raised the blouse to her nose. It smelled of sheep's milk soap. She had scrubbed Mr Grimani's scents out, and all that remained of him were the faded brown bloodstains. His blood on her blouse. It was the first time she'd saved anyone's life, and though part of her said she was being foolish, even vain, she wanted to keep this. Mr Grimani would eventually have to return to wherever he'd come from.

The thought of the house empty again, those lovely hands gone, and those keen eyes no longer on her, made her feel hollow. This cloth would be all the memory she would have left of him.

Katharina folded it and pressed it to her before raising the lid of the chest. The scents of pine, leather, flaxen cloth, and her father's shaving soap rose around her. The smells of unfulfilled promises.

The blouse went to the bottom under the stack of baby clothes. She reached for her father's leather shaving kit and remembered the Christmas when Mama had given it to him. She could remember the shop in Innsbruck and the scent of herbs and flowers—a meadow caught indoors. That was when her family had been prosperous and doing well. That was just before they'd moved to Arlund because Opa needed help with the farm. That was a long, long time and whole wide world ago.

She clicked the shaving kit's snap open. Each item was secured in place in its separate compartments. Inside the lid, leather straps held the cutthroat razor and the shaving stick. In the main pocket were the soap container, the razor strop, and a clothes brush. There was a place for two more things, but they were no longer there, and Katharina could not remember what should have been there. A lot of things were out of place these days.

She put the kit on the floor. Mr Grimani could use it, and when she pictured handing it over to him, or shaving him herself, her stomach felt weak. Without another look inside, she dropped the lid of the chest shut and went to the wardrobe.

Opa was waiting for the doctor to come down from seeing Mr Grimani, so Katharina stirred the whey soup again to prevent it from burning at the bottom.

"Sunday best?" Opa muttered.

Katharina glanced down at her light-blue smock, one of two dresses she owned. "Hardly. It's my work dress."

Opa grunted. "Weren't wearing that when Toni Ritsch came courting."

Katharina was about to say something sharp about Toni Ritsch, but footsteps sounded in the hallway above, and Opa stood up from the bench.

"Thanks to your fine nursing, Katharina," Dr Hanny said as he came down the stairs, "Mr Grimani is doing quite well. He's having his shave now and then needs to rest."

He looked at Opa. "We'll have to report the incident, and that means going to the barracks. I'll take him to Captain Rioba myself. In two or three days, I could move him to the hospital in Meran."

Two or three days. Katharina's heartbeat tripped over itself. "But—"

"Thursday, then," Opa said.

"Latest." Dr Hanny slid behind the table. "Mr Grimani lives in Bozen now, but some of his family's originally from Arezzo. I was there once, while travelling. Francesco Redi was from there."

Katharina placed the bowls on the table and the pot of whey in the middle. Opa stood, and they joined him in prayer, and then he broke the bread. When they were seated again, she asked, "Who was Francesco Redi?"

"Francesco Redi was an Italian physician, naturalist, and"—Dr Hanny wielded his spoon—"poet."

Jutta had once told her that Dr Hanny had a whole room at his *Schlößl* filled with books, and not just in German but also in Latin, in Greek, in French, and even in Italian. Jutta and Dr Hanny would have been a much better couple than his brother Fritz and Jutta had been. It was hard to believe the two men stemmed from the same family.

As if believing he'd lost her interest, Dr Hanny turned to Opa. "Yes, so, Redi. Very fascinating man. He was the first to recognise and correctly describe the details of many important parasites. They call him the father of parasitology."

Her grandfather looked up from his soup. "And this Mr Grimani comes from the same place? How fitting."

The doctor's smile disappeared. "Mr Grimani works as the chief engineer for the Ministry of Civil Engineering in Bozen."

"Government man." Opa sniffed. "In our mountains."

Dr Hanny motioned for the bread basket. Katharina wanted to know more about Mr Grimani now. Instead, Dr Hanny finished his breakfast and pulled out his pipe and a tin of Modiano tobacco.

"Fetch mine, Katharina," Opa said.

When the pipes were filled and lit, the men puffed for a few moments.

"You were right," Dr Hanny said. "He's here about the river."

Opa's eyes narrowed behind his pipe, but he said nothing.

"He was surveying the land," Dr Hanny said. "The Italians are resurrecting the plans for the dam. They'll have to find ways to divert the river and the creeks for it, like last time. That's what he's here for."

"How long will the old laws stay in effect? The Austro-Hungarian laws?" Opa asked.

"My best guess? At least until the annexation to Italy. 'Til Italian laws take effect. Rome will have no interest in upholding our old ones. Not if it means obstacles to building up our industry."

Opa clamped down on his pipe. The smoke curled and rose— a little sour, a little fragrant. Katharina could hear their teeth grinding on the wooden stems as if they were chewing on silenced ideas. Talk of a dam had trigged an uproar in the whole valley, but that was over a decade ago. At school, on the blackboard, Mrs Blech had drawn their rivers and creeks, then the two lakes and shown how they could be connected to create a reservoir for electricity, but Katharina hadn't understood how people could build something like that. Then Mrs Blech had shown how much of the valley between the lakes would have been affected and said the project would not go through because diverting the waterways would destroy too many of the farmers' lands. The kaiser's laws had been written to protect against such things. That was the last Katharina had heard of it.

Opa sniffed. "We appealed that project before and won. We'll do it again."

Dr Hanny did not look convinced. "We can't complain about

not having enough electricity in the hinterlands and then not allowing for progress either. We're starting to sound like the Viennese. They complain about the weather when it's cool and complain about it when it's warm. However, I believe there's a compromise to be made here. There's a good stretch of land that's not fit for agriculture. The farmers won't miss it. Even Jutta might see the bright side of things this time around. She'll be closer to lakeshore property and can sell that to the tourists."

"And what?" Opa glowered. "Rename the Post Inn the Lakeview?"

Dr Hanny waved his pipe and smiled apologetically. "Maybe you're right. It's not a matter to joke about. But I'd still be interested in ideas on how to produce more electricity. To be honest, my concerns are about how this is all being communicated to us, or not at all for that matter."

"But what happened to Mr Grimani?" Katharina insisted. "Who stabbed him?"

Opa and Dr Hanny looked at her as if seeing her for the first time.

Opa shrugged. "Do you think the two things could be connected, Frederick?"

Dr Hanny shook his head.

Katharina looked to Opa for confirmation. "Hans thinks it might have been a smuggler."

"We followed the tracks," Opa said. "They went over the border."

Dr Hanny scratched his head. "Mr Grimani said he was working when he heard someone behind him in the woods. He said a big, raggedy fellow came out. It didn't take long for the fellow to see a chance at changing his fortune. He tried to rob Mr Grimani, demanding the surveying tools and any other valuables he had. When Mr Grimani refused, the man pulled the knife and attacked."

"Opa, something has to be done about this."

Her grandfather grunted. "What if it's one of *our*...poor fellows?"

"You mean from our valley?" Dr Hanny said.

"The smugglers are organised," Opa said. "The ones to the north of the pass hide the contraband, and then the ones from our side of the pass pick the things up. Who can blame them, Frederick? It's been good business so far. The Italians take everything from us. Even some of the border patrols get something out of it for turning a blind eye. If there's violence though..." Opa glanced at Katharina, then turned back to Dr Hanny. "Frederick, if this man who attacked the Italian was someone on our side of the border..."

"Then it would be someone we know," Dr Hanny finished.

"But who?" Katharina asked.

Neither of them looked at her.

Opa was reflective. "If you take Mr Grimani to the *carabinieri* to report this, we'd be getting one of our own people into trouble. The Italians won't show that poor fellow any mercy."

Dr Hanny tapped out his pipe. "Will you be at the meeting in Graun? We could talk to Jutta and ask her to get the word out before I take Mr Grimani to Captain Rioba."

"If that's enough time," Opa said.

He laughed softly. "We're talking about Jutta—postmistress, innkeeper, and the woman whose finger is on every pulse in this valley and beyond." Dr Hanny stood up. "I have to go. Thanks very much for the breakfast." He turned to Katharina. "It might be a good idea to let Mr Grimani come down into the sitting room. It's a bit warmer, and he won't be doing anyone any harm." With those last words, he looked at Opa.

"Goodbye, Dr Hanny," Katharina said.

"Let me pay you something for your time," Opa said, reaching into his pockets. "I mean, if the man up there hasn't got anything..."

Dr Hanny put a hand on Opa's arm. "Don't think of it. Besides, the breakfast was very good. You have good cows, Johannes. Still the best around." He snapped his medical bag open and took out a bottle. "And this is for you. Take care of that cough. Anyone asks, that's all I was here for."

As she was clearing the table, Katharina realised that nobody had mentioned about getting word back to Bozen. Nobody had mentioned Angelo Grimani's people.

4

APRIL 1920, GRAUN

S t Katharina's church was packed with townsfolk from the whole valley, but Jutta pushed her way to the front. Every hamlet was represented, and not just by the leaders. Farmers with their wives and children had come early from their fields to hear the news. The Prieths, who usually got up at three in the morning to begin baking, had postponed going to bed to take part. Even two of the travelling craftsmen, the tinker and the barrel maker, were present.

Near the sacristy, the councilmen flanked Mayor Georg. He called for everyone to quiet down, but nobody heard.

"Mayor Roeschen wants to speak," Jutta shouted above the din. When it was quiet, she nodded at her brother-in-law to continue.

"Welcome," Georg started. "In my capacity as the mayor of Graun, I want to thank you all for being here. Especially when our Tyrolean delegates are still protesting the treaty, I'm afraid tonight's news is not good at all. The regime has informed us that the names of the villages will be changed to Italian ones and all official government business must be conducted in both German and Italian."

Voices rose in protest, and when the volume finally died down, Georg continued, his voice grave. "The list of name changes are as follow: Reschen is now officially Rescia. Graun is now Curon Venosta. Piz is now..."

The protests escalated, and Jutta stared at the group of leaders at the altar. Nobody had to state the obvious. None of the men up there spoke enough Italian to handle any official government business. Except maybe Frederick. Her other brother-in-law, the good doctor, was rather fluent.

By the time Georg finished, the people had been stunned into silence, but the air was charged with tension. The mayor scanned the crowd, cleared his throat, and lifted his hat. "Well, that's all I have to say, folks. Thank you for coming."

"Mayor Roeschen! What about the farmers who have no alp left to go to this season? The ones who took their livestock north of the pass and now can't get over the border?"

Everyone turned in their pews, but Jutta had already recognised Martin Noggler's voice. The redheaded blacksmith rarely raised it, and Jutta pricked with curiosity. He had but maybe four cows left, some goats, but where should he graze them in high summer when he planted his crops in the valley?

Georg started to speak, and the people turned back to the altar. "Martin, I am still negotiating new parcels for you. I promise to have an answer for you in the next couple of weeks. In the meantime, it would be good if those of you who have some land within the border help your neighbours with a solution."

The farmers grumbled amongst themselves. Grazing was serious business too, but they were being dismissed, and the fact that the villages were being renamed still stung over everything else. Surely the farmers would lend one another a helping hand, but who would stop the tide of injustices the Italian regime was imposing?

Outside, as people gathered beneath the oak tree, Jutta walked along the edges of the groups. Their whispers sounded like a kettle about to boil over, the outrage just below the surface. The longer they talked, the louder they grew.

"We're Tyroleans."

"This is Tyrol."

"One hundred years of autonomy! How can they?"

"It will always *be* Tyrol. It's *our* land!"

Father Wilhelm's usual tactic: "I'll write to the Bishop of Brixen."

Jutta looked up at the sky. The clouds looked threatening, and the wind picked up. "That storm is here," she called to the priest. "There's no stopping it now."

She walked over to Georg, standing with some villagers. Mrs Blech—nervous as a hovering wasp—clung to his arm.

"But Mayor Roeschen," Mrs Blech said, "how much longer before the world's leaders realise their mistake?"

Georg looked polite, his voice weary. "I already said, my dear Mrs Blech, I don't know."

"But surely they won't be replacing you in October with some *Italian*?"

Jutta touched Georg's other arm. "May I have a word with you? Excuse us, Mrs Blech."

The schoolteacher muttered something, and Jutta led Georg away.

"How was I to tell her," he said, "that by October she should be as worried about her job as she is about mine? The teachers will be affected too."

"She has no reason to be so solicitous. She cosied up to those Italians in no time, she and Klaus Blech. I heard him bragging about how he was going to make a fortune by importing real Parma ham up here and selling it to all the incomings." She watched Mrs Blech standing with her husband and a number of the valley folk Jutta had seen warming up to the new Roman administrators. "I'll wager she'll be starting her Italian lessons tonight before she risks losing her job at the school." She patted

Georg's arm. "Everyone's coming to the *Stube*. Will you join us? Where is Lisl?"

"She's taken the news quite badly. She's waiting for me at home."

Jutta nodded. She'd not expected her sister-in-law to be happy about any of this. Georg's long run as their community leader was surely in jeopardy. "I'll visit her tomorrow. Give her my greetings."

"I will. And"—Georg made a slight gesture towards the retreating Mrs Blech—"thank you again."

She watched him heading home, but then he turned.

"Jutta? What do you really make of all this?"

She forced herself to smile. "We can all rest easy, Mayor. Every child here knows that Austria won the war, but who would have guessed we would get all of Italy to boot?"

At the door of the inn, Jutta saw that she had her own delegation to attend to. The way Frederick Hanny, Hans Glockner, and Johannes Thaler watched her come up the stoop, she knew the three of them had something important for her. The noise from the *Stube* also told her they would have no privacy there.

"Right, gentlemen. Get out of this wind and come into my office." She returned Hans Glockner's shy smile before unlocking the door to her apartments.

Inside, Johannes Thaler moved to the shelf where she kept her photos. She glanced at Frederick. Did the good doctor notice that she had removed the photos of his brother, Fritz? She hoped he would not mention it if he did. Every time Frederick was at the inn, the unspoken questions about Fritz's disappearance lay between them like a fallen boulder they could find no way around.

"How's Katharina?" Jutta called to Johannes Thaler, and opened the credenza with her key.

"She's fine. She sends her greetings."

Jutta heard his hesitancy and left a question mark to check on later. From the credenza, she pulled out the bottle of schnapps she kept for serious matters and placed four drinking thimbles on the table. Each man took a seat, all three in a row like a jury on judgment day. They said nothing as she filled the glasses. Outside, the wind tore around them, a windowpane rattling somewhere in the next room. She pushed three thimbles to her guests and then raised her own.

"To Graun," she started, "and to Reschen. To Spinn. To Arlund. May our Austrian leaders do right by us before the new village signs arrive."

They tipped their heads back, and Jutta tasted the hazelnut on her palate. Her schnapps was still the best in the valley, and from the looks on their faces, the men believed it as well.

When she was seated across from them, she said, "Now then, what's troubling you?"

Frederick leaned forward. "There's been an incident near Graun's Head."

"Near Karl Spinner's hut," Hans Glockner said.

Jutta turned to Johannes Thaler.

"Katharina found him," he said.

With that, she checked off her earlier question mark—the reason Katharina's Opa had sounded so hesitant. "Found who?"

"An Italian surveyor," Frederick said. "An engineer. He was stabbed."

"Stabbed? Wait. Katharina, is she safe?"

"She's fine," Johannes Thaler said.

"But," she said, "what is a land surveyor doing here?"

Jutta listened as Johannes Thaler told her how Katharina had rescued the Italian stranger and how Frederick had questioned the man about the attack.

"We think it might have been a desperate smuggler," he finished. "Which would most likely make that someone from our valley."

"Someone desperate enough to be stealing and robbing people," Hans Glockner said.

Jutta straightened, curious. "You can say that again. You promised to install that new lock on the cellar door. He's been here again last night, that thief. A sack of potatoes and some preserves gone missing. Lisl's been good enough to take some of the things to her place, but I want to know who this ruffian is. The Italians are doing enough of their own pilfering. I don't need anyone else—"

"Sorry. I was busy with the new lambs coming in. I'll come down tomorrow and do it."

"Much obliged if you would, Hans." She looked hard at them. "This Italian, however, well, he's another matter altogether. Thieving is one thing. Trying to murder a man is another issue entirely."

"That's why we're here," Frederick said.

"You want me to get the word out to the smugglers that you're onto them," Jutta said. "But is that the right thing to do?"

"This is our problem, not the Italians'," Johannes Thaler said. "You know who to talk to. Let them know we're looking for the one causing trouble. Want to clear this up. Might be that the Italian provoked him. So, you can say that before the *carabinieri* get a hold of a fellow Tyrolean—"

"Whoever stabbed Mr Grimani," Frederick cut in, "deserves to be punished, and we'll make sure there's justice."

Jutta shook her head. "You three are unbelievable."

Hans looked down at the edge of the table, his beard pressed up against his chest.

"Hans?" she asked. "Do you really want to take this into your own hands?"

"It seems the fair thing to do," he muttered.

"There's one more thing, Jutta," Frederick interrupted again. "You wanted to know why Mr Grimani is here. He's here about the reservoir."

"That's nonsense," she scoffed. "That project was deemed unfavourable. The laws—"

"Our laws will *not* be adopted by the Italians, I expect," Frederick said. "Like many that were written to protect our autonomy."

She fingered the key ring at her waist. "No, the Italians will pass laws that will give them rights to whatever they want."

Hans moved his hand towards her. "Your inn."

"Yes, my inn." She glanced at Frederick, but he did not react to her calling his brother's inn her own. "I need to think about what you have all said. If you'll excuse me, I should check on Alois."

When she reached her son's bedroom door, Johannes called to her. "How is the boy?" His look was on the photograph on the shelf, the one of Johi and her. The memories of the day the mountain took Johi came back to her. When Fritz had beaten her for the last time and disappeared, it was Johi who came down from Arlund, declared his love for her, and asked her to marry him. Said he would help her with Alois's disabilities. But marrying had been an impossibility because nobody knew where Fritz was and she had to wait five years before she could claim his death. But Johi had promised to wait, and Johannes Thaler had never said a word against what his son wanted. No, he had not. More than the church, Johannes Thaler and his family had opened a place for her son and her.

"Alois is fine," she said. "I'll tell him you were here."

She looked at Frederick and Hans Glockner. "Give me until tomorrow before you take that Italian troublemaker to Captain Rioba."

5

APRIL 1920, ARLUND

The air smelled of new snow, animal shit, and soured milk. Angelo stood in the doorway of the sturdy wooden house, built to fit at least three generations, a monument to rustic living. In awe, he watched the dark clouds that moved across the valley, the wind whipping up the dead sticks and leaves. By the end of the night, the ice would recapture them. The first time he'd encountered the insanity of the foehn wind was when he'd fought on the Marmolada Glacier. First the temperatures rose, then the wind would come in, almost desert hot, eating away at the snow and ice. Bean-shaped clouds would appear, and soon enough the storms would start and the temperatures would drop again. The speed at which the weather changed in the Alps always amazed him.

He heard the girl moving behind him, and he turned to find her holding a blanket, which she motioned to put over his shoulders. Her mothering was becoming irritating, or it was the stiffness and the soreness or a combination of all those things. Christ, just two years ago he had swum naked in the glacial waters, competing with Giovanni for who could remain in the water the longest, and here was this Katharina behaving as if a chill could kill a strong man.

It wasn't pneumonia that had killed Giovanni. Or any of his men. But he couldn't tell this girl that. Hell, it wasn't just the language barrier; he would never tell anyone about the deaths of his comrades.

She lifted the blanket again just as a sharp pain in his head made him wince.

"*Der Föhn*," she said. "*Meine Mutter hat immer Migraine bekommen.*" She bit her lip.

"Your mother might have had headaches from this wind, but someone also cracked my skull."

She looked at him blankly, and he sighed, smiling his thanks as he let her put the blanket over his shoulders. He stepped out onto the doormat made of woven twigs. Where had the old man gone off to again? With the oncoming weather, he felt mildly alarmed for the grandfather. Below them, he could see a few lights from the town. That must be Graun, and to the north, Reschen. He could not make out the lakes from here. He wondered where the rest of his possessions were, but then he thought of the attack on him and felt the anger rising again.

When a gust of wind swirled more debris in his direction, he ducked back indoors and dropped the bolt into place, then went into the simple kitchen. These houses were dark. Gloomy and dark.

He noticed something else. She was wearing a dress now. Earlier, he'd seen her splitting wood with big, strong swings, wearing those too-big britches. Had he not seen her with a rifle too? Or had that been the old man?

"Where's your grandfather?" he asked. "Katharina?"

She looked up and gave him the same apologetic smile she always did when she didn't understand. As she put out bowls—soup again—Angelo smelled a hint of something like garlic. What he wouldn't do for a plate of rich ragu. Or a veal cutlet and a good glass of red wine, not the grape juice they served here. He sniffed the steam coming from the bowl. Wild leek and well water would have to do.

"*Setzen Sie sich.*" Katharina indicated the bench.

He sat down at the wooden table, smooth from years of use. She was across from him, her brown eyes always just a bit lowered. She was young, maybe early twenties, and she was handsome with dark-blond hair tucked away in that crown of braids, and good teeth. There was a lot that was non-Tyrolean about her. Most of the women he had seen in the villages or encountered on the way up here were short, dark, and rugged. This one, however—this Katharina, despite the perplexing choice of clothing and her man-like strength—had the feminine quality that reminded him of—

"You like beer?" she said.

Her Italian startled him.

"I get you beer."

This time his smile was genuine, and she seemed delighted as well. He nodded, and she poured him a mug from a glass bottle.

"I'd love some ragu too," he said.

"Ragu?"

"Yes. Pasta with tomato sauce. Real garlic! Something I can bite into." He chomped down on his wooden spoon.

Katharina looked baffled but laughed. "Hunger?"

"Yes, yes. Lots of hunger."

She laughed again, something she did more easily than the first time, and pushed the loaf of bread towards him. It was a dark rye with caraway, dry and sour, and made his gums ache, but for the love of God he needed something to bite into, so he reached for the loaf. He had heard how the people here baked bread only two or three times a year, hung the loaves in their rafters, and let it dry like beef. It was flat, and when fresh, it was fine. But this was from an old batch, and he had to saw through the crust. She smiled at him when he had a slice, then dunked her piece into the beer. Good idea.

She said something, the lilt and cadence of her dialect so foreign he understood nothing. Chewing, his face blank, he listened anyway. She was a mystery, and yet somehow familiar. Or easy to know. Maybe it was because he owed her his life. He remembered how an engineer he worked with—Stefano Accosi— had fallen in love with a Tyrolean nurse. He'd married her, Angelo thought, but he couldn't remember. Did Stefano fight on the Tyrolean side? He was half-Tyrolean, half-Italian. Angelo gave up trying to recall, and when he realised that Katharina had stopped talking, he felt he owed her an explanation.

"I was thinking of someone I know. An engineer in Bolzano."

"Bolzano," Katharina repeated, and she made a slight face before looking interested again.

He shrugged. "Bozen."

She smiled a little.

"Anyway, he was injured in the war. Married a nurse. I just can't remember if she's German or Italian."

Katharina pointed to herself. *"Tirolerin."*

"Yes, all right. Tyrolean. But who knows—maybe she was Prussian."

Katharina shook her head, as if she were apologising and wanting to put an end to the topic.

From outside, a crashing noise sent them springing from the bench. They ran to the door, and when Katharina yanked it open, Angelo saw nature in a glorious rage. It sent a thrill through him, and he almost laughed when something flew from the barn and across the yard. It looked like a crate.

Katharina shouted, "Hund! *Wo bist du*, Hund?"

Angelo remembered the dog and joined her at the door, but he did not see the animal. Another violent gust came in, and he tried to close the door, but Katharina would not budge, still calling for the dog. Then Angelo heard it.

The barking was coming from behind the house. Then from the front of the house. Like a demon, the foehn was playing tricks on them.

Katharina yelled something at him, then pushed past and ran towards the back of the house. He followed her, the wind and the rain like a torrent of shrapnel against his face. As he rounded the corner, he saw her bending over the cowering, stiff dog. She tried to pick it up, and he moved to help get the terrified animal out of the weather, but a loud smacking of wood from above made him look up.

"Oh hell!"

A shutter from his bedroom window had come out of its bolt, and now it battered the wall in the wind. On the next strong gust, it tore away, and Angelo ducked as it flew over his head and behind him.

He felt a ripping sensation and then a hot pain. *"Madre di Dio!"* He dropped to the ground, trying to get his breath.

Katharina had the dog by the scruff of the neck but bent down low enough so that Angelo could grasp her arm and pull himself up. They stumbled, bent over, back into the house, and the dog scrambled under the table for safety.

Above them, Angelo heard the sound of glass break, and Katharina sprinted up the stairs. His side still burning, he followed her. In the bedroom, he saw the broken windowpane, grabbed a rag from the dresser, and stuffed it into the hole. When the window was sealed, he dropped onto the edge of the bed and pressed his hand to the wound. A warm stickiness left streaks of blood on his palm.

"Stitches be damned," he muttered.

Katharina pulled his vest away to reveal the seeping wound. He had no idea whose clothes he wore, but he felt badly about ruining them. She bit her lip, as if trying to hold back a good scolding. She motioned for him to undo the shirt's buttons, and she poured water from the jug into the washing bowl. Then she took a new rag and dropped onto her knees to examine his side. He watched the top of her head.

Why wasn't she married? She was a handsome woman, maybe even beautiful if she could invest in it. Most of all, she was practical and valiant. Perhaps the reason she had no husband was because all she cooked was soup.

He chuckled at his own joke, and she looked up.

"*Das ist nicht lustig. Es ist sehr ernst.*"

"Have more soup for me?" Angelo asked, laughing now.

She shook her head and looked at him as if he were touched in the head. She began washing the wound, biting her bottom lip, as if to keep from laughing.

Stinging pain. "Damn it."

Katharina smiled wryly. "Damn it, Signor Grimani. Damn it. *Die ganze Zeit nur,* damn it."

He chuckled and looked around the room as she cleaned him up. Wooden floors, low wooden ceilings, small windows with wooden shutters. The bedrooms were purely functional and not in the least bit decorated for aesthetic purposes save for the handiwork on the most practical pieces of furniture. The wardrobe was intricately carved. The dresser too. The bed, however, was simple with a headboard and footboard. Crucifixes hung in every room. And animal skins. The girl even wore wooden clogs with cowskin uppers.

When she finished, it was clear he would have to lie still, at least until the doctor came back to restitch him, and from the looks of it, that was not going to happen for a while either. The wind had died down, but outside the broken window, snow was now falling.

"Katharina." Angelo looked from the window and at the girl

again. "Katharina. Katharina. Katharina." He pointed at himself. "Angelo. Angelo. Angelo. Call me by my Christian name. We're in the wilderness for Christ's sake."

Her smile was uncertain, and she finished cleaning up, then pulled out dry clothes from the wardrobe. He unbuckled his trousers, looked up, and saw that she had turned her back on him. "Someone has to get the doctor. Where's the old man? Is he your grandfather? Or your father?" Christ, he hoped the old man wasn't her husband, but in these hinterlands...

She shrugged and shook her head.

Wherever the old man was, he hoped he was all right. It was awkward being here alone with the girl. He wondered again why the house was so large but empty. Downstairs he had seen a number of photos of young men, an older woman, and another woman who looked very much like Katharina and who Angelo could only presume was the mother of the girl. But where *was* everyone? It was as if a plague had swept through the house.

"Right. I'm done."

Katharina turned and came to him, holding out her arm.

"I thought I would just stay here."

Her smile remained patient, and she waved her elbow up and down. "Angelo."

He laughed softly and took her arm, and they slowly made their way downstairs.

"Warm," she said in Italian when they had reached the room with the tiled oven.

She was right. It was a lot warmer down here.

She pointed to a worn green upholstered chair and took the one across from it, an ugly chair covered in a rough blanket. He stayed standing. She watched him expectantly and he looked around on the shelves and mantel for something printed in Italian that he could read. He gave up on that idea almost immediately. In the far corner of a shelf, next to a tin of tobacco, he found a pack of playing cards and lifted them.

"May I?"

She nodded.

He opened the carton and took them out. These were not regular playing cards. There were strange pictures—of hot-air balloons, of acorns, of pigs, of kings, of what looked like a leaping lord. Sometimes the suit—a hot-air balloon, a heart, an acorn, or a leaf—were located beneath one of the figures. Pigs on playing cards was truly odd, especially ones with saddles on them.

"What is this?" he asked.

"*Watten*," she said.

She may as well have spoken Chinese. Indicating the table, she sat down at it, and he across from her. Katharina gestured for the cards, then shuffled them. What followed was a fruitless attempt on her part to teach him the game. Each time he thought he had a winning trick, she placed her hand over them and took them to her side of the table. He challenged her, and she would laugh. Explaining again, with the patience of a school teacher, and in that dialect, that lilt, that he had it all wrong.

He figured the game was similar to *briscola*, where one could trump someone else's card, but he did not understand the rules, and his head was fuzzy. After a half hour and losing two games, he indicated he intended to give up and went to the chair to rest. Katharina followed, a little shyly, and once settled, she plucked out a ball of wool and some knitting needles from a basket next to her chair and began knitting. He recognised the start of a sock.

It was very late before Angelo felt that Katharina also missed the old man's presence. Her grandfather, he had decided. She moved occasionally to the window and watched the snow fall, her brows pinched together. At one point she looked at Angelo and hurried to him and put a hand to his forehead.

"*Du hast schon wieder Fieber.*"

A few minutes later she was back with tea, and the thyme smelled of home. He finished the mug. Shivering, he lifted the blanket up to his chin. He wanted only to sleep.

Katharina's worried expression was now on him instead of the outdoors. She lifted a finger as if she wanted to say something and then disappeared upstairs. A few moments later, she returned with something in her hand.

"What?" she asked in Italian. "What, Angelo?"

Angelo held out his palm, and she placed his war medal into it, her fingers pressing lightly before retreating again. He remembered how the thief had searched his pockets. He'd believed the man had taken everything.

"Where did you find this?"

She pointed at the floor.

"At the hut? Where you found me? This was there?"

She nodded. "What?" she asked again.

Angelo held the medal up for a moment, then closed his fist over it. He shut his eyes. "It's just a medal, that's all."

He heard her moving away, and when he opened his eyes, she was standing at the window once more.

"Opa," she said and hurried to the door.

"Opa," Angelo whispered. It seemed the old man really was the only person Katharina had left in her world.

He hears himself breathing, feels the wool of his blue-grey collar scratching his face, and feels the droplets of sweat rolling from underneath his armpits. Under his feet, the explosions from the dynamite throw him off his feet, and pieces of debris fly by his face. The peaks begin to crumble.

Angelo knows these mountains. He has skied them since he was a boy, and that is what he is now, a boy on the day his father took him straight onto the steepest Dolomite slope. When Angelo cries, his father slaps the back of his head, sending him sprawling into the snow.

"Get up," the Colonel orders. "Up on those skis, Angelo! You're not a girl!"

46

Angelo bites the bottom of his lip and gets up, tasting blood. He learns. He wins medals in ski championships, earns medals in school, and receives medals in the war for the dynamite he plants.

Father is never satisfied.

He sends Angelo to tunnel under the Austrian watchtowers so that Angelo can win the war for Italy.

"We're going to flatten the whole of the Marmolada," Angelo tells his battalion, laughing on the outside, terrified inside.

His breathing becomes heavier. He hears the bullets whizzing by before they hit the snow. The glacier is steep, and the Austro-Hungarians have the deadly advantage—aiming their shots down from their forts. His comrades materialise as he flies down the mountain on his skis. He's afraid that he will hurt them; they're so fatigued and malnourished. Giovanni, the Roman who makes them all laugh with his crass jokes and hides pornographic postcards in his helmet, looks like a skeleton. Angelo twists to the left, but then the theologian from Calabria appears from behind a fir. Angelo shakes his head at him, gaining speed, swearing at him. The Calabrian laughs and shouts after Angelo, "How the navy ever sent me to fight in the Alps, I'll never understand!"

The bald Gasparo is standing in the snow, playing his guitar. He opens his mouth to sing and reveals the meaty stub, the remains of his tongue. The air is filled with the sweet breath of death.

On the valley floor, the snow is melting at Angelo's feet. He is in a valley, this valley, and his skis are gone. He is climbing the path along the Karlinbach. He stops to survey the ground below him. He checks his compass and then continues to the next clearing. There it is, the Etsch River and the villages of Graun, Piz, Gorf, Reschen, Spinn, Arlund.

Arlund!

The Reschen and Graun Lakes are still covered with thick steel-coloured ice. He measures. He checks the map. He records. The two lakes crack, they grow, and they fill up the fields and houses between them. Angelo watches, and his heart is racing. Someone is missing. Someone is supposed to be here. Something is wrong, and his heart feels a pain he has never felt before, a longing and sadness. Whoever this person is, he must save them.

As the water rises, a terror builds in him, but before he can turn to run, he feels an impact, sees an arm in ragged clothes. The person swims before him, but Angelo struggles to focus. If he fails, he will die. He feels a punch to his ribs, then a burning sensation and sees the glint of steel. The impact leaves him breathless.

He grabs his side, and blood seeps between his fingertips. He sees the man lunging towards him again. He moves to duck the attack, but in slow motion. He has to raise his arm to protect himself from the knife. There is a sharp pain in his head.

On his knees, he crawls and scrambles. Through the grey fog, Angelo sees the man kicking the snow like a maniac, laughing in absolute silence. Angelo struggles to his feet, stumbles, falls, gets up again, uses the trees to brace himself, and runs for his life.

In the darkness, he calls for his wife. His light.

When the dark broke, it was the blond woman who stood there.

~

In the night, long after Opa had retired, Katharina was awakened by muffled sounds from the farthest room down the hall.

Angelo.

Half-awake, she lit the night lamp and passed her grandfather's room, where he was snoring. The flickering light cast long shadows in the hallway on the way to Uncle Jonas's room.

Angelo was muttering in his sleep, the blankets in a heap on the floor and his forehead burning hot to the touch. Wide awake now, she hurried downstairs and out the door to the well outside. The snow had ceased, with only a few centimetres of it on the ground. That storm had been more bark than bite. With the water, she hurried back to Angelo and applied a wet cloth with one hand while arranging the animal skins over him.

He awoke and stared at her.

"You were so brave. You ran out into that storm to help me, and all you get in reward are torn stitches and another fever. The doctor will come tomorrow, Angelo."

He reached for her with a shaking hand. *"Mia cara."*

Blood rushed into her ears. She sat down on the edge of the bed and covered his hand with hers. *Mia cara*, he'd said. My love.

She led his hand to her heart, and when she looked at him, his eyes were closed again. Through her nightclothes, she could feel his fingers moving. They were on her left breast; she leaned into the touch, dizzy with anticipation, to kiss the top of Angelo's forehead. She allowed her lips to linger, her breath on his warm skin.

The door creaked, and she jerked back. Hund nosed her way into the room. She and the dog stared at one another before Hund lay down with a sigh, her eyebrows twitching as if to avoid looking in the direction of the bed.

Katharina had to leave. She moved to go, but Angelo moaned, calling for her again. She leaned in to kiss his forehead, to comfort him, but it was his mouth she kissed and his lips that opened against hers. Her insides stirred, and a fluttering in her middle made her ache. She wanted those beautiful hands to touch every part of her.

At first she gently kissed his cheeks, his eyelids, then more eagerly the tip of his nose, his lips again, the base of his neck, something wild trying to break free. When she took his chin between her teeth, he jerked his head away with a soft moan, and when he looked at her, she sought his lips out again. His warm and dry lips. The scent of thyme and the soap from her father's shaving kit overrode the smell of fever on him.

"Cara?"

"My love," Katharina whispered.

"Katharina."

"Yes," she breathed.

With half-closed eyes, he arched beneath the covers, and she lifted the sheepskin and the blankets and slipped next to him, aware of his masculine scent, of his heat, and of his nearness. What if he rejected her now? She held her breath, closed her eyes, but opened them again when she felt his hand on the back of her head. He led her to his mouth, and she felt his tongue slip between her lips. The taste of him was medicinal.

Angelo moved his hand along her belly, then reached between her legs. She carefully draped a leg over his torso.

Butterflies. Fields and fields of butterflies.

Beneath her, he was fumbling with his soft trousers. She slipped her nightdress up to her waist, aware of how her breathing was changing. Angelo held her hips as he moved under her, his eyes closed, his hardness between her, and she ached for more of everything he had.

A burning sensation made her suck in her breath, and he opened his eyes to her as if seeing her for the first time.

Her wounds were like his now. Silently, she pleaded for him to be gentle, but he groaned, an angry sound that sent a cold shiver through her. She tried to pull away from the tearing, hot pain. She dug her fingernails into the soft skin in his shoulders, but he did not stop. He pushed against her, his grip on her thighs strong, until he tensed beneath her, grunted, and grew still.

When he released her, Katharina gasped, falling over him. A mixture of wonder, pity, and relief washed over her. The darkness of his skin and the black hairs in the curve of his neck swam before her. She tasted an unfamiliar scent between them, and a bead of sweat rolled down her back, as the pain in her throbbed. When she stood away from his bed, her nightgown fell over her legs, shrouding her shame.

Angelo slowly shook his head, then turned his face to the wall.

"I must go," she choked.

There was no reaction. Her heart racing, she kissed the tips of her fingers and placed them on his cheek. He made no sign that he'd felt it.

As Katharina left him to go back to her own bedroom, Hund scrambled up from the floor, padding close behind her, her nails on the floorboards. *What have you done? What have you done? What have you done!*

6

APRIL 1920, ARLUND

The chirping of birds and the slight creak of the door were what woke him. He opened his eyes, saw the rag poked into the broken windowpane, the crucifix on the wall, and Christ looking tired. The light outside was a white-grey fog. He rolled over and caught sight of the girl's figure before she scurried out the door again. A mug of tea was on the dresser. It had not been a dream. He'd broken more than the window last night. God forgive him.

When he heard Katharina approaching again, he pretended to still be asleep, but even behind closed eyelids he saw her youthful figure, her innocence, and those moments of raw boldness. He threw an arm over his face.

"*Morgen.*" The grandfather.

Angelo's heart leapt, and he opened his eyes to the old man looming over him.

The man's face was scrunched up as if he smelled something bad. In Italian, he said just one word: "How?"

"How what?" Angelo struggled to sit up.

Katharina took a step into the room, as if she'd been waiting outside the door. "How you feel? *Gut?*"

The double entendre of her question in any other situation—
for example, if he were not married—would have made Angelo
laugh. Instead, he kept his guard. "*Gut*," he said.

The grandfather grunted and moved to the window.

Angelo let his eyes linger long enough on the girl to take her
in: the dark-blond braids, her brown eyes, the toned figure of a
hard-working woman. He thought again of her in his bed. As if
reading his mind, she dropped her eyes to the floor.

Once more footsteps treaded in the hallway, and Angelo was
relieved when the doctor walked in.

"Good morning, Signor Grimani," Dr Hanny said, his manner
authoritative. "Signor Thaler tells me you've been taken to bed
again."

Angelo frowned, but Dr Hanny was speaking to Katharina in
German now. What had the girl told the old man?

When the doctor turned back to Angelo, he said, "She says
you were quite a brave fellow, helping her out in the storm." He
looked towards the grandfather, measuring the window.
"Herr Thaler will fix that right up. So shall we take a look at those
stitches? I'm afraid I feel rather badly about that. Usually my
quality of work is much better."

Angelo forced himself to relax. "It's not your fault."

The grandfather and Katharina disappeared behind the
doctor's back as Dr Hanny examined him. "She said you were
quite feverish last night." He put a hand to Angelo's head.

"I'm afraid I was not myself," Angelo muttered.

"Your temperature is normal now."

Old Man Thaler said something to the doctor. Dr Hanny
nodded and replied. The grandfather's tone was then gruffer
with Katharina, and she hung her head, then followed him to the
door. Her eyes locked briefly with Angelo's before she closed it.
He knew that look, and it was too late for him to signal any
semblance of an apology to her.

Angelo braced himself for more pain as Dr Hanny threaded a

needle. The poking and yanking was uncomfortable, and Angelo watched the doctor as he closed the wounds again.

When he finished, Dr Hanny put his things away slowly. He finally snapped his bag shut. "So, Signor Grimani, I am scheduled to pick up some medicines in Meran today, but I can wait. I would suggest one more day in bed, and then I will bring you to the *carabinieri*. Captain Rioba will want a full report about the incident on the mountain."

"By all means it was a crime, not an incident. That thief must be brought to justice. My papers are gone, the ministry's equipment, my money—"

"Yes, yes. All in good time."

"I have to go today." Angelo sat up. At the foot of the bed was a pair of newly knitted socks. He stared at them. "Your stitches are certainly strong enough now. I want to take care of that report as soon as possible. My family has no idea where I am, and I should be back in Bolzano already."

"Bolzano. Of course." The doctor scratched his brow. "Where did you say your hotel was?"

"In the next village. On the way to Meran. I'll need to fetch the rest of my things there."

"Yes, yes. Thing is, I really don't want you bouncing around in my wagon for too long. You need to rest and let the stitches close that wound."

"How far are the barracks?"

Dr Hanny hesitated. "Just down the hill, in between Graun and Reschen."

"I'm very grateful to the Thalers here, but..." Angelo cleared his throat, determined. "I'd like to get down to the barracks and make the report. Then go. Today."

"I don't recommend—"

"Doctor, I insist."

Dr Hanny pursed his lips.

"I'll say my goodbyes," Angelo said, "and then we can go."

"The Thalers have gone into Graun." The doctor indicated the window, "To pick up glass and supplies."

What luck! "Then I ask you to please give them my apologies and my thanks. Give me a hand please."

Before Dr Hanny could hesitate again, Angelo added, "I will make it up to them. I promise."

At the wayward cross, Opa turned towards Graun, but Katharina hung back. She did not want him to see her, could not let it show that she had been changed. The whole village would probably be able to see her desire for Angelo, her guilt pouring out of her.

When Opa spoke, she jumped and picked up her speed to hear him properly.

"These Italians have no sense of taking care of things," he said. "Why didn't he just close the shutters before the storm? First that man breaks my window, and then he's going to build a dam that breaks our backs."

Maybe it was the dam that was bothering Opa then, not her. What a dam would mean to the villages of Reschen and Graun, Katharina wasn't sure. Surely the Italians would find a way to salvage the valley and still get the electricity they were in need of. Either way, the men would take care of it. After what had happened last night—a night that had put her somewhere between legitimate and illegitimate womanhood—she had no room in her head to worry about a dam.

At the memory of lying next to Angelo, she sighed.

Her grandfather's step faltered. "You're right. No use talking about it now. That's all we do around here anyway. Talk, talk, talk. And write letters to newspapers. And what have we learned? That the outrage of a few hundred thousand people who've been fleeced by foreign politicians is of no concern to the rest of the world, that's what."

They walked on awhile before he spoke again. "It's good that you came with me."

"I was meaning to visit Jutta anyway," she lied. She was in love and there was no one to tell, except maybe if she told Angelo how she felt he would... She shook her head. He was Italian. After all that had happened here with the Italians, it was impossible.

At the glassmaker's, she touched the objects on the shelves, but all she wanted was to look Angelo in the eyes again and know what last night had meant to him. A glass figurine of a dancer tipped and nearly dropped to the floor.

"Quit your fidgeting and go to the seamstress," Opa said. "See if she has some cloth for a new blouse."

Katharina did as she was told and eventually found the fabric she would need. She met Opa near the miller's again and looked up the hills towards Arlund, towards home. Where Angelo...waited?

Opa frowned at her. "Go on to the Post Inn." His voice was irate. "I'll meet you there."

On her way to Jutta's, Katharina avoided making eye contact with the few *carabinieri* loitering under the oak tree that stood between the church and the inn. Could *they* tell what she had done? Could *they* see that she was a woman now? One of them muttered something, but she hurried past. It was Jutta she was anxious to see. Jutta, who knew everything.

Katharina had once overheard her mother talking about Jutta to another friend. "She's got sharp eyes, that Jutta, a sharp mind and a sharp tongue," she'd said. "She can be your best friend or your worst enemy, but rarely is she something in between."

To Katharina, Jutta was her best friend, had indeed become a second mother to her since Katharina's mother's death. If Jutta asked why Katharina looked so different—if Jutta noticed—Katharina would tell her everything. Wouldn't she?

When Katharina reached the inn, she saw Jutta standing in the garden out back, examining the cellar door. She was so deep in thought that she barely greeted Katharina in return. From the barn came the sound of hammering.

"Who's in the barn, Jutta?"

"Hans is building a fortress for me. Would you just look at this?"

"Why are you looking at boot prints?" Katharina handed Jutta the kilo of butter she'd brought with her and peered closer to the ground. Goosebumps ran up her arms. She recognised the pattern of the soles. "Jutta, who is this?"

"I have no idea, but he's a big man. This is the second time this week he's stolen from my pantry. Broke the lock, see?"

Katharina's mind reeled.

Gathering up her skirt, Jutta marched to near the barn, shouting, "Hans, I'd put a hunting party together and start looking for lost relatives of yours. These tracks out here could only belong to a yeti or your folk."

The hammering ceased, and Hans stepped out with that rocking gait as if his hips were welded to their joints. He walked past them to the cellar door, and Jutta brushed her hand on his arm as he passed, but Hans did not seem to notice.

She put her hand to her cheek. "Why am I so cruel to him?"

Katharina was struck giddy by all the revelations. "You're not unkind, Jutta. You love him."

"Nonsense."

"Come now. It's true. He only provokes you because you must feel something for him, but you're just too wrapped up in…"

Jutta's look was challenging but not hostile. "Wrapped up in what?"

"I don't know."

"Oh-ho. Don't start something you can't finish, child, especially if you're going to claim expertise in love."

Katharina opened her mouth, but Jutta was already moving to the kitchen door. Jutta was right. What did Katharina know about love?

In the kitchen, Jutta said with a lowered voice, "I heard that you found an Italian man. Stabbed."

Her heart missed a beat. "He's doing better."

"Well then. What's he like?"

Should she tell her? Now? She sat down at the table and picked up the saltshaker. "He's very nice, Jutta. Whoever hurt him deserves to be punished."

Jutta half smiled and huffed, "Is that what you think?"

"Yes." Why would anyone defend a thief, and a violent one at that? "Wouldn't you like to know who is stealing your things and bring him to justice? Because I'm very certain it's the same person."

Jutta raised an eyebrow and moved to the table. "Why would you say that?"

"The footprints outside," Katharina said. "They're the same boot sole I saw in the snow, up on the mountain." She told her about the day she had found Angelo Grimani.

Jutta cocked her head. "I wasn't really joking when I told Hans he should begin looking for lost relatives of his. The Glockners were all big and, well, so are the Hannys."

Katharina laughed. "Dr Hanny? That's ridiculous."

"No. Fritz Hanny."

"Fritz? Your husband? But you don't really think…"

"That would be pretty amazing, wouldn't it?"

"But he's—"

"Nobody knows what *he is*," Jutta said. "Alois's father disappeared, but that doesn't mean the coward's not lurking about, profiting from the smuggler's way."

"What are the chances…"

Jutta grimaced. "I'm going to find out. Coffee? I've got to use up this roasted barley. The fruit seller is coming next week, and I'm going to buy up his fig coffee this time."

Jutta went into the pantry and brought out plum dumplings before putting the coffee on. Watching her, Katharina remembered Fritz Hanny and the conversations Jutta and Katharina's mother had had about how Fritz did not behave like a God-fearing man. But there had been no sign of Fritz Hanny in almost five years. In fact, Jutta awaited the day she could get the township to officially register his death. Then the inn would be hers.

"Who else has tall people? Big people?" Katharina asked.

"Not many of us here," Jutta said. She tested the enamel pot. "Your mama was tall, like you."

"Jutta, don't joke about this. This person almost killed Angelo."

"Angelo?"

"Mr Grimani."

"You used his Christian name."

Katharina swallowed. "He made me call him that."

Jutta put her hands on her hips. "What else did he make you do?"

"Nothing."

"Don't bite your lip like that. I know there's something wrong when you bite your lip like that."

Katharina looked down at her hands. Jutta's shoes came into view at the edge of the table.

"Look at me, girl. What else did he make you do?"

"Nothing." He'd not *made* her do anything.

"You were alone with him up there for some time during the storm. Katharina, did he touch you?"

She blinked. "No." Too soft. Not enough outrage.

Jutta looked at her as if she'd already known something Katharina had told her. "But you like him, don't you? Is he a good-looking man? Handsome? Exotic? Like our Captain Rioba?"

"Captain Rioba is old."

Jutta's smile had something cold in it. "Distinguished, we could say. He's distinguished, but you're right, too old for you."

Her voice dropped a decibel. "If there were ever thieves or killers in this valley, it's those Italians. Don't you go falling in love with any of them." She folded her arms. "Not our old settlers, mind you. They were always good people. These new ones is what I mean, the ones who think they have a right to our land—those are the ones we don't want to appease. In any way. Do you understand me? Even Marianna would agree with me."

Katharina looked down at her lap. Why did Jutta have to bring up Katharina's mother? She was feeling ashamed enough as it was.

"Being smitten with a man whose life you've helped save," Jutta continued, "well, there's nothing wrong with that, but he's going back to Bozen. No, sorry. It's called *Bolzano* now. He's going back to Bolzano, and if he's smart and even a smidge honest, he's going to take a message to his big boss. The Reschen Valley is no place for a dam. Those Italians have yet to see how we really fight."

Katharina didn't care about the dam. She wanted to get back to Angelo. When Opa came through the kitchen door, she leapt up.

Jutta's eyebrows arched high on her forehead. "Someone light your chair on fire, Katharina?" She turned to Opa. "Greetings, Johannes. Come in and have a bite."

"No thank you, Jutta," Opa said. "Work's calling. Katharina can stay awhile. She knows the way home."

"That's all right." Katharina hurried to him. "I'll come with you."

"What? So soon?" Jutta put her hands on her hips and looked at Opa. "Johannes, I think the girl is smitten by that Italian man in your house. You keep him on a short lead. 'Specially how pretty she's made herself look today."

Opa scowled but did not look in Katharina's direction, which was good because now her face was burning up.

Instead, he asked, "Jutta, did you warn the smugglers?"

"We have a problem, Johannes. I suspect the thief that's been raiding my cellar is the same one who"—Jutta jerked her head at the window—"you know, tried to rob your Italian guest up there."

Opa looked at both of them and stepped into the kitchen, the door closing softly behind him. "Any ideas of who it might be?"

Katharina wanted to say something, but Jutta started first.

"Someone big. Like a Glockner. Or a Hanny."

"Fritz," Katharina said.

Opa stared at Jutta.

"That's what my gut is telling me," Jutta said. "It'd be fitting for that man to come and steal from me, from the chapel. And the violence, well, that's telling, isn't it?"

"That's a serious accusation, Jutta," Opa said. "And we haven't seen hide nor hair of him in what? Three, four years?"

"Four," Jutta said. "Five next March."

"That long?"

"That long."

Opa scratched his head. "But someone would tell you. If anyone saw him, they'd tell you."

"Maybe." Jutta shrugged. "Maybe not. But if anyone in this valley knows that Fritz is about and they don't tell me, they'll be sorry for it."

"We need to report this to the authorities," Katharina said. "Mr Grimani's attacker should be brought to justice."

Opa was still acting as if she weren't in the room. "Jutta, did you talk to Hans about this?"

She shook her head. "Katharina's the one who recognised the tracks outside. I'm just thinking aloud."

"Well then," Opa muttered. "If Fritz is out there, we'll find him."

~

On the way back to Arlund, the sun was high in the sky, and Katharina's stomach felt empty despite the plum dumplings and coffee at Jutta's. Her grandfather lagged behind, so she had to wait at the wayward cross for him.

"You bought a bag of *Riebl*," she said when he reached her. Now that they were heading home, she felt lighter, as if she could skip all the way back to the *Hof*. Angelo waited there. "I'll make the porridge with some of the applesauce from the other night."

Her grandfather nodded and continued walking up the slope.

"I could kill a chicken?" she said, following behind him. "Signor—I mean, Mr—Grimani could use the meat."

Her grandfather shifted the basket on his back. "You needn't bother about that. Saw Dr Hanny's wagon going south with Mr Grimani in it."

No! Katharina choked. "When?"

"On my way to Jutta's."

He couldn't. He wouldn't. When she managed to get her voice back, it sounded too desperate. "Surely he isn't able to travel already?"

Her grandfather jutted his chin. "It's for the best. He needs to get back to his family."

They were just beneath the *Hof* and Hund came running from the yard, barking. Opa spoke to her. But Katharina had stopped in her tracks. Her stomach stirred dangerously.

Family. Of course Angelo had family.

She had lain with a man who was most likely married, maybe even had children. As she trudged behind Opa and the dog, everything seemed louder. The swish of her skirt. The crunching under her boots. When they reached the crest of their drive, her heart fell. Dr Hanny's wagon was indeed no longer there. She closed her eyes and held her breath, afraid she would crumple from the sobs inside her. Her grandfather knew how she felt about Angelo—she was certain of that. Perhaps he knew even more.

Without a word, she stumbled through the doorway, smarting from the falls she was taking. On the chair next to the tiled oven was the blanket Angelo had used. Upstairs, the bed was empty, the sheepskins neatly folded. Her socks. Her heart lurched. He'd taken her socks.

She ran down the stairs as her grandfather hung up his hat. This morning he had behaved like a stone-faced, distant stranger, but now she saw the way his mouth turned downwards and how his eyes glistened when he looked up at her.

Her chest heaved with the crying she had to do. He was not angry with her. He was grieving for her. If he really knew what she had done, her actions from the night before would have serious implications. This was not child's play, her affair with Angelo. Nobody in this valley would tolerate such a thing.

"Opa," she whispered. "I must see him...I have to..." The words "just once" were barely audible in her own ears.

Opa shook his head as if it hurt his neck, and she thought he would crumble before her, her bull of a grandfather, but Katharina could not apologise for what she was about to do. She had to find Angelo. She ran past Opa and into the barn where their old bicycle leaned against one of the posts. She pushed it out of the barnyard, flinching at the thought of her grandfather coming behind her, his hand raised to her, bringing it down on her. But he did not come after her, and she did not look back at the house as she mounted the bicycle and pedalled down the drive.

How long ago had Angelo and Dr Hanny left? They must surely be as far as St. Valentin by now, if not farther. She knew how she could get to them, and fast. She steered the bicycle towards the steep fields, every rut and stone bumping and jarring her thoughts. She just wanted to touch him, just one more time really. She wanted to look Angelo in the eye and wish him well, to let him know that despite what they had done, she would not be ashamed of it. The folks be damned. *Let he who is without sin...*

As the muscles in her thighs burned and her breathing turned into great gulps of air, she fell into a trance, saw Dr Hanny's wagon in her mind, with Angelo at the doctor's side. She would shout at them to stop. Angelo would be the only one to hear her, and before the wagon could even halt, he would leap off and meet her, relieved that she had come. He would embrace her— she pedalled faster and her heart soared—and she would lay a hand on his heart and feel it beating. The picture in her mind was so real that the tears it caused blinded her for a moment and she saw nothing. What would happen after they said goodbye?

Katharina stopped pedalling and coasted for some metres, clutching the handlebars so hard it hurt.

There was nothing after that, she thought. Just a void. A big, black, unforgiving void.

A police transport passed her, a number of *carabinieri* inside, and Katharina heard the taunting shouts, but it was the wagon she saw beyond them that made her cheeks burn. She pushed on, riding the bicycle at a dangerous speed through the fields of St. Valentin.

When the wagon slowed down and Dr Hanny turned in his seat towards her, her own voice startled her.

"Stop! Stop! You forgot something!"

The wagon rolled to a halt, and the horses pawed the ground, snorting. Angelo was indeed next to Dr Hanny, but he was not turning to her. He did not get off the wagon and run to her. When she reached them, the bicycle fell clumsily from her and thudded to the road. She stood, straddling its frame and gasping for breath.

"You…you…forgot something," she said, staring at the back of Angelo's head.

Dr Hanny turned and said something in Italian to him.

Angelo shrugged, then turned to her, his face calm and only the slightest bit curious. Her legs shook as if the ground were crumbling beneath her. It did not matter one bit to him that he'd

had to leave without saying goodbye, even with the assumption
that they would most likely never see one another again, never
touch each other again. She ripped her gaze away, the ground
swirling beneath her tears. She heard something and saw Dr
Hanny's lips moving.

"Katharina? What did Signor Grimani forget?"

She turned this way and that. Only the bicycle was to be had,
and it was certainly not Angelo's. She looked at her dusty fists.
Now Angelo softly said something to Dr Hanny, and she heard
the squeaking of the wagon's seat, but she did not dare look in
the direction of his voice. She was making everything worse for
herself. Struggling to lift the bike up, she only wanted to flee.

"Katharina," he said. Water over a creek bed.

She felt him standing between Dr Hanny and her. She saw his
hands reaching for the bicycle handle to help her with the
contraption. She shook her head. *Let it go. Let it go.*

"Katharina."

Mia cara! Why not *mia cara* now?

Her black leather shoes burned her feet and faded in and out
before her swimming tears. If she looked up at him, she would
throw herself at him.

"Katharina, *la mia famiglia…*"

In his words, she heard such regret that she looked up. He did
not feel what she did.

Angelo rolled his eyes in the direction of Dr Hanny behind
him and held out an open hand. In it was his war medal.

Understanding the charade he was asking her to play,
Katharina reached into her dress pocket, laid her palm over his,
and gave him nothing.

7

MAY 1920, BOZEN/BOLZANO

P anting steam, the train slowed down as it neared Bolzano, the engine's exhaustion reflecting how tired Angelo felt. It had been an ordeal: the hospital in Meran, the questions he'd had to answer, the lies he'd had to write in his telegrams home.

He craned his head to look out the window and watched the city sign grow nearer. Out with *Bozen*. In with *Bolzano*. As if painting over the German names of cities here was as easy as changing a pair of shoes. Eighteen months since the Armistice. The nationalists were not wasting any time.

He gathered his bags and prepared to get off, but sat back down when he saw her. Picking Chiara out in even the most crowded places was easy. Some might claim it was because of her red hair and fair, northern-Italian features, but he knew it was more than that. Chiara drew people to her, just as she did him now. She was his light.

He watched her standing on the platform in a pale, shimmering green dress. Her hand shaded her eyes from the sun, and despite her hidden face, he could see she was worried. His chest constricted. He'd been wrong in thinking that he'd put his mistake behind him. Now that he saw his wife again, Angelo was overwhelmed by the guilt of what he had done, of what he was about to do.

He opened his bag; in the inside pocket was the pair of socks Katharina had knitted for him. He glanced around, felt ridiculous as soon as the idea of giving them to one of the Tyrolean mothers crossed his mind, and slipped them onto the baggage hold above him as discreetly as he could. They did not fit into his story in any way.

It was only as he stepped off the train that Angelo realised his in-laws were also waiting for him. Pietro, Chiara's father, ran his hand over his silver hair and straightened his already impeccable suit. Beatrice, Chiara's mother, was on his arm. She left her husband's elbow and marched up to Angelo.

"Mama," Chiara called after her. "Be careful."

"Of course I'll be careful," Beatrice said as she palmed Angelo's face. "She thinks I will hurt you. Welcome home, Angelo. We've been so anxious." She smiled and rose on tiptoe to kiss his cheeks before telling Pietro to take the bags.

When Chiara reached them, she put her hands in Angelo's. "You look exhausted."

"You look wonderful."

"We've been so worried." Her smile did not erase the frown.

He leaned into her and kissed her cheeks, then brushed his lips against hers. The scent of her, delicate and sweet, was so familiar that he took in a deep breath to stop the threat of tears.

"You're here now," she said and lightly kissed him. "Let's get you home."

Pietro clapped him on the shoulder and embraced him gently, then bent down to retrieve the bags.

"Pietro, about the equipment," Angelo started.

"Never mind the equipment. We're just happy nothing more serious happened to you."

Chiara took Angelo's elbow. "What did the doctors say?"

"Some deep cuts. A concussion. But mostly bruises."

"That must have been quite a fall," Pietro said.

Angelo smiled at Chiara. "You've got quite the scarred man, I'm afraid. First, war scars, and now, this silly accident."

Beatrice squeezed his arm. "Never mind. They're the stories you'll tell your children."

He doubted it.

"Papa's brought the car," Chiara said. "Let's get you home. We'll talk about everything later."

They drove the brown-and-red Ansaldo the short distance to Villa Adige, and he had the feeling again that the events in Arlund were fading away from his consciousness the way a dream did when one awoke. They turned into Selig Heinrichstrasse, lined with large Austro-Hungarian villas with gables and towers and decorated, tiled rooftops. Theirs came into view—a more Italian-looking structure with a two-storied veranda facing a small vineyard in the southeast garden. The iron fence was lined with oleander and Chiara's rosebushes. He let his eyes roam over the details: the massive cedar in the northern part of the house, the rose trellis at the front of the walk, the front stoop with the rounded, heavy wooden door and cast-iron knocker. Before the d'Oros had bought it, the villa had belonged to an Austro-Hungarian merchant who appreciated Roman architecture. Either way, it was nothing like the farmers' houses up north, and Angelo was happy to be back; it was time to establish some normalcy again.

They unloaded the car, and he watched Chiara stop at the trellis and examine the buds, thin pink stripes hard to miss.

"Look, darling," she said. "These will be blooming by the end of the week."

He reached for her hand, and they walked up the stoop. Beatrice announced that dinner would be served at six before disappearing with Pietro into their downstairs apartments. Angelo and Chiara climbed the stairs to their floor, and he went directly to his dressing room. When he stepped out, Chiara stood at the vanity table.

"I found something of yours," she called through the mirror. When she turned towards him, one hand was behind her back. "You thought you'd lost it, remember? The last time we were at the baths?"

"My ring?"

She opened her fist. "Your ring."

He reached for it, but Chiara snapped her hand shut.

"Don't ever lose it again," she chided. "Or I'll have to think you're up to no good when you're travelling." She kissed his cheek, then pressed the ring into his hand and moved to finish undressing him.

No good indeed. He sucked in his breath, and she looked up at him.

"Does it hurt?"

He shook his head and watched her face as she lifted the bandage on his chest. Alongside the scabs, two angry red lines flared on his skin.

"Good God, Angelo—"

"It's just a scratch really." And he remembered his shirt and the coat. They had been ruined, Katharina had told him, so she had disposed of them. He turned away from his wife. "My head hurts more than anything."

"I'll run you a bath."

"Chiara," he said, slipping his wedding band onto his finger. He heard the water running and went to the door. "Chiara."

She looked up from the faucet, her fingers splayed out under the running water.

"I will never leave you again. Ever."

Chiara smiled and kissed him. "I knew you would come home safely. And these," she said, tracing her index finger just above the lines of his scabs, "they will heal in no time."

Though Chiara's eyes were a light green-blue colour, when

something moved her, they turned dark, almost black, whereas Katharina's eyes, even when pained, remained a soft amber brown. With a sting to his chest, Angelo pictured Katharina standing over the bicycle, how small she'd grown before he turned around and forced himself to put her behind him.

"What are you thinking, my love?" Chiara said. "Where are you?"

"I'm sorry." He faced her. "I shouldn't have left you."

"Since when have you worried about me on my own?" She rubbed his arms. "You're home now, and everything's fine."

Angelo escaped into the tub, the water still rushing from the tap.

His wife moved behind him, took a sponge, and began washing his back. "You seem terribly sad. Tell me what's wrong?"

Chilled, he took Chiara's hand from behind him and placed it over his heart. "You're beautiful," he said and kissed the inside of her wrist. Lily of the valley.

"Angelo? There is something I must ask you."

Blood rushed to his head, and he closed his eyes. He was giving too much away. Her hand came under his chin and lifted it. When he opened his eyes to her, he was prepared to lie.

Over the sound of running water, she said, "Would you be happier today if I told you we're expecting a baby?"

A gate slammed shut between himself and that image of the girl in the Reschen Valley. He now stood on the side of salvation. An opportunity to make this up to Chiara. He'd be the best possible father, the most loving husband...

He rose and pulled Chiara up with him and into his arms, but she lost her balance. He held on to her tightly. It was too late. One foot of hers, still in a boot, landed in the tub, and as she wavered in his arms, the second one followed. Her laugh was like nothing he'd never heard from her before—unburdened, gay.

He held on to her. In that tub full of water, he held on.

Before dinner, Angelo endured all the chatter and news over champagne. By the time the family was served their main course, however, talk turned to his trip and the accident. He was ready for it, easily weaving his half lies as if observing the scene from outside himself. He gave honest answers as long as they were not directly related to the attack or the events thereafter.

"It's remote up in the Reschen Valley, not like around Bolzano or Merano," he said when Chiara asked what the landscape was like. "After the convent in Wattles, it gets rough. High plateaus, high mountains. Lots of woods and meadow. Not like the apple orchards and vineyards here. Ideal for what they do, I suppose, which is dairy production, cattle breeding, farming."

"Some of the best cattle around," Pietro said, cutting into his veal.

"And the people?" Chiara wanted to know. "What are they like?"

Angelo shrugged. "They're people."

"I mean"—she put down her fork—"is there unrest amongst them? The Tyroleans are such an industrious folk. How are they dealing with the economy? And the new government? What are people talking about up there?"

Beatrice cleared her throat. "Your husband has just come home. Your father and I are celebrating the coming of our first grandchild. Must we discuss politics now?"

Pietro chuckled. "That's my daughter."

Beatrice turned her scowl on her husband. "And you're always encouraging her. You know what that Mussolini character says. It's the Socialists, he says, those liberals, who are destroying Italy."

"You don't honestly believe that, mother," Chiara said. "Tell me you don't believe that."

Beatrice looked down at her plate.

"Of course she doesn't," Pietro offered. "We raised you to be kind and good to people. Which is what you are."

"Mama, remember that we used to be the foreigners here once," Chiara said. "And we were never treated with anything but respect. I simply don't understand why—"

"Darling." Angelo stroked Chiara's shoulder. "I'm awfully afraid that with my rudimentary German, I couldn't pick up on much."

He saw her fist clench under the table as she stared at her plate. "You're right. How silly of me." She picked up her fork again and raked her greens.

What had the people been like, his wife wanted to know. Unrest indeed. Someone had nearly killed him. But there was no reason to cause them any more worry than necessary. They would inevitably want to know more, and he was not about to volunteer more.

Someone chimed a spoon against crystal, and Angelo looked up to see Pietro holding up his wine.

"I propose a toast, to our lovely daughter and favourite son-in-law."

"I'm your only son-in-law," Angelo said. Thank God they were changing the subject.

Pietro beamed. "Fine, then to my favourite employee at the Ministry of Civil Engineering."

"I'll drink to that," he said.

Beatrice raised her glass towards Chiara. "I'm sorry for my harsh tone, my dear. I'm proud of you. Really, I am."

Chiara raised her glass, but her mouth was still drawn tight. Under the table, Angelo reached for her, and without turning to him, she slipped her hand into his.

After dinner, Angelo and Pietro moved to the deep leather chairs in the study as the women retired to the salon. A bottle of grappa in his hand, Pietro poured for them both and then raised his glass to Angelo. "To your future child."

"To your first grandchild."

When they had each taken a sip, Angelo sensed a change in his father-in-law's mood.

"The Colonel was here shortly before we received your telegram."

Angelo's father. Of course. Who else could dampen a festive spirit so quickly? "Is that so? Did you tell him about my circumstances then?"

"I have assured both your parents that you were well enough to come home." Pietro raised his grappa to his lips. "I'm sure they'll come by tomorrow."

"Wonderful," Angelo said sarcastically. He twisted the stem of his glass. "What did the Colonel want from you?"

"The usual. He wants the Electrical Consortium to control the terms of the damming project in Gleno—who gets to bid on it, who will run the project, and so on."

"I asked him to stop pushing this. Just because he's the consortium's president, he can't go about dictating the terms of state-run projects. You're the minister, Pietro. He needs to remember that."

"Your father is a self-made man, Angelo. A representative of the rising middle class. He didn't get that way by following the rules. Besides, he believes in rebuilding this country. He's just doing his job, and"—Pietro smiled—"like any military man, the Colonel feels the bureaucrats stand in the way. Like most of the country does these days. I'm used to that."

"Doing his job? You mean ensuring that his cohorts and power seekers get all the work. I don't mean to play with the word power here, Pietro, but these supposed philanthropists want to set up a monopoly. Anyone can see that. You needn't defend him. Besides"—Angelo leaned forward—"the Colonel won't be happy about being in the middle of any class. He wants the top, Pietro."

His father-in-law put his glass back on the side table. "Since the war, we've been putting everything into question. The Crown. The parliament. Our armies. Our colonies. The capitalists and the Communists. The schools and the churches. That castle of idealism we built to convince ourselves that the war was righteous and good is crumbling right before us."

"We might have bowed out, Pietro. The Colonel claims we settled on the goal of losing as little as possible. That said, I do believe we must Italianise our newly gained frontiers as quickly as possible."

"Not without a struggle from the Tyroleans," Pietro said. "They're not going to give up their autonomy just because we say so. This treaty, Angelo, is forcing a new world order on us, and everyone is trying to make sense of it. In the meantime, men like your father are snatching the opportunity to position themselves in a way that people of your—I'm so sorry to say this— background have never had before. The old families are in a panic because they can't stop the changes that are coming." He swept the room with his arm. "To be perfectly honest with you, son, I don't know how much longer this will all last. We must all find a new way for ourselves now."

Angelo glanced around the room. The almost ostentatious way he lived now, thanks to the d'Oros' money, the decorum he'd adopted, was absolutely contrary to what he'd grown up with, not to mention what he'd just left up north. He pictured the Thalers' rustic wooden house, the absolute simplicity. The storm. Katharina.

In the Reschen Valley, he realised now, he'd felt something. Free?

Angelo's head swam as if he'd just been shaken upside down

and set upright again. The new Italy in the making. He was now a part of all that, but where was his place really?

"Angelo? You look rather unwell."

He was. "You know what's wrong?"

His father-in-law's face remained blank.

"The nationalists accuse anyone who does not stand with them of being traitors, whilst the Communists and liberals beat up war veterans. The middle class is terrified of the workers. The workers abhor the middle class. The monarchies and noble families are collapsing, as you said. And my father? He and people like him are the Trojan horse.

"He was the supervisor at that power company in Milan before the war, and since we've moved here, he's got the consortium thinking we can keep up with the Americans in building up our industry. Whilst everyone else is too busy fighting one another, people like my father are manoeuvring—"

"Some people call him a visionary."

"Did he try to bribe you? Try to convince you to sell the Gleno project to a private enterprise? Because that'd be his way."

Pietro raised his eyes and made a dismissing gesture. "Angelo, come now. It's not all so dramatic as that. If I got upset every time a politician or some official tried to twist the process, I'd have given up long ago. You must learn to play their game, Angelo. Believe it or not, Colonel Nicolo Grimani is not exactly the only calculating man around. Take Herr Schneider from Schneider Electric. He approached me, months before your father did, wanting to know how they could secure the bid as soon as the Gleno project was approved."

This was surprising. "Survival of the fittest, I suppose."

Pietro chuckled. "Don't be so hard on people. Beatrice and I have been living here for three decades, and since the invention of *Speck*, the Tyroleans know how to oil the wheels of government."

Angelo laughed a little.

"I believe they even pay their penance with that bacon."

Angelo took the bottle and poured each of them another grappa. "So what are Schneider's chances?"

His father-in-law turned serious. "I trust Schneider. I know their work from years of dealing with his company. In fact"—he raised a finger—"they were the original winners of the bid when the Austrians first put the Reschen project forward. This is another matter I'd like to talk to you about tonight. As for people like Schneider, things are changing. They would have been a sure runner in the Gleno Dam project, but they don't have a chance now, I'm afraid."

"The Colonel will get it. My father always wins."

Pietro leaned back and sighed. "Some of my good colleagues —talented men—are being pushed out of the ministry not just because they don't *speak* Italian but because they're *not* Italian." He shook his head and downed his glass. "I don't like it, to tell you the truth. It speaks against everything the Versailles Treaty promised. And this Italianisation program? They change the names of the rivers and mountains, then the cities, and now the people."

"What do you mean, the people?"

Pietro tapped his chin. After a moment, he said, "You're to keep this to yourself. It would only upset Chiara. You know how she feels about her Tyrolean friends being alienated. And Beatrice is nervous about the *fascisti* and their threats against the liberals, so, naturally, she's worried about Chiara."

Angelo nodded.

"It seems that, after the official annexation is to take place in October," Pietro said, "all the German family names ought to be changed into Italian ones."

Angelo turned his thoughts to Katharina, again. What would such a woman do if she were told she would have to change her name? She probably would if it meant a better chance at snagging him. She had chased after him! What had she believed? That he would take her with him? That he'd have stayed on with her because of one night?

Angelo shook himself away from the events in the Reschen Valley. "What does this mean for someone like Schneider then?"

"Regretfully, he'll be called Tailor Electric." Pietro smiled and lifted his palms, as if in surrender. "If you ask me, I would prefer to see Schneider get the upcoming projects. Yet, the consortium—"

"Is made up of Italians," Angelo finished. "They won't let it happen."

Pietro nodded and folded his hands into his lap. "Listen, your father—"

"My father." Angelo slumped back into the settee.

"Your father came to talk to me about the Reschen Valley project as well because he's got some other ideas for it." Pietro seemed to be choosing his words carefully, and this put Angelo on the alert again. "He asked to see the results of your work before you officially report them to the ministry."

"He has no right."

"I told him that he'll receive the project specifications publicly just like everyone else. And he accepted my word."

Angelo smirked. "That's quite generous of him. So what grand idea has my father got now?"

"Automobile factories, airplanes, heavy machinery."

"He's interested in manufacturing now?"

"No, he's interested in selling the electricity to the factories."

"Sell it? How? He'll *earn* from building the Gleno Dam, from the other projects we have in the works. But selling electricity? That's a power company."

"He's been offered a position on the board of a new electrical enterprise. He's been asked to scout out possible reservoirs to buy off the state."

Angelo stared at him. "What does the Reschen Lake project have to do with this?"

"Your father wants us to consider adjusting the proposed height."

Angelo set his glass down. "I'm chief engineer, not him. I went up there to see whether the project would even be feasible as those kaiser lovers had proposed it, and he's already changing it?"

"First tell me what you know."

"What I was able to survey before I was, well, injured was that the original plan would be sufficient."

Pietro nodded. "Five metres then?"

"Yes, five metres would be more than enough to connect the two lakes of Reschen and Graun and create enough electricity all the way south to Bolzano. The problem, like it was for the Austro-Hungarians, is the waterways. I don't have a solution yet, but if we can find a way to minimise the damage to the wetlands and to the agricultural fields, well, we have a chance. Compensation and relocation would cost some, but I believe it will be worth it." Angelo remembered Dr Hanny's surprise. "The locals don't seem to know we are bringing this project up again."

His father-in-law nodded. "We're keeping it low profile for now. No need to irritate them until we've made our analyses. When the annexation has been signed in, we'll get the process started."

"You said the Colonel has some other proposal."

"He would like," Pietro started, "to see the Reschen Valley provide electricity to the entire state."

"Of the Tyrolean province."

"Of Italy."

Christ, his father was either ambitious or thought he was above the laws of nature. "Pardon me, but how?"

Pietro looked cautious. "By connecting Lower Lake to the Reschen and Graun lakes."

"The Lower Lake? You mean in Haider?" Angelo saw an aerial of the valley in his mind. "Wait a minute, Pietro. There are seven towns and villages up there around those lakes. We would have to do some major work on the waterways then." He could see it, that nightmare he'd had, watching the valley fill up, the water rising. And that feeling...that feeling that someone important was missing, someone he had to save. His skin prickled, sweat broke out on his forehead, and his head ached.

"It's a proposal—"

"It's preposterous, is what it is. Just look at what's at stake here. We'd have to flood out the whole valley. Where does he— where do *you*—plan to relocate hundreds of families? Farmers with land?"

"The Colonel suggested sending a new surveillance team. With some experts from the consortium to do a complete collateral damage analysis." Pietro sat back. "Angelo, when you've recovered and rested—"

"No. No. No. I am not going with them. I want nothing more to do with this. Send someone else from the ministry. A risk assessor. Better yet, send one of the more assertive Tyroleans. That will keep my father busy."

A sharp pain throbbed in his head again. He placed a hand over where his wound was. When Pietro did not respond, Angelo stood up again. "Chiara's expecting our first child. I'm not leaving her now. Besides, I already know what it's like to be commanded under my father, remember?"

"That was war, Angelo. You were just following orders."

Angelo bristled. More than anything, he hated that excuse. He turned to Pietro. "You don't see it. The Colonel's sneaking behind the backs of the people who live there. We have people in our own ministry who are blocking the way to a fair and civil process. We don't want to add my father to the list of conflicts. As minister, you must put a stop to this."

Pietro stood up. "I'll do what I can. In the meantime, I would encourage you to put yourself into a position where you can keep an eye on things. That is, if you really care about what's going to happen to that valley. Being there yourself may have its advantages."

"If he gets his hands on me again..."

Pietro sighed and leaned on the arm of the settee. "You can handle your father. You're a good man, Angelo. The people in the Reschen Valley would trust you."

Angelo felt doomed. Certainly he could have built up trust amongst the people, but he had just left *her* without an explanation. What if Katharina came after him or, worse yet, her grandfather did? The other men in that valley. He'd seen them. He did not want to cross them in the least.

"Pietro, I know how the Colonel operates."

"When he gets the contract...not *if*, Angelo—when." His father-in-law's voice became gentler. "Listen, you have a chance to give that organisation some soul."

"He'd never give me that much power."

"Every father wants his son to succeed, Angelo."

"If you believe that, then you do not know Nicolo Grimani."

8

MAY 1920, GRAUN

F rom the *Stube*, a man burst into laughter. Jutta stopped stirring the goulash and handed the spoon to Sara.

"Sara, watch Alois for me. I'm going to check and see what all the raucous is about." She rubbed a hand over her son's shaven head, the dark stubs already softer, and went to check on the men in her dining room.

When she'd last left them, Martin Noggler and Kaspar Ritsch had been in deep discussion about the dam, word having got out that there had been a surveyor in the valley. But when she walked into the *Stube* now, Johannes Thaler was at the *Stammtisch*. The playing cards were in the middle, still stacked, and someone had fetched glasses of wine, which were now mostly empty. They were oblivious to her.

"Let them," Martin Noggler cried and slapped his knee. The blacksmith's nose was red, and one earlobe had also turned pink, bright against his copper-coloured hair. "Just let them. They'll spend all their money just to find that the ground beneath us is too porous. Those Italians think they're smarter than us. They think we're just a bunch of provincial peasants and don't know our land."

Kaspar Ritsch lifted a finger, his face rugged with worry lines. "We already paid the geologists from Munich once. All the ministry in Bozen needs to do is ask for those reports."

Johannes Thaler waved a dismissive hand. "Let it be. Stubbornness is the wasted energy of fools."

Martin Noggler howled again, and Jutta stepped in.

"All right, let's get you home, shall we?"

Kaspar Ritsch gave her a sorrowful look. "His would be the first to go," he whispered.

"First of what to go?" Jutta asked.

"His house."

"I know that, but the dam will never be built." Her words sounded hollow, even to her.

"I'll take care of him," Johannes Thaler said.

"I'll get you all some water. You're wasting yourselves away with this wine." Then she whispered closer to his ear, "Did you and Hans find anything? Any sign of, you know, that thief?"

Johannes Thaler shook his head.

Jutta sniffed. "He's out there. I can smell him."

Late afternoon, the postal wagon rolled up past the church, and Jutta wiped her wet hands on the kitchen towel before going out to meet it. The postman would probably need a room before continuing on south. She called David Roeschen over to help unhitch the horses and watched a man jump off the back of the wagon. The stranger shook hands with the driver and dropped the sack of mail on the steps of the guesthouse. His clothing was foreign, almost everything from head to toe in black: His black jacket reached just below the waist and was adorned with two rows of silver buttons. His black britches had red piping that ran the length of the leg, but at the middle of the thigh was a handsomely tooled leather carpenter's strap.

When he removed the broad-rimmed black hat, he revealed a head of curly brown hair and an open smile on a sun-browned face. This was what she called a special delivery.

"*Grüß Gott*," she said.

"*Servus*," he replied less formally and offered his hand.

She took it, feeling a surge of unexplainable happiness.

"Florian Steinhauser, from Nuremberg."

"Nuremberg? That's way up in Bavaria. What in heaven's name are you doing all the way down here, Mr Steinhauser? And how on earth did you get across the border?"

"My mother's from Tyrol. I still have my papers."

"And she dragged you all the way up to Bavaria?"

Mr Steinhauser laughed. "No, my father did. She met him when he was working on the Arlberg Tunnel."

"The Arlberg Tunnel. Ah. What God divided by nature..." Jutta started.

"Should not be joined by man," he finished. "But if it weren't for that tunnel, I'd never have found my way back here."

Jutta smiled with him.

Mr Steinhauser turned and looked around. "It's nice here. Very clean."

"What did you expect?"

He gave her a sly wink. "Italy?"

She had to laugh. "Well, it's a miracle you found the place now that everything's being Italianised." For her, Graun would always be Graun, no matter what the Italians were calling it.

"So I've heard," he said soberly. "The postman tells me this sack of mail is the lightest he's ever seen."

"No room for the mail anymore anyway. He delivers Italian border guards these days. They want to make certain we know our place." She shifted her weight with the change in subject. "And now what? If you're a *Sommerfrischler*, you're a bit early for the season."

"A what?"

"*Sommerfrischler*. That's what we call the tourists. They come here in the summer to get some fresh air, take their chances climbing mountains and the like. Or are you a *Kärner*?"

Mr Steinhauser scratched his brow, then grinned again. "I don't know what that is. I'm going to have to relearn the dialect. I was afraid you would all be speaking Italian by now."

Jutta wagged her finger at him. "Don't you go talking like that to the folks around here, Mr Steinhauser. That's not going to make you any friends."

His grin vanished. "I'm sorry if I've offended. I didn't mean to."

She looked him up and down. "So why are you here if you're not a sneaky salesman, a *Kärner*?"

"The war postponed my apprenticeship," he said. "I'm a journeyman, a carpenter."

"Is that what you carpenters in Nuremberg wear?"

He looked down at himself. "In Nuremberg, yes. It makes me stand out, does it?"

"I've heard of you city carpenters before, but never seen one come through these parts. You're supposed to travel for about a year—*walzen*, you call it?—and work for your food and lodging, is that right?"

His grin returned. "Supposed to make my masterpiece before I return to nail a hole in my ear, that's right. Then I'll be a master carpenter." He took a few steps back off the stairs and looked up at the inn, then at the Prieths' house across the road. "I'd like to stay here awhile. I like the feel of it."

He smiled again, and this time Jutta noted how the creases of his eyes tilted downwards. This one feature made her decide that he was someone who would be keen to listen and slow to judge.

"There's plenty of work around here, don't you worry," she said. "Come in and get settled."

Inside, she arranged the room for the postman and for Mr

Steinhauser and then led him to the door of the dining room. The men at the *Stammtisch* had switched from wine to wedges of cheese and smoked bacon.

"Don't worry, boys. He's no *Kärner*," Jutta said by way of introduction. "Mr Steinhauser's got nothing to sell except an extra pair of hands. Go ahead and make some room for him."

The men slid over and shared courteous greetings, and she brought him a glass of wine and water. "I'll put this on your bill."

He looked crestfallen.

She winked. "Like I said, I'll put it on your bill. Tomorrow, first thing, you get to work."

"And may I now know your name?"

"Mrs Jutta Hanny."

With this, Mr Steinhauser held up his glass. "To your health, Mrs Hanny. To your health, gentlemen."

Before the men could get a good drink down, someone tugged at Jutta's skirt. Her son. "Alois, I thought you were with Sara."

Alois held up a piece of paper. "I finished my picture. It's for Mrs Blech. She can hang it up in the schoolhouse."

"That's a nice picture," Jutta said, glancing at the usual scribbles. "You go do your chores now. The chickens need feeding."

Alois was not listening. He was looking at the men, and Mr Steinhauser wiggled his fingers at her boy. She stroked Alois's head, conscious of how her son looked more different than ever with his shaven hair. The bout of lice had infested more than half of the schoolchildren, but Alois was not concerned about his hair. He was copying Mr Steinhauser's wave.

The half-Tyrolean stranger directed his question at Alois. "Who are you?"

Alois sniffed and pushed his spectacles up his nose. "I'm the son."

"What's your name?" Mr Steinhauser asked.

"Alois," Jutta answered at the same time her son did.

"I'm Florian. And how old are you, Alois?"

Her boy looked up at her, squinting behind his glasses. His almond-shaped eyes. The thick legs. She searched the newcomer's face for the usual look of morbid curiosity mixed with pity or repulsion, but she could not find any. "He's nine."

"How many is nine, Mother?"

"It's this many," Mr Steinhauser said. He held up his right palm and the first four fingers of his left hand.

Alois giggled. "Oh, that's many." He looked at her again. "That's many, Mother, isn't it?"

"Say goodbye to Mr Steinhauser," Jutta said. "And go do as I said."

The newcomer stood up from the table and crouched eye level with Alois. "Do you want to sit with us? When you're done with your chores, I mean."

"Yes—"

"No." Jutta jerked her boy away and glared at the men at the table. She knew the others were pretending not to notice the conversation, except Johannes Thaler. He was watching her, and he'd intervene the moment she might need him to do so.

Her son's eyes were filled with tears, and she pulled him to her. "You didn't do anything wrong, Alois, but you know that this area is just for guests."

"I want to talk to Florian," her son whined.

"Mr Steinhauser," she corrected.

Alois sniffed, wiped his runny nose, and plodded back to the kitchen.

She pressed a cool hand to her face, but Mr Steinhauser rose, opening his mouth again. Apparently he still hadn't got the message.

"You've just arrived, Mr Steinhauser. I suggest you learn how things have been built around here before you begin renovating them."

"I am sorry for that. He's just a child. He just wants to be a part of—"

Jutta pulled away from the table so that he had to follow her. "Headstrong and naïve, that's what you are. Perhaps where you come from mongoloids are embraced as functional members of society, but I sincerely doubt it. I know all about institutions that lock children like Alois away. Now, you sit back down over there and just stay still. That is, if you want to stay on my good side, Mr Steinhauser."

She was gone, but his voice followed her around the corner. "It's Florian. Just Florian."

In the kitchen, Sara had given Alois the first bowl of goulash and was slicing more bread.

"Did you feed the chickens, Alois?" Jutta said. "I told him to go feed the chickens first, Sara."

Alois pushed himself from the table and ran out, nearly crashing into Hans Glockner, who was coming in from the yard. Jutta watched the two through the window. Alois's voice carried into the kitchen, but it was unintelligible. Hans patted Alois's shoulder then and pushed him gently towards the chicken coop.

She watched Hans lumbering up the back steps to the kitchen door.

"Look," Sara said. "He's brought the eggs already."

Sara did not need to smile like that. Jutta was not a young girl. "Thank you, Hans."

"Jutta." He tipped his head and headed out towards the *Stube*.

Sniggering, Sara poured herself a glass of water. "He walks as if he got stuck that way from ducking through your doorframes all too often."

"There's nothing to make fun of when a man is as big as his heart."

Sara's smile grew wider. "I wasn't making fun of him. I was teasing *you*."

Jutta flipped the dishtowel in her hand against her skirt, about to give Sara a piece of her mind, but instead she took the pot of stew and returned to the *Stube*.

Hans spoke with Florian Steinhauser, and everyone at the table listened attentively. The sociable carpenter, already carving out a place at the *Stammtisch* for himself.

"So you took care of the home front," Mr Steinhauser said, clapping Hans's great shoulder. "A man like you? Why, you look like Andreas Hofer himself."

Hans shrugged, flushing. "Had to. They wouldn't take me because of my leg."

Jutta could not tell whether he was reddening from the comparison to Tyrol's biggest hero or because indeed he'd not been able to defend their homeland.

Martin Noggler put a hand on Hans's other shoulder. "They didn't take him, but they took his twin brother, Hugo. He was killed on the Marmolada."

The men shared a knowing look, and Jutta interrupted them. "Can I get you anything, Hans?" she asked.

"If you have beer. Please."

Martin Noggler jerked his head at her. "Give him some goulash, Jutta."

She served him a bowl and was about to serve the others, when Alois ran into the *Stube* again.

"Hans," he cried happily. "You missed one egg, but I found it!"

Hans opened his arms and engulfed her child.

Jutta protested. "Alois, I thought I made it clear that—"

"Oh, leave him, woman," Hans growled. He broke into a weak smile. "He'll be fine. Won't you, Alois?" He hoisted the child onto his lap.

She flicked the dishcloth against her skirt again, considering.

Florian Steinhauser, that cheeky stranger from Nuremberg,

was grinning. He looked at Hans, then at her, then back at Hans. She glowered at both of them before walking out. Somebody burst into laughter, and the merriment of it followed her all the way into the kitchen. When she stepped back into it, she grinned too.

9

MAY 1920, BOZEN

Angelo fitted the phonograph record of *Nabucco* on the Victrola, remembering the British officer he'd received it from. He'd raced the man to a Red Cross station after his leg had been blown off. A few weeks later, the machine was delivered with a thank-you note: *You were humming Verdi during your last visit to me. Cannot possibly take this back to England. I'm putting it into your capable hands.*

He rested in the settee, head back, listening. Just before the end of the second act, Chiara walked into the salon, dressed in pale blue and cream. Angelo had never seen the gown before. It was modern, scooped out at the front and the back, and she wore a long string of pearls. He wondered how the common workers would react to seeing their wealthy Socialist champion in such elegant dress. The rich patroness taking the less fortunate Tyroleans under her wing.

Perching on the settee, she laid a hand on his shoulder and tipped her head towards the music. "What did I miss?"

"The first two acts. Nabucco is begging Abigaille to spare his daughter."

"Fenena."

"Yes."

They listened like that, he on the sofa, she next to him. In the middle of "Deh, perdona," one of the servants announced that the Colonel was downstairs.

Angelo scowled at the record player before standing up to receive his father. He just wanted to enjoy one day without any interruption. Just one day to return to the world he knew well. The chorus began to sing "Va, pensiero."

Gloves off already, the Colonel strode in and greeted Angelo first. "Captain."

"Colonel."

Angelo leaned into his father just as the voices of the Hebrews defiantly rose.

Greet the banks of the Jordan

And Zion's toppled towers

The Colonel turned towards the record player, his arm slipping around Chiara's waist. He led her to the machine. "The infamous British gift," he said.

The Hebrews sang, *Oh, my country so lovely and lost!*

The Colonel raised his head. "And *Nabucco*. Verdi is our nation's hero, my dear. A man who supported the *Risorgimento*— our rebirth. Did I tell you that my father worked as an usher at the Milano Teatro de la Scala? He was there for the opening. Eighteen forty-two. He worked thirty-two of the seventy-six performances that autumn."

"You don't say." Chiara was being awfully obliging. "Would you like a glass of wine?" She slipped gracefully from the Colonel's hold.

He turned to Angelo. "He sneaked in a different woman backstage every time. But alas, he met Angelo's grandmother."

"At the thirty-second show?" Chiara guessed, back at Angelo's side.

She was really being a good sport.

"Not quite." The Colonel's gloves, in his left hand, twitched against his thigh. "Afterwards. My father never went to another opera again, I can grant you that. Does Angelo ever take you to the opera?"

Angelo removed the stylus from the recording, the silence in the room like a vacuum until he said, "We had plans to travel to Milan, but we've postponed all that now. Where's my mother?"

The Colonel waved a hand over his face, his tone regretful. "One of her headaches. She sends you her love. You're both to come to dinner tomorrow."

Angelo had hoped they could tell his parents the news of the baby now, in their own home. Dinner at their house was another matter altogether. He hoped his mother would still have a headache tomorrow.

"Right after church service," Chiara said with a cheeriness that Angelo knew was forced. "Are your girls back from school?"

"Francesca and Cristina are arriving this afternoon," he said. "Weren't you offering wine?"

"Certainly. I'll fetch one of the servants. Will you gentlemen excuse me?"

Moving himself to Angelo's settee, the Colonel seated himself and laid the white gloves on the table. "You're looking well." He plucked a Turkish delight from a pink crystal lily-shaped bowl that lay between them on the table.

Angelo sat across from his father on the divan. "I'm fine, thank you."

"So what happened up there, up north?"

Angelo gave his father a brief version of his made-up story.

"Alpine Rescue party, eh?" the Colonel said. "Seems an irresponsible thing to happen to a man who led his troops up the Marmolada."

"Accidents can happen to anyone. Even to seasoned alpinists."

"Yes, well. I'm glad to see you're all right. When you didn't come back as planned, I thought maybe you'd got caught up with some milkmaid or a butcher's wife." He winked at Angelo and took another Turkish delight. "Right good these are."

Before Angelo could take in what his father was saying, Chiara returned with the servant and a tray of wine.

"Lovely." The Colonel smiled.

She handed Angelo a glass. "Darling, you look pale. Are you feeling well?"

"I'm fine. Please. My father and I have important issues to discuss."

Her eyes flashed but the rest of her demeanour remained compliant. "I'll go for a stroll then and leave you to it."

When she'd gone, Angelo steeled himself against any further surprises. "No. There was no butcher's wife, nor farmer's daughter," he said.

The Colonel raised his glass, grinning. "Of course not. You don't take after your grandfather, do you?"

Or you. "What brings you here?"

The Colonel set his wine down. "Two reasons. One, to see about your condition. Make sure you're healthy."

"I'm recovering."

"I see that."

"And two?"

"And two, I'm here to talk about the dam."

"Which one? The Reschen Valley or the Gleno?" To hell if he was going to ask about his father's new venture. The Colonel would have to tell him himself.

"Let's start with the Gleno."

Angelo was on solid ground then. "The ministry is responsible for it, and there is no reason why the consortium needs to begin manoeuvring around us."

The Colonel sighed. "Angelo, I admire your belief in the system, but there's a lot of chaos in our political arena."

"Like the Colosseum during the Roman games."

The Colonel paused his reach for another sweet, his hand

hovering over the crystal bowl. "Italy, my dear boy, is facing a new day, and out of this chaos, we will have order, but it will not be our current administrators who pull us out of the ashes."

Angelo shrugged. "I don't believe there's anything to discuss, yet. The treaty may not stand. The Austrians will not allow their people to go without a fight."

"Of course they'll fight." The Colonel smiled. "I would lose any little respect I have for them already if they didn't. But these people will have to learn their history properly. Our deal with the borders was prophesied by Dante and is dear to every Italian heart." He pointed his finger into the air and began drawing a line from top to bottom. "The Brenner line, the Biulian Alps, the Illyrian Alps. Fiume and Dalmatia. Those are our borders. Every Italian man, including myself, must examine his national conscience."

Angelo stood up and walked to the window. "Before we went to war"—he turned to the Colonel—"you said that the European conflict would show which race was the supreme one. *You* prophesied that Italy would come out of this and be seen as one of the leading nations of Europe."

"And that is what will happen."

"No, Colonel." Angelo stood before his father. "No, it won't. At least not yet. Do you remember Giovanni?"

The Colonel's face remained blank. "Giovanni? Yes."

He smirked. There was no Giovanni. Just himself. Angelo. "He didn't believe in your war, Colonel. He wasn't convinced by these supposed historical facts, as you call them. But do you remember how he fought?"

"That is why we won the war, Captain. Because of discipline."

"Because of blind obedience," Angelo corrected. "There is a cure for that. It's that conscience you're talking about."

The Colonel rose and jabbed a finger into Angelo's breastbone. "We built a spirit of solidarity in that war. It was deep, Angelo, and alive. That solidarity built our army and our families. A high spirit of duty and sacrifice was the rule!"

"And now? Where's that spirit of duty, now? We're fighting each other because we have no Prussians left to fight. Or is this why we're turning the fight onto the Tyroleans? The Ladins in the south? The gypsies? The Jews!"

The Colonel released his finger from Angelo. "Order is on its way again," he said. "And once we have it, we will expose the saboteurs of this country, those who cloak themselves under the banner of humanitarianism. Those people talk of national rights, and this to a population that has been, for centuries, an instrument for oppressing the Italian elements. Under Austria, a despotic empire! The Austro-Hungarians never had a consciousness, never had a dignity of nations. I promise you, Angelo, sentimentality—especially coming from other Italians— will not rule the day. It's important that you remember that. It's important that your *family* remembers that."

"Another attempt to disband a government of centuries," Angelo said. He walked to the door, checked the hallway, and found it empty. He closed the door again. "You talk of treason as if it were easy."

"Treason? You dare to accuse me of treason? I talk of finally removing the traitors."

"Of course, because the Blackshirts are going to convince the king to step down?"

"We're negotiating with him."

"Who is? Battiste? Last I heard, he was tripping around Trieste, high on drink and drugs, shooting his pistols like a madman."

"You defame our national heroes by spreading that gossip, Captain!"

"What this country needs is stability, Colonel. Leadership with dignity."

The Colonel shrugged. "You might be right, but it's too late to stop the momentum." Then he smiled. "Your pessimism is not really becoming for a man who's about to be a father."

"What do you mean?"

The Colonel clapped him on the shoulder. "Your mother bore three children into this world, but she carried five. I know what a pregnant woman looks like. Come now. This is good news. Congratulations are in order. May I?" The Colonel seated himself again and popped another sweet into his mouth. "I didn't hurt you, did I? Because you winced."

"No. I'm fine."

When his father motioned to the divan, Angelo sat.

"Let's talk about something more regional," the Colonel said. "Perhaps less abstract for you. Did Minister d'Oro tell you of my vision?"

"You mean regarding the Reschen Lake project? He did."

"And?"

"It's hard to say," Angelo started.

"Speak up, boy. You're mumbling."

"It's hard to say. Raising all three lakes will cause a great dent in those livelihoods. It will cost a lot of money in compensation."

The Colonel smacked his lips and rubbed his hands before reaching for the last Turkish delight. "Indeed. But those livelihoods are replaceable."

"With what?"

"A modern world, Angelo." He began counting on his fingers. "Industry. Development. Design. Research. Culture. And even"— the Colonel raised the palm of his other hand, a coat of sugar on his thumb—"war machines."

"Another war."

"It will come, Angelo. It will come, and next time, they won't catch us with our pants down."

"In that case, I'll ask you again. Who are you going to put in Rome to lead your school of fish?"

"Fish. Indeed. There are a lot of washed-up politicians now."

The Colonel chuckled. "Perhaps you're right, Angelo. Politics stink, no matter who is at the helm."

"And the Tyroleans? The ones we're going to flood out up there?"

The Colonel laughed, as if Angelo had told him a funny joke. "*We*, Angelo. All in the same boat. That's good to hear." His smile vanished. He crossed his arms and leaned back, as if to assess Angelo. "Change tends to bring out the worst in people, son. Progress is always met by resistance. Yet the human being is an interesting creature. It quickly gets used to the luxury of advancement; actually *believes* that it needs that luxury to survive. Take it away, and those same people will fight you twice as hard, forgetting they never wanted that thing in the first place."

10

JUNE 1920, ARLUND

K atharina dreamt of going to the barn, lamplight illuminating the heifers and cows. Standing in the doorway, she watched a row of them roosting in the hay, softly blowing through the dark-black nostrils that reminded her of the swollen pads of dog paws. The middle animal rose slowly, heavily, and pawed at the ground with her left foreleg, rocking and swaying, unbalanced by the weight of the calf in her middle. The cow nearest Katharina rubbed her head against the stall trough, the chain tinkling in rhythm, eyes closed slightly and groaning with pleasurable relief. A sound like the gushing of a fountain pump came from the standing cow, yellow liquid followed by clear water. The other cows turned their heads towards Katharina, chewing mouths stilled, and stared at her. Aloof, challenging, judgmental even. And then the pregnant cow bellowed.

Alma!

Katharina leapt out of bed.

Alma was already on her side in the stall when Katharina came in with the lantern. Opa crouched nearby in a ring of yellow light. The only sounds were those of Alma's rhythmic huffs and a lone cricket chirping in the far corner of the barn. The stable was warm and heavy with the sticky, primal smell of blood and birthing fluids.

"Opa?"

Her grandfather looked up from the brown heifer. "The hooves just pushed through."

Katharina set the lamp on an upturned crate next to his and crouched in the hay to watch Alma. The heifer bellowed at her, a plea, not a greeting. At the vulva, the calf's hooves pulsed out with the heifer's contractions. The amnion sac, milky white and shining in the light of the lanterns, was still intact. Panting, Alma twisted her head towards her middle and pushed again.

"There's the nose," Katharina encouraged the mother.

"She'll manage this one on her own," Opa said.

Katharina felt relief. Yesterday, she'd been up in the middle of the night as well, helping turn a calf. Blood had poured out of the cow, and Katharina had been afraid they would lose both mother and calf. After the birth, the cow had been too exhausted to get up, and Katharina had cleaned the placental membrane away herself before giving the babe its first milk. Both animals had been fine by dawn.

As Alma pushed again, dark, wet streaks ran from the heifer's eyes along the side of her broad face, and Katharina winced as more of the calf's head appeared beneath the stretched-out skin of the vulva.

"There you go, Alma," she said. "You're just about done, girl."

Through the open door at the east end of the barn, the sky was a pale sulphur colour when Alma dropped the calf. The heifer scrambled to her feet and cleared the sac from her baby with wet licking noises.

Katharina stood and smiled at the calf's first calls. "That is a very healthy one."

"Sure is," Opa said. He clapped a hand on her shoulder and shook her a little. "And a heifer."

"This makes six this season. Four bull calves, two heifers."

They weren't supposed to keep them. They needed money, and fast. Yet something about this particular calf made Katharina yearn to keep it. Maybe because Alma was her favourite cow, gentle and docile. The calf had the same fawn colouring, but there was a little white streak on her forehead, an unusual trait for the Braunvieh.

Quickly, Katharina calculated what they might make at market for the others, how much of that would go to paying off debts, how much to the dairy man, how much to food, whether it would be enough if they should just sell five of the newborns. She thought it might just work if they incurred no other expenses.

Her stomach rumbled, and she felt sick, as if she hadn't eaten in years. She also felt as if she could sleep for months, but Opa was already going about cleaning the stall.

"I may as well get dressed," she said, "and get the milking started. Alma's the last one." They would all get some sleep tonight, finally.

She left Opa to clean up Alma's stall, dip the umbilical cord in iodine, and get the first colostrum into the calf before separating it from the mother. More than anything, Katharina hated that part, but the longer they allowed the calf to stay with its mother, the worse the crying was through the walls of the stables. One cow had nearly destroyed the entire fence trying to get to her calf because Katharina had let it stay for two days.

Opa had chastised her, told her it was certainly not her place to question age-old traditions, the centuries of animal husbandry. Opa also claimed the herd stayed healthier this way.

The herd. Over half the stalls were empty, but with seventeen, their number was still the largest in the valley. People like Hans Glockner, though, were struggling a lot more, and just this week the price for fodder had soared with the immorally low exchange for krone to lira.

In the pale dawn light, she observed how shabby the

neighbours' homes were looking. It was as if people were losing the will to get back on their feet after each new crisis. Or to ask the Farmer's Bank for more credit. Materials were costly, and most farmers were too proud to ask for more money. Making repairs was necessary in this mountain climate. Something would have to give.

She went inside and climbed the stairs to her bedroom, opened the wardrobe, and removed her smock. Just as she was about to slip it on, she noticed a tear in the armpit and sighed.

"Not now," she mumbled but went to the dresser and fetched the sewing kit. She examined the dress in full and ran a hand along the sides. The cloth was worn and faded. It was time for a new one. This or the calf? She got to mending.

Opa and Kaspar Ritsch talked the night before about the signs of inflation. Opa had tried to get her involved, a gallant gesture she could have appreciated more if Opa and she weren't so ill at ease with one another. Especially if the discussions were beer infused, Katharina remained wary of participating in any conversations that might make it seem she no longer knew her place. Whatever that meant. But that was the state of things since Angelo Grimani had left.

It was the calving that had helped keep her mind off Angelo until now, and with the last calf here, she faced the emptiness of the big house once more. Six weeks since he'd left. It frustrated her, all the pining she did for him. At nights, it was worse. She remembered his hands, the warm eyes, the handsome face. His laugh. And if she dreamt of him, it was to make him return to her, send some kind of word. Change his mind. Anything.

She always awoke feeling bitter and cursing herself for being so weak hearted.

She was about to tie off the knot when she found a tear near the waistband. With an exasperated scream, she snapped the thread, tossed the dress onto the bed, and put on the trousers and her last clean blouse.

She closed the bedroom door and hurried down the stairs and back into the yard. Opa came out of the barn and scrutinised her.

"Something wrong?" she challenged.

His eyebrows shot up. "No. Go on back to bed. Still an hour before you need to be up."

Katharina shook her head. "Maybe you're the one who needs some rest."

"I still need to put the calf in the pen."

"I'll do it." She had to learn to be tougher with what nature threw her, anyway.

It surprised her when Opa so readily agreed, and only then did Katharina notice how tired her grandfather was. Promising to wake him in a couple of hours, she watched him go into the house, then went back into the barn and milked the first few cows.

She dragged each of the milk tins to the scales and measured them. When her stomach rumbled again, she dipped a tin cup into one and drank a little. It made her gag. She frowned and pressed the back of her hand to her forehead. She was coming down with something, and if that was the case, she had better get on with it. Maybe the baking could wait, or the garden, but she did not want to have to fetch Opa out of bed to finish up for her.

She took the halter down, fastened it to the calf, and led her out the barn, around the side to where the other five were already nipping at the wooden planks of the pen. She pulled a tin of the colostrum out and placed a teat on it and began feeding the babies, Alma mooing from her emptied space inside the stable.

"Resi," she said to the newest calf. "That's what you're going to be called." If they kept her.

The others nudged up against Katharina, and she laughed as one sucked at the edge of her scarf. She'd keep them all if she could, these sweet, dewy-eyed babes. Resi drank the longest, and Katharina considered all the possible ways she could convince Opa to hold on to the biggest of the bunch.

She had loads of ideas for the farm, and not just to help them but maybe others too. As much as she wanted to share her thoughts with Opa, she couldn't. His temper had become shorter and easier to discharge ever since she'd gone running after Angelo. He had never asked where she'd gone, what had happened, and that made Katharina wonder what Opa really knew. Or whether Dr Hanny had told him everything—his version of it, real or imagined. That alone prevented her from broaching the subject. She could only tell a filtered story anyway, one that would most certainly lead to lying.

The only way then was for Katharina to keep her head low and her mouth shut. Every morning, she was up without Opa having to come to the bedroom door and knock. Outside, the woodpile had become her job without him saying anything. She swung that axe every day. She looked for the next chore and did what needed doing. Meanwhile, she let her ideas simmer, wishing for more than the exchange of idle words during the milking or at meals.

Miserable, she scratched the calf's ears. The only man Katharina should care about was the one whom she'd offended the most: her grandfather. How was she to bridge that gap between them? No matter how much she tried to bury the events of that night with Angelo, she knew its secret stood right in the middle of the way back to Opa.

Opa fell asleep in his reading chair that night. It had been a long day for them, and Katharina gently prodded his shoulder as he softly snored.

"Opa, go on up to bed."

She tried a second and a third time, but her grandfather was deep asleep. She sighed, eager to get to bed herself.

At dinner, Opa had remarked at her colouring, saying she

103

looked pale, and Katharina replied that she guessed she was coming down with a cold or a fever. Her stomach rumbled and churned no matter what she ate. Despite her intentions to rest, she had worked all day except for the six times she'd run to the privy behind the house.

As if reminded by her thoughts that she was not well, Katharina's stomach clenched once more, and she hurried to the privy for the fourth time. Inside, she unrolled a bit of newspaper and waited for the discomfort to dissipate. This time, it was a wave of nausea, and she feared she'd eaten something bad. Sweat broke out on her brow, and she dabbed at it with a bit of the paper. Finally, it ebbed away, but as she stood to leave, she heard something just behind her, outside the toilet.

"Opa?"

There it was again. A rustling, and then a noise, like the licking of chops. How did Hund get off her lead? She reached to turn the latch open, when Hund, from the front of the house, began barking like mad.

Whatever was outside picked up speed, moving through the grass and towards the back of the stable.

A predator.

Cold fear ran from the pit of her stomach into Katharina's extremities.

Certain the animal had now gone a safe distance, she quickly unlatched the privy door and scrambled to the front of the house, straight to the workshop. Outside, Hund growled, straining at her lead. Katharina dropped to the slats under the far end of the workbench, pulled up the loose floorboards, and removed the rifle from the protective canvas wrapping.

With the rifle in hand, she went outside, yanking Hund to her and hissing for her to stop. Hund whined, her growls lower and deeper. Katharina shushed her again, glanced at the window of the *Stube*, and could just make out Opa's sleeping figure.

"Stay," she said to the dog and swung in the direction of the stable with the rifle aimed, listening. It was pitch black out, and she cursed the night. She heard the usual sounds: bells softly tinkling from cows chewing their cuds, the chains latched between the troughs and the cows, scraping against the wood if one moved her head. Katharina sniffed the air and detected just a little of the scents left over from a week and a half of birthing.

A wolf—a desperate one—would be drawn to that, would take advantage of the calves penned up outside.

She could release Hund, let her chase the predator away, but the wolf would return as soon as it felt it was safe again. She had to be tough. To protect the livestock. They came first. And that meant getting rid of the danger now. She locked the dog in the workshop.

Inside, the dog whined and scratched, but Katharina ignored her, going to the enclosure next to the stall and sliding over the top rail before dropping softly to the ground. The predator—it had to be a wolf; what else would go after something as big as a calf?—would come from the other end, from the privy, from behind the adjacent house.

With the lack of moonlight, Katharina could not make out any shapes in the calf pens. She heard no movement from them, but what did they know of predators? Maybe Hund had already scared off the wolf. Or maybe the wolf was assured by the fact that the two had not already encountered one another. It was also protected by the blasted darkness.

Katharina crouched, scanning the surrounding area with the rifle point, trying hard not to let the sounds behind her distract her. The noises from the barn were muffled, a comfortable ignorance shrouding them all. At the sound of something bumping up against the wall of the calf pens, Katharina nearly jumped out of her skin. She steadied the rifle and listened. The calves were rising to their feet, jostling against the wooden slats. So they did understand something was wrong.

Unsure whether the rear sight lined up with the front sight,

Katharina strained to listen. From around the corner and in the yard, Hund's scratching and whining turned into frantic, snarling barks. Oh yes. The wolf was definitely still here.

Her brow felt damp, and a cramp started in her stomach again. Her arms shook.

"Jesus." She sucked a breath in. To steady herself, she tensed her muscles. She should have woken Opa before coming out here. What was she trying to prove?

At the sound of a low snarl followed by panting, and that wet sound of tongue on teeth, Katharina froze, her spine tingling, blood rushing to her ears. She swung the rifle to the right of the pen in the direction of the noise. Squinting, she tried to catch the sight in her line of vision. A movement again. This time closer. In the pen, a calf bawled and skittered. Katharina swung her rifle towards it. Where was the cursed wolf? For the love of God, she couldn't shoot towards the pens!

Another snarl. Right in front of her! The trigger. The blast. A howl and then the sound of gnashing teeth. She aimed at the sound again and shot again.

Behind her, Hund's barking, louder than ever. The sound of metal clanging onto wooden boards. She grit her teeth and pulled the trigger again. Something from behind dashed by Katharina, and she shrieked.

"Hund! No!"

But Hund fell on whatever was before her, barking and snarling like Satan's hound.

Then a light from behind, and Opa shouting her name, his voice higher than usual. He scrambled over the railing of the enclosure, lamp held high, and Katharina caught a glimpse of Hund snarling at a fallen animal.

"What in God's name?" Opa shouted. He reached her and swung the lantern at the dog and the wolf, shone it on the pen of calves, who were scrambling to get as far away from the open as possible. Back to the wolf. Then to her. He stared at the rifle in her hands.

In the distance, the slamming of doors, Kaspar and Toni shouting Opa's name into the darkness.

Opa stalked over to where Hund was still excited, Katharina following, and pulled the dog off by the scruff.

Before them, the dead wolf, shot twice—once between the ear and the eye and once on the hind.

"Jesus," Opa breathed, eyes wide. He looked at her, then the animal. "And I thought you were in trouble."

Katharina stared at him in disbelief, but when his mouth cracked into a wide smile, she laughed and sobbed at the same time. And when he put a heavy arm around her shoulder, she fell against him, weak with relief. He righted her up just as Toni and Kaspar rounded the corner from where the wolf had come. Katharina nodded at Opa in the lamplight, brushed away the stray tears with the back of her hand, and handed him the rifle.

She went to the spooked calves to calm them, while Kaspar and Toni gathered in the ring of light before the wolf carcass, Hund now sniffing and growling intermittently. She blocked out the excited chatter, stroked Alma's calf for a little while, and then joined the men as they dragged the wolf carcass to the barn.

They talked at her and around her, and her head spun with the excitement and energy. But when the excitement dissolved into faint relief, Katharina felt woozy. She took a step back from the gathering of men and smiled apologetically.

"I have to go inside, sit down," she said. Surprised by the revelation, she added, "And I'm absolutely starving."

Toni, eyes bright, whether from excitement or spirits, Katharina could not tell, looked her up and down.

"Yup, killing whets the appetite," he said.

She turned away, not wanting to reveal how disgusted she was by him, and took the rifle from Opa.

"I took it out—I'll put it back into hiding."

"Thank you, Lord Father, for keeping my livestock and my granddaughter safe," Opa said soberly.

She smiled a little, put a hand on his.

"Amen," she said with the others.

That morning, Opa was in a finer mood than Katharina had seen him in months, as if the excitement from the night before had lifted spirits. He whistled while he worked, acknowledged Katharina whenever she passed by, and it became so contagious that she even smiled back at him.

As they sat down to their breakfast, she handed her grandfather the basket of soft-boiled eggs, some fresh bread, and slices of cheese. He was still silent, but the air between them had lost its tension. Still famished, she ate quickly and piled her plate again with another helping. When Opa was finished, she watched him fill his pipe, more relaxed than ever.

"You know," he drawled, concentrating on getting the tobacco in nice and neat. "We'll have to explain the shots to the *carabinieri* this morning."

She shrugged.

"You'll be a real hero in the valley," he added. "By the time Toni tells the story, anyway."

Katharina scoffed. "I doubt that."

Opa raised his eyes and tapped the pipe down before closing the lid of the tobacco tin. "Might attract new suitors, that act of heroism." He pointed the pipe at her, indicating her outfit. "Might even find that getup attractive."

He'd caught her off guard. "You're not bringing up marriage again, are you, Opa?"

"Well..." He dragged the word out. "Toni Ritsch didn't seem to know whether to admire or admonish you, but I did sense some envy on his part. You missed your chance there."

"You know darned well how I feel about Toni Ritsch."

The corners of his mouth jerked upwards. "I do. But if you rejected him, who else is there?"

"Well, Patricia agreed to marry him, didn't she?" Katharina retorted.

Opa's look softened, "I was talking about you. Who else is there for you?" He stuck the pipe into his mouth and jutted his chin at the shelf behind her.

Angelo, she thought. She might have married Angelo.

She stood up, her back to Opa, and reached for the tin with the matches. The box was on top, but she pretended to fish for them, trying to blink away the sudden onset of tears.

She took in a deep breath, removed the matches, and set the tin back on the shelf, then lit one and held it to Opa's pipe.

"I don't need a husband."

"Well…" he said again. Same tone, same drawl.

Katharina sat back down and waited as he sucked in and puffed out. Her knee bounced, making the bench beneath her shake.

"I was thinking," he finally said, "about what's going to happen to the farm when I'm gone."

"Where are you going? On holiday?"

"Your sarcasm is not attractive," he said. "You know what I mean."

The morning had emboldened her. "Well, I'm not getting married just so you can feel assured you've got an heir for the farm. Why can't I just take it over?"

Opa removed his pipe and held it. "You'd want the *Hof*?"

"Oh, Opa! You know I do. More than anything."

"No harm in making sure. Well…"

"Well what? Come out with it already."

He leaned in towards her, as if the room were full of eavesdroppers. "I spoke with Mayor Roeschen some weeks ago.

And it seems he can help arrange the documents necessary to put the *Hof* in your name—"

Weeks ago? "Really, Opa? Truly?"

"Now hold on. There's one condition."

"All right. What is it?"

His eyes darted around her face. "You're a beautiful girl, Katharina. It'd be a shame for you not to get married."

"Is that the condition? To be ugly?"

"It is," he said, not giving in to her sauciness. "You'd have to be unmarried for the Thalerhof to be in your name."

"Done." She stuck out her hand, but Opa did not move. She frowned at him and reached over the table further. "I'm serious, Opa. I don't want to get married. I won't."

"At least for as long as I'm alive," he said, and there was an unmistakable sadness there. "And that can be a very, very long time. Think of Jutta, child. You know the hardships she has being a single woman."

"I'm not worried about it," she started.

"You aren't now, but in a few years, you might regret it. I might live to be a hundred."

"I hope you do," she said, meaning it.

"And then?"

"If I change my mind, then I know the consequences," she finished. "That's all. I know I'll have to give up the Thalerhof in my name if there is a husband first."

Opa smiled that quick smile again and nodded. "Then it's settled. We'll go see Georg about the process, make sure he gets it all down on paper."

Katharina sprang from her bench, wild with love, and threw her arms around his neck. Though he tried to pull away, indignant, she managed to pepper his face with a few kisses, thanking him over and over.

He pried her off and pressed her to the bench next to him. "Now sit down, and listen—"

"I have such ideas, Opa, of what we can do. Just think of this. I could begin experimenting with the herbs. You know I love learning about them and their properties and mixing them into the cheese. In a magazine, I read how we might cover the rind with alpine flowers. And the butter! You could make some more decorative moulds for me for the butter, and I'll go to market with them and sell them for their prettiness."

"What makes you think someone wants pretty-looking butter and cheese?"

Katharina sat back and grinned. "Look how drab everything is around us. It's a dark time. People yearn for pretty things when times are dark."

Opa scratched his head. "I'll be damned," he muttered.

But the ideas rolled out of her head and onto her tongue and she could not stop to consider what he might think. "And then, Opa, you know the valley is short of hands. And the farmers, Opa, who've lost their access to the alps up north. What if we offer to take their livestock up to our alp? Lease them some of our land?"

"And what then?" he asked, but his face lit up.

"We get their livestock's milk to make more cheese, but only up to a certain point, as return for rent on our meadows, for example. And, Opa, you can decide what that amount will be, what's fair," she said. "Whatever extra amount the cow produces, we pay up. They get some money back for it so they can earn something too."

"Now that—" He didn't finish but just stared at her, wagging the end of the pipe at her.

"Just think, Opa. If we put our heads together, we could help a few others get back on their feet. We can rebuild the Thalerhof to what it once was."

"Yes." He nodded and squinted with admiration.

It was a look Katharina had sorely missed.

He stood up and brushed the front of his vest. "We'll do all those things, Katharina, but first I need to do something about that wolf's pelt."

When Opa left to go outside, Katharina—lighthearted and almost dancing through the room—cleaned up the dishes, stuck them in the sink, and began washing them up. Her mind whirled with all her ideas. She had to write them down.

Shaking her hands dry, she went to the small desk in the *Stube* and pulled out a piece of paper, jotting notes and people's names to whom she could turn to with her ideas, collaborate with, help.

She would be a landowner. She would have a farm. Who needed a man? She could shoot, hunt, chop wood, fix fence posts, help birth calves. She had Hans Glockner as a neighbour, when things got really difficult. Patricia, whom she liked even if she was married to one of the most unpleasant men Katharina could think of… Yes, even Patricia would be helpful. Katharina might yet manage to make good neighbours out of the next generation of Ritsches.

She would handle it all. Absolutely and certainly.

When the cramp clenched and took hold of her insides again, Katharina shot up from the desk chair and doubled over in pain. The wave of nausea rolled over her middle and her back, and sweat broke out on her brow. She ran to the washing pot at the sink and heaved. Two helpings of breakfast tumbled out of her.

After she vomited once more, she sobbed, saliva hanging from her mouth, and moaned softly. Pressing her palms against the sink, she raised herself and came face to face with the calendar. The moon showed that it was waxing, that today would be a good day to fertilise the garden, to do the wash. She lifted it off its hook on the wall and flipped the pages back from week to week until she came to April.

Yes, six weeks since Angelo had left. And eight since she'd last bled.

11

JUNE 1920, GRAUN

The chiming of scythes cutting grass was the sound Jutta associated with the beginning of summer. She looked up from her lettuce garden towards the hills to see a couple of workers loading hay into the rivets and wagons. She stretched her back and scanned the freshly raked greens, blooming like small peonies, before choosing a head for its crunchy, tight-fisted curls.

On the other end of the garden, Alois was pulling weeds.

Jutta pointed to a clump in front of his right foot. "You can take those there too."

Alois pulled them out, turned the plants in his hand, and watched the dirt fall away when he shook them. "And these?" he asked, posed over the carrots.

"Not yet. Those are to eat, but they're not ready yet."

Her son knelt on all fours and brushed his face against the feathered tops, then tipped his head back, his mouth wide open, and giggled in that way that made many people look away.

She picked a second head of lettuce and caught sight of a bent figure making her way towards the church. "Good morning, Mrs Winkler."

The old woman raised her cane, then disappeared around the corner. Jutta recognised Lisl's voice coming from where the Widow Winkler had gone, and she straightened up to greet her sister-in-law as she rounded the corner. When Lisl reached her, Jutta examined the shawl Lisl wore. It had bright-red poppies stitched onto a green background, and the edges and fringe were cream. Lisl had crossed it over her chest and tucked it into a matching green frock, the colour of winter sage.

Jutta lifted the fringes of the shawl and examined both sides between her thumb and forefinger. "Is this cotton?"

Lisl smiled. "I bought it in Meran."

"It's beautiful."

"Trust me, Jutta—everyone will be buying cotton soon."

"And what will we do with the flax?"

Lisl shrugged.

"It'd be sad, wouldn't it?" She released the fabric. "Just another thing for us to toss out on the doorstep, like dirty bathwater."

"But it's so much better than flax."

"That's what we'll be saying about Italian food, Italian fashion, the Italian language."

Lisl looked hurt, and Jutta sighed. "Never mind, Lisl. It's a beautiful shawl. You'll be the most elegant woman at the Corpus Christi procession, as befitting the mayor's wife."

Her friend did not look convinced.

The church bell signalled half past ten. "Come in. I have to start cooking," Jutta said. Over her shoulder, she called Alois to come in as well.

He squinted at her behind his glasses. "I want to play with Florian. He promised he'd play with me."

"Mr Steinhauser's working at the Planggers. He's in Gorf."

"But I want to play with him."

"Alois, I'm not going to repeat myself."

He pouted. "I want to stay outside."

Jutta gave in to him and instructed him not to pull out any more plants before sweeping Lisl towards the kitchen.

When she had a pot of stew on, she sat next to Lisl to review the task list for the Corpus Christi festivities. "If everyone shows up on time, we should just need a couple of hours to set up. I've asked for a few extra pairs of hands."

Lisl leaned back and crossed her arms. "Speaking of extra hands, Alois has taken a real liking to Mr Steinhauser, hasn't he?"

Jutta felt her cheeks flush. The newcomer was already accepted relatively well by the community. "He's a hard worker. Helpful and polite. Some of the villagers rib him about his dialect, but he's picked up quite a few of our words."

"You mentioned he's at the Planggers," Lisl said. "They're building a new storage house, right?"

Jutta was not about to answer a question Lisl already knew the answer to.

Lisl cleared her throat, her smile turning sly. "So how's Hans?"

"He gets on well with Florian too."

"Really? Florian?"

"Hans comes as often as possible to keep an eye on Mr Steinhauser, it seems."

Lisl laughed. "He's a very handsome man, that Mr Steinhauser. I think you enjoy provoking him."

In response, Jutta whipped the dishtowel at her. "He's a boy! Mr Steinhauser would have nothing to do with an old woman like me."

"I wasn't talking about Mr Steinhauser's attentions, but Hans's." Lisl winked and stood up. "Besides, Jutta, a woman is never too old as long as she has at least one suitor in her life."

Jutta led her to the door. "How's Georg?"

"He's working. But we're on tenterhooks. He tries to stay out of Captain Rioba's way and is trying to learn Italian. Frederick is helping him, but I'm afraid Georg doesn't have much talent with languages."

"I'll pray he won't need it. The annexation isn't finalised yet. Tell him I said hello, and I'll see you tomorrow."

After she had finished with the lunch rounds in the *Stube*, Jutta went back outside to put the final touches on some linden branches that were placed outside of the house for the Corpus Christi parade. The temperatures had risen, and the peaks to the south blended in with the white clouds, making the valley look more hilly than mountainous.

Outdoors, her neighbours were tidying up their gardens and flower boxes in house-proud fashion. Those who were able to, whitewashed their homes and painted the shutters with fresh coats of paint. Any eyesores, whether a pile of cow manure or unrepaired bits and things, were covered up or hauled away. Early in the morning, someone would be responsible for spreading fresh-mown hay on the street to make a fragrant, spring-green carpet for the procession.

She tied the branches of saplings off with a gold ribbon and leaned them against the wall just as Katharina appeared.

Jutta embraced her. "Where have you been hiding? It's been at least a month since I've seen you. You haven't been to church either. Your grandfather says you've been taking communion at the chapel."

The girl looked down. "I've been feeling unwell."

"Are you better now?" Jutta asked.

Katharina shrugged. "I am to see Lisl about her boys helping us move the cattle to the alp. If her Paul is going away to study, I'll need to see about another hand or two elsewhere. Maybe she has some suggestions. But I need to speak with you, Jutta."

"Come inside then."

They climbed the stoop and went through the post office and into the living quarters. Inside, Katharina went straight for the shelf of photographs. She picked up the photo that had captured one of Jutta's happiest moments: the day Marianna and Josef had taken Jutta and Johi on a hike to Graun's Head. The youngest Thaler boy, Jonas, had also tagged along with his new camera.

"You look so beautiful in this photo," Katharina said. "Look at you and Uncle Johi." She held the photograph towards Jutta. "You were very much in love with him, weren't you?"

Jutta did not have to look at it. She knew it as well as she knew the image that faced her in the mirror these days. She had been dressed in a *Dirndl* and new buckled shoes that had pinched her feet and caused a blister on her heel. Her black hair was set in a crown of braids. Next to Marianna, Jutta's compact mountain-woman figure and round face were in stark contrast to Marianna's exotic height, fair hair, and fine-boned features.

The girl brought the photo over to Jutta and traced a finger over Josef's dark, swept-back hair. Katharina's father had his arm around Marianna's waist, and a guitar in the other hand. His feathered cap lay in the grass next to the wool blanket. Beside Jutta, Johi stood with his thumbs hitched in the straps of his *Lederhosen*, and Jutta remembered that the tassels on the knee socks had been red. His teeth were clamped over his favourite pipe. She had just said something to him—she could no longer remember what—and Johi had turned to her, his gaze meeting hers. Just as Jonas snapped the photograph, Johi had laughed, and the result was that his head was slightly blurred in the photo.

"We were very much in love." Jutta put the photo back on the shelf.

Softly, Katharina asked, "How did you survive a broken heart?"

Jutta noticed the tears. This had nothing to do with Jutta's heart, but with the girl's. "What's happened?"

Katharina's face contorted as she sobbed. "I've tried so hard to be strong. I tried to forget him. I know it would have been impossible between us, but I can't forget him now, can I?" She sank down on the sofa.

Jutta reached for a handkerchief in her pocket and offered it to the girl before sitting down next to her. "Forget who, girl?"

"Angelo Grimani," she cried.

"The Italian? The man who was attacked?"

"I wanted to tell you, Jutta, remember? I wanted to tell you, but you warned me against him. By then it was too late."

"You said he didn't touch you."

The girl sobbed into the handkerchief, and Jutta tensed, waiting, remembering.

"I went to him," Katharina whispered, her gaze in her lap. "The night before I saw you, I went to him. He didn't do anything to me that I didn't want him to do."

"What did you *do*, you stupid, stupid girl? Blessed Jesus, child." She grabbed the girl's shoulders and shook her. "When did you last bleed?"

Katharina shook her head, as if she were denying the answer. "Not since he left."

Jutta made a mental calculation. April. May. June. She released the girl. "Jesus, Mary, and Josef. Thank God Marianna is not here for this. History repeats itself, she used to always say. Marry someone from the valley, that's what she wanted for you. She felt it was hard enough to hold a marriage together without being an outsider too."

She stared at Katharina, sobbing. There was no question of marriage though, was there? And this Mr Grimani and Katharina were not writing love letters back and forth. As postmistress, she would have already known.

"Will you contact him?" Jutta said. "Give him the chance to do the decent thing?"

The girl wiped her face and pulled up straight. It must have taken all of her effort to speak as soberly as she did. "He has a family."

Jutta drew in a sharp breath and pounded her thigh. The keys at her waist jangled.

"I didn't know, Jutta. I swear it. I didn't know until afterwards."

"You're a fool!"

"Jutta, help me. Please. What will I do?"

"Well, the villagers aren't going to stone you to death," she snapped.

"That's not funny," Katharina shot back. "You know what they're like. They never forget a scandal."

"You're right, and it's made me into a hard woman."

"But you've managed," Katharina pleaded. "Look, you've got the inn, and the people respect you here."

Jutta scoffed. "Katharina, I don't even rightfully own this inn. As long as Fritz's corpse hasn't been found, it's still his establishment. And the people only respect me because the mail goes through me."

The girl sniffed. Then she looked desperate again. "If Opa finds out, Jutta." Bent over, she wailed, "He wants to give me the Thalerhof. I told him I wouldn't marry so it could be mine." She looked up, sobbing. "He'll never forgive me, Jutta. This is the worst thing I could do to him. He'll send me away!"

"Oh, stop it. It's the twentieth century. We won't send you to a convent, and we won't put you in stocks either. What do you mean, Johannes is giving you the *Hof*?"

Katharina nodded, misery caked on her face. "It could have been mine. As long as I remained unmarried, he said, it would go to me. In my name."

Katharina, a landowner! Jutta felt something swell in her. Pride? Hope? She looked the girl up and down, and something in her sank to the pit of her stomach, lost as if she'd dropped a stone down a deep well.

"Jutta?"

"Just give me some time. I need to think."

Hannelore, the midwife, who had certainly been called in for dozens of similar situations, was discreet. Maybe there was something they could do to save the foolish girl. Maybe it was not too late. But it was dangerous.

"How do you feel about the child, Katharina? Have you thought of maybe... It's early enough. You see, I might know someone."

Katharina looked stricken. "No, Jutta. I couldn't."

Of course not. Getting rid of the baby was not an option. Using the past tense about the Thalerhof was already proof enough. The silly chit loved this Angelo. Why would Katharina want to get rid of the one thing that would remind her of him? Memories were like sand, slipping through the fingers when one tried to hold on harder. But a child. Katharina could hold on to a child, and even though its existence would be a constant reminder of some phantom love, it could also numb the disappointment of it.

The silly chit!

If Jutta thought about all the experience she had harvested over the years... It made her ever so weary. The girl knew, surely, that the villagers would tear her apart. The menfolk—driven by jealousy more than virtue or social justice—would wreak havoc on Katharina's future. No greater sin than to bring a bastard into this valley. Infernal hypocrites.

Jutta went to her and clenched the girl's arms, forcing her to sit upright. "Go to Lisl and get the boys to help you herd the animals up to the *Vorsäß*. Leave the worrying to me for now. I'll figure something out. Now, go."

When she awoke the next day, Jutta felt so disoriented by her exhaustion that she needed to check the calendar on her nightstand: June 7, Corpus Christi. It was going to be a long day of festivities, but she had stayed up late to make sure everything was ready. Her plan was to go for a long walk before church. She needed time to think about what Katharina had told her yesterday.

Before leaving, Jutta instructed Sara to wake Alois in time for church and bring him with her. Outside, she listened to the noises around her: the opening of doors; someone coughing, then clearing their throat with a loud hacking sound. A horse called for attention from its stall, and two dogs barked in the distance. Leaning out the window to water her geraniums, Mrs Prieth raised her hand to Jutta in greeting, while Mr Prieth propped the picture of Jesus in the windowsill, the Sacred Heart painted in a beating, thudding red. With the bakery closed for the day, the Prieths must have enjoyed sleeping in until now.

Jutta headed north on the road to Reschen, passing the Blechs' butcher shop, where a white cat meditated on a pile of wood. She passed the Farmer's Bank, the sundries shop, and the miller. Martin Noggler's hammers were hung neatly on the wall of his barn, along with his other blacksmithing tools. At the crossroads, she turned west towards Gorf and took the road that led between the lakes of Reschen and Graun. It had not been something she had planned, but she was going towards the Planggers' place. Florian was there. She heard a teasing voice in her head saying that she didn't just think she would see him—she hoped for it. She reminded that voice of the purpose of her walk, and that was to find a solution for Katharina and her baby.

These things happened. When Jutta had found out she was pregnant with Alois, she remembered the terror and uncertainty, then the dread when she had to face her future. Fritz married her to avoid a scandal, but he had always made Jutta feel as if it had been her fault that he had lain with her. He'd conveniently forgotten that he had forced himself on her. When it became apparent that Alois was different, Fritz had blamed her, saying that it was because he had married beneath him and that made his boy only half of what he could have been. She did not really blame her husband for having abandoned them. It made her love for Alois all the more whole. Her feelings for Fritz had never included any sort of real affection. Still, she needed reminding to stop blaming herself for her son's incapacities. And not all the people were bad to Alois. Hans was gentle with him. The Thalers accepted the boy. Sara was a good child minder when Jutta needed her, even if the girl was a silly chit herself sometimes. And Florian. He treated Alois no differently than anyone he came into contact with. Florian was as patient with Alois as he was with his carpentry. Under his touch and attention, things just took their best form and true potential.

Gorf was just straight ahead, its boundaries marked by the single tree they called the Planggers' Tree. It was where the children played and swung from to splash into the pond. She stopped, feeling as if she'd been walking for hours, and even though that could not be possible, she checked the sun's position over her shoulder. It was starting to come over Graun's Head.

When she turned again, Jutta recognised the Planggers' house and the distant figure of Maria Plangger dumping water from the front stoop, scattering the chickens. A man dressed all in black stepped out from behind Maria and adjusted his broad-rimmed hat. Jutta's heart jumped. As if her thoughts had produced him. Florian.

She was still some distance from him, but when he looked up, it took only a moment before his arm went up in a wave. She waved back, and they started towards one another.

"What are you doing here?" He smiled down on her when he reached her. "We were all leaving for church."

"I needed a walk before I get trapped behind the food stall."

"May I escort you to the service, Mrs Hanny?"

Before taking his arm, Jutta looked back towards the Planggers' house. "What about the others?"

"They'll be along. They'll see us anyway."

Jutta took the arm he offered her, his muscles taut under her fingers. They started back towards Graun, and Florian told her about his work on the Planggers' farm.

When he was finished, Jutta said, "You've managed to make yourself quite comfortable here."

"I like it here."

"Would you consider…I mean, would you stay on?"

"Why not?" he said without looking at her. "I'd planned to come back to Tyrol before the war. I've been to Bozen many times, as you might imagine."

"Do you still have family or friends there?"

"Not many."

"What about your mother? Will she visit?"

"She is not well."

"I'm sorry to hear that." Jutta fingered the key ring attached to her belt.

"I'd have stayed on with her, but she insisted that I do my year's travelling. All of that was postponed with the war. She said I've had enough delays to my happiness. My aunt is taking care of her now."

A breeze rippled through the barley fields, and the sheaves bowed their green heads. Florian took his hat off before wiping his brow. He stood with his face directly to the morning sun, eyes closed, as if giving himself up to the light.

So that he could not catch her trying to bore into his soul, she turned to the field, the edge dotted with red blooms. "The poppies are beautiful. They're my favourite this time of year."

Florian seemed to have returned from wherever she had pushed him with her questioning. "They're funny little flowers." He bent towards them. "They look as if the slightest breeze could tear them apart. But it doesn't."

He held a finger under one of the red petals, and it fluttered against his skin. It reminded Jutta of butterflies that did not quite dare to land.

"Don't pick it," she said when she saw him reaching for the stem.

He tipped his head her way, the brim of his hat shading his face. "I thought you could pin it to your dress for church."

"It won't make it to Graun." When he looked uncertain, she placed a hand on his shoulder. "They wilt and fade too quickly when plucked."

Florian straightened up and smiled. "We'd better leave it where it is then."

They walked the rest of the way into town. In their silence, she regretted not letting him pick a flower for her.

Before the final benediction, Jutta watched Florian move to the front of the church to stand with the rest of the *Schütze*, or what remained of the riflemen. The territorial regiment was now an *omnium gatherum* of older men and scarred war veterans. The brass band, too, had more women than men now.

To finish the Mass, Father Wilhelm faced the congregation. "And may the blessing of almighty God, the Father, and the Son, and the Holy Spirit, come down on you and remain with you forever."

"Amen," Jutta said.

She saw Florian pick up the Graun banner. Ironically, it featured the same colours as the *tricolore* of Italy: three vertical stripes in green, white, green, and a red eagle in the centre, its wings stretched out like Father Wilhelm's robe when he raised his arms in blessing.

The regiment marched ahead. Florian smiled at her as they passed. Hans Glockner lifted his hand and waved at her, elbow at his hip. The altar boys led Father Wilhelm, who had the Book of Gospels raised above his head. As soon as the official part of the procession was outside, the sound of shuffling feet and muttered greetings from the townsfolk spilled together into the aisle between the two rows of pews. Sara and Alois joined her when they reached the door.

As the congregation spilled out onto the church square for the Corpus Christi procession, Alois pointed to beneath the oak tree.

"Look, Mother."

Captain Rioba and two *carabinieri* she'd never seen before were lounging on the rim of the fountain. Reinforcements. They straightened up when Florian raised the gonfalon but did not step in to follow the procession.

Jutta took a close look at the three men. Captain Rioba was grey haired, looked gentlemanly and cultured, but he was also very military-like in his uniform and stature. In fact, all the Italians she encountered strutted about like peacocks on parade, as if they had truly won the war with their own two hands instead of just on paper.

The other two men were much younger. One had curly sand-brown hair and light-green eyes, giving him an ethereal look against his darker skin. She thought of Katharina. Had her Angelo been this handsome? If so, Jutta could understand the attraction. When she focussed on the third *carabinieri*, Jutta hardened. He looked of farmer stock, heartily fed and strong, with a broad forehead and wide-set eyes. He was watching the men at the front of the procession, and when Florian passed by with the gonfalon, this one spit into the fountain. Jutta grimaced. This man was cold, like her husband, and likely prone to brutality if need be.

Once everyone had gathered, the procession headed for the first of four altars placed around Graun, and the brass band played the "Tyrolean Eagle" march. At first the music was hesitant, as if with the three *carabinieri* looking on, the musicians were not certain whether their instruments would be confiscated like the regiment rifles a year ago. Only the official hunters were allowed theirs, like Johannes Thaler. Nobody said much about that aloud anymore, but they all felt it. The citizens in the valley felt stripped bare, helpless.

She stole one last glance at the three policemen before moving on with the others, and Alois, next to her, craned his neck to look back at the *carabinieri*. She felt as if predators were stalking them.

The congregation went from one altar to the next, stopping at each one for the prayers and blessings Father Wilhelm led. Florian had built the altars from fresh saplings and pine, and some of the women had decorated them with flowers. As the procession came full circle and returned to the square, Jutta tore herself from the crowd. Everyone would head to the Post Inn after the last prayers and blessings had been given, but there would no longer be a forty-gun salute that signalled the opening of the festivities.

The stands were already set up under the oak tree, with beer kegs and pitchers of apple cider. Jutta gathered Sara and Lisl together and started a relay of pots filled with boiled white sausages. She had boards piled high with sliced cured bacon, cheese, bread, pickled cucumbers, and the first fruits of the season. She searched the crowd for Katharina and noted that, like in the last few years, the festivities had taken on something of a forced cheeriness. It used to be that the townsfolk dressed up, cleaned up, and readied for a good party until the morning, but now there was an oppressive air about them. On the outside everything was orderly and clean, but the people looked leaner and harder. The children ran around in their *Lederhosen* and *Dirndls*, but some had no shoes on.

Remembering to check on her own child, Jutta set out to find Alois. She discovered him with a group of mixed-aged children in the back garden, under the apple tree. They were whipping the rock-hard green apples into two lines. Alois was in the middle, in no man's land. She moved swiftly to shield her son from the next onslaught.

"Those apples are not to be used as grenades," she ordered the children from the two fronts. "The war is long over!"

Alois pulled away from her and ran to one of the groups, giggling. He picked up a handful of the stray apples and slung one at a boy.

"You bum," the boy cried.

"Alois! Put those apples down!"

The rest of his gathered apples tumbled to the ground.

"But, Mrs Hanny, those apples are so sour, nobody's gonna eat them." It was Robert Federspiel, one of the few who was kind to Alois.

"I don't care. They're good for something, but it sure isn't for whipping at each other. Alois, come with your mother now."

Alois started to put up a fuss, and when the Federspiel boy assured her that he would watch over him, she let him stay on. "Whatever you may think"—she glared at the rest of children— "my son is not the enemy."

When Jutta returned from the garden, Katharina was coming towards the stand, wearing Marianna's *Tracht* from Innsbruck. The blouse was new however, with the sleeves fitted just above the elbow and the bell-shaped lace down to her wrists. Instead of wearing a scarf wrapped crosswise over the chest, as Jutta and Lisl did, Katharina had on a red bodice with small white roses printed on it. The collar was piped in green, and her apron was a dark-green calico. In her hand, and swaying with her every step, she had a broad-rimmed red hat. It reminded Jutta of Florian's black one.

When Katharina reached her, Jutta hugged her close. "You look very pretty. Are you enjoying the day?"

"I'm fine, I suppose."

Jutta smiled. "You will be."

Katharina looked cautiously hopeful, but Jutta handed her a tray. "Stop biting your lip. We'll talk later." She watched the girl disappear around the corner, heading to the tables that had spilled out onto the street. Jutta could not tell her that she still did not know how to handle her predicament, but she would have to tell Johannes Thaler. Katharina's grandfather would have to know. Somehow.

Someone poked her waist, and she expected to find Alois, but it was Florian. He wore a boyish grin and held an empty beer mug. "Can I help, Mrs Hanny?"

She was immediately cheered. Florian Steinhauser had that effect each and every time. "Thank you. I'm fine. You look like you could use a refill."

"Have I paid off my bill yet?"

"Yes, sir. Yes, you have. The altars are beautiful. And I haven't yet thanked you for building the stand here."

Florian reached to top off his mug of beer. "That wasn't me. That was Hans." He poured another glass and gave it to Jutta with a wink. *"Prost!"*

"To your health." From the rim of her glass, she watched Captain Rioba and the two new policemen. "Did you see the reinforcements?"

Florian nodded. "Vincenzo something, that's the short one. And the other one"—he indicated the younger, handsome one—"is Ghirardelli. Georg told me."

Everyone moved aside, as if the *carabinieri* carried some sort of force field around them. They greeted no one as they made their way to Jutta's food stand.

"What can I do for you?" she asked when they reached her.

Rioba spoke Italian, sounding as if he were making a grave request.

"I don't understand," Jutta said just as someone touched her elbow. It was Frederick.

"Dottore Hanny," Rioba greeted him, then repeated the request, his eyes on Jutta.

She heard him say *Signora* Hanny and then *Signor* Hanny.

Frederick slipped around the table to the two officials and motioned for the two men to follow him.

"What do they want from me?" Jutta asked.

Frederick turned, his face troubled. "It's nothing." Her brother-in-law walked away with the police.

"But they wanted to speak to me," Jutta called after them.

Florian was the only who heard her, for the band had begun to play.

She watched as Frederick stopped near her garden gate and turned to face the two *carabinieri*.

"It's a good thing Dr Hanny speaks Italian," Florian said.

"Look at him," she said. "He's even beginning to talk with his hands like them."

Florian chuckled. "The language must demand it."

Jutta watched her brother-in-law. He nodded and looked concerned, even from where she was standing.

"What are they going on about?" she wondered aloud.

Frederick then put a hand on Rioba's shoulder and leaned in closer, but the police chief glanced in Jutta's direction. Her stomach went weak when Frederick offered his hand and Rioba shook it before they parted, but instead of returning to her, Frederick disappeared into the inn.

Jutta fingered the key ring on her belt. "Least he could do is come back here and tell me what that was about."

"Maybe it has nothing to do with you," Florian said. He wiped the beer that had pooled under the tap, and his grin was good-natured.

Signor Hanny, they'd said. She thought about the smugglers. "I just have a gut feeling," she muttered. "Something's wrong, and I mean to find out what it is."

"Well, Dr Hanny is a good man. If he can divert trouble, he will. We're lucky to have someone who speaks Italian and be so well respected and liked."

"Everyone liked his brother, Fritz, too," Jutta snapped. "Besides, I don't need the good doctor meddling in my business."

"Who's Fritz?"

She did not answer him.

"You can't throw them all into one pot, as you folks say here," Florian continued. "Besides, Lisl's a Hanny too, before she married the mayor, anyway. She's also your best friend, no? Why hold something against an entire family because of maybe one bad egg? That is, if this Fritz was a bad egg."

She grabbed the rag from Florian and shoved it under the counter before facing him. "There's a lot of history here, Mr Steinhauser, and it's going to take a long time before you figure out who's who. A long time."

Florian looked satisfactorily put into his place.

She jerked her head towards the inn. "Maybe you'll never really get to know us. You mark my word. There's going to be barrels of new secrets to cover up before you'll have time to unearth most of the old ones."

She was about to say more, but a high-pitched scream had Jutta moving. Florian shouted for Alois behind her. When she reached the apple tree, Jutta threw herself on the boy who was pummelling Alois with the small green apples.

"Stop it! Stop it! You nasty thing! How dare you?" She yanked the boy by the ear and pulled his face to hers. It was the blacksmith's son. "Martin Noggler's Thomas! You just wait until I tell your father about this!"

She turned to the crowd that was gathering and searched out the blacksmith. "Martin! Where are you, Martin Noggler? Come fetch your son!"

The blacksmith shouldered his way through the crowd, his fiery hair standing on end. His normally good-humoured eyes glistened dangerously as he grabbed the boy.

Jutta turned her attention to Alois, who was crying in Katharina's arms now. Before she went to her son, she stopped.

Florian was standing above Katharina, the expression in his eyes one that Jutta recognised. It was the same look of adoration Johi had given her for two happy years.

She studied the girl she had grown to love like a daughter, and watched as the German hovered over her and Alois. Katharina was oblivious to the stranger, even as Florian bent before her to put Alois's spectacles back on, and putting them on askew because all Florian had eyes for was Katharina.

Sniffling, Alois pushed the glasses up his nose, the frames still sloped across the bridge. Katharina helped him up. When Florian bent down and wrapped his arms around Jutta's son, he tickled the boy, and Alois let out a peal of laughter.

Katharina turned to Jutta, her expression mystified. "Well, that was quick. Who is that?"

"A friend," Jutta said. She watched Florian lead Alois away, and when he cast a look over his shoulder back at Katharina, Jutta glanced at the girl to see whether she noticed. But Katharina was already helping the children collect the apples into crates.

You don't see him yet, Jutta thought as she watched Florian walk away, *but that will change, girl. That will change.*

12

JUNE 1920, BOZEN

Angelo was knotting his tie when Chiara walked into their bedroom, an envelope in her hand.

"Your sister, Francesca," she said. "And if you'll notice, even she knows that our street name has changed."

The letter was from the boarding school in Milan and was addressed to Via B. Arrigo instead of Selig Heinrichstrasse.

"How nice," Angelo said. "We didn't even have to pack."

Chiara tugged on her gloves. "This is not a joke."

"I didn't say it was."

She came to him and straightened his lapel, which did not require straightening, then laid a palm on his chest. Her blue-green eyes flashed dangerously. "The Tyroleans are good people, Angelo. Hard-working Christians whose freedoms and identities are being taken away. Ettore Tolomei's Italianisation program is oppressive, don't you see that?"

Angelo kissed her hand. "And that's why I am meeting some of your friends today, so that I may hear for myself. Though what you have to gain from this, my dear, I'm not certain." He reached to tuck a hair behind her ear, but she turned away.

"I'm not on one side or the other," he said.

"Angelo, my friends, the people I've grown up with, are being treated appallingly. There's talk that Tolomei even wants to have the Tyroleans change their names into Italian ones. Can't we even wait until the annexation is official? He and his Fascists are scaring them." She sat at her dresser, facing him. "The tactics. That's what I'm trying to change, Angelo. What do I want from this meeting? Your understanding, I suppose. Your acceptance for my cause."

He went to her, trying to shake the feeling that he was in competition for her affection. "You have my love, Chiara, and that means my acceptance and understanding. I needn't meet your Tyrolean friends to offer you that."

"Then I'm wrong. I suppose what I hope is that you do eventually choose a side, and that is my side. I would very much like you to be more present in my campaigns. I should have my husband next to me when I speak out against the Tyroleans' enemies."

What she was asking for was a different matter altogether.

He lifted her chin and kissed her forehead. "Since when have you needed anyone at your side to fight your causes? I don't feel the need to do battle, Chiara, not like you." He wanted to chide her about her fiery temperament having to do with her hair colour, but when she looked up, her disappointment in him was clear.

"On the other hand," he said, "I'd be honoured to meet these friends of yours."

She rose. "We'll be late."

When she had her hat on, he offered his arm, but she did not take it with her usual warmth.

They left the villa and headed up Bindergasse. The street sign now read Bottai. They turned left after the ministry offices in city hall, and Angelo stopped to let an oxcart go by. It was piled with hay and led by a peasant woman with two dirty-faced children following her like ducklings. He thought of

Arlund for a second before escorting Chiara across the cobblestoned street.

In the square, street hawkers cried out their prices, and customers haggled over them, sometimes with vehemence. He pinched his nose at the smell of fresh horse manure piled near the kerb and steered Chiara away from it. Moments later, the yellow facade of the Laurin Hotel appeared. He led her through the garden to the back of the hotel.

On the terrace, patrons basked in the almost-summer sunshine. Porcelain cups chimed against saucers, and the clatter of silverware competed with the chatter in Italian and German. A waiter recognised the Grimanis and motioned them to a table where two men stood up to greet them, one dark haired and tall, the other shorter with sand-brown hair and a soft face.

"You look radiant," the shorter one said to Chiara, then turned to Angelo. "Sir, if I may say so, your wife looks absolutely radiant."

"This"—Chiara clasped her hands together—"is my dear, dear school friend. Peter Innerhofer, my husband, Captain Angelo Grimani."

"It's an honour to meet you, Captain Grimani," Peter said. He clicked his heels and bowed his head in that Austrian military manner Angelo didn't know whether he detested or admired.

She offered her hand to the darker one, and he held it a little longer before she turned to Angelo. "And this is Peter's brother, Michael Innerhofer, the journalist at the *Meraner Zeitung* I told you about."

"A pleasure, Mr Innerhofer." Angelo received a firm shake from the journalist, a grave man with an unkempt beard and frayed suit cuffs.

Chiara folded her parasol, and Angelo pulled a chair out for her, then sat down next to Peter.

"So you're the teacher?" Angelo asked him.

Peter nodded.

"I hope you don't mind speaking Italian," Angelo said.

The journalist, Michael, crossed his arms over his chest. "We are all learning Italian, Captain, as it seems that we must."

Angelo raised an eyebrow.

"To keep our jobs," Michael added.

"They're closing Michael's newspaper," Chiara said.

"I'm sorry to hear that. It's a poor economy at the moment."

The journalist frowned. "It is always easy to blame anything but the real source, is it not?" He then spoke in quick German to Chiara.

Peter leaned towards Angelo. "They close the paper so that we have no voice, Captain. There is no reason other than that."

"Then you must have been writing provocative things," Angelo said to Michael. "Now is not the time to twist the knife."

Michael did not understand, and when Chiara translated, he chuckled. "Certainly, we were writing—how did you say?—ah yes, provocative things. When else should we stand up and defend ourselves? First, when we are already chained to the walls?"

Chiara leaned in to Angelo, her jaw clenching. "Do you understand now? Their voice is being extinguished." She leaned back and fanned herself. "Michael is losing his job in Meran, and if Peter doesn't learn to teach in Italian by next winter, he too will be without a position."

"That's unlikely," Angelo said. "The Italian government is not interested in an uneducated population. Of course the Tyroleans need to learn Italian; are we all to learn German for them? Besides, I know the governor-general's mind, and he supports handling the integration peacefully and democratically. A bilingual society has its benefits, and we have a responsibility to all our new colonies to integrate them."

Chiara turned to the Innerhofer men and spoke slowly. "My husband believes the governor-general will be more powerful than the Fascist movement." She glanced at Angelo. "More powerful than the movement to Italianise the Tyroleans."

Michael laughed drily and reached into his coat pocket. He pulled out a cheap varnished cigarette case, flipped it open, and indicated that Angelo should take one. He declined.

They waited as Michael lit his cigarette and inhaled. "Bilingual, you say? We should all learn English and Russian as well so that nobody can write secret treaties that bargain for our land. But tell me, Captain Grimani. If we should have a bilingual society, when will you learn enough German to hold a conversation? Another question. Why do you still—after all the experience you must have from the war—lay your trust in weak leadership? Do you not recognise a puppet when you see one, such as your king?"

Angelo stood up, but Chiara stayed put. "That is treason, Mr Innerhofer!"

"He is not my king," Michael said. Next to him, his brother turned pale.

"I daresay, Chiara, your friends are quite out of line. Dangerously so, and I will not allow you to—"

She grabbed his arm and jerked her head towards the terrace entrance.

When he looked, Angelo found the Colonel waiting at the landing for the maître d'. His companion, a rotund man dressed in the latest fashion, sniffed at the passing waiters, himself stinking of money and corruption.

Chiara squeezed Angelo's arm again. "Go to them," she whispered. "I don't want them to come here."

He lifted his hat at the two Innerhofer men. "Will you excuse me, gentlemen?"

Michael had his eyes on the Colonel, "We already have, Captain Grimani."

Angelo felt a twitch in his neck, and his arm tensed, but it was his father's voice that kept him from punching Michael

Innerhofer in the face. He turned on his heel and went to the table where the Colonel and his companion were being seated.

His father stood up again when he saw him. "Angelo, it's been some time." He indicated his companion. "This is Luigi Barbarasso, from Piedmont."

"I've heard much about you, Captain." Barbarasso smiled. A wolf.

The Colonel's voice was like silk. "Chiara looks quite engaged."

Angelo kept his eyes on his father's face. "She's fine, Father. She and the baby are doing well."

"Baby?" Barbarasso grinned in Chiara's direction. "Your wife is expecting? How nice. And you two are out and about, enjoying the sunshine. Back in my day, women had to stay home when their constitution was so fragile. But"—he sighed—"these are modern times."

Angelo felt the vein in his neck spasm again.

His father made some noise about being a grandfather, then gestured towards Chiara's table. "And the two men?"

"Friends of ours."

Barbarasso's face darkened. "Really? Is not one of them a journalist?"

"I believe a printer," Angelo answered.

Barbarasso narrowed his eyes.

"And the other one?" the Colonel asked.

Angelo said lightly, "A teacher."

Barbarasso's face lit up. "After the newspapers have been closed, Colonel, the teachers will be next. Just you wait"—he smirked—"we will see to that."

Chiara had been correct in her earlier forecast!

"Your plan to turn this into a backwater of uneducated folk," Angelo said, "would be like shooting the Italian nation in the knee."

"My dear Captain, nobody wants to make this into a

backwater. It's already a backwater. We plan to integrate these people into the Italian culture, the Italian language, and the Italian ways. Only Italians can accomplish that."

"I see. By running the Tyroleans into the ground and hoping that Italians sprout up in their place?"

Barbarasso smiled. "If you mean it will take a generation or two, you're right."

That was not what he had meant.

"Not running them into the ground, Angelo," the Colonel said. "Introducing them to progress. Industrial progress."

Angelo ignored him. "And what do you do in Piedmont, Mr Barbarasso?"

"Lumber."

"Now I understand the interest you two have in one another," Angelo said.

His father was studying him. "Signor Barbarasso and I became acquainted through our common political interests. Perhaps it's time you join the fold. Those who will make an indelible impression on our, I daresay, landscape."

"Yes. The Colonel and I were just discussing some matters which could be of great interest to you, but your wife..." Barbarasso looked behind Angelo. "Perhaps she will protest?"

"I do not understand what you are referring to," Angelo said.

"Your father tells me your wife grew up here and does not share the ambitions of the Italian nation. Perhaps sympathises too much with her unfortunate friends. Certainly you can convince her that, as a real Italian, it would be best if she left the politics to the men."

The Colonel leaned back. "I don't think we need to concern ourselves with that, Barbarasso. Once she's had the baby, she'll quickly remember her role. If my son can't keep her on a lead, the child will certainly occupy her."

Barbarasso burst into laughter and patted his mouth with a

napkin. "Indeed. Tell me, Captain Grimani. Will you and your wife send your child to a German-speaking school?"

"Certainly not," Angelo snapped.

The lumber baron opened his hands. "Now you understand the need for replacing the teachers with Italian-speaking ones."

"And separate schools?" Angelo asked. "The Tyroleans would be won over more easily if you allow them to at least keep their language."

"My dear boy," Barbarasso said, "you're beginning to sound like the hopelessly liberal governor-general. We have just won the greatest war ever so that Italy can finally be what it has been all along: a ruling power."

"Angelo fought in the Marmolada," the Colonel said.

Ignoring him, Angelo said, "The Alto Adige—this province—was handed over to us like the others we are now trying to unify. We entered the war because the English convinced us that we were fighting for a safer and greater world. A peaceful world."

When Barbarasso laughed, his middle bounced and a button strained against the tide. "Yes, that's what our leaders told us to get us involved." He leaned in, fumes of coffee and tobacco wafting from him. "The truth is, our great war was just the beginning. Many people have profited from it, and now we need to continue moving forward. Industry. Machinery. Weapons—"

"I don't mean to be impolite, but my wife and friends are waiting for me."

The Colonel grabbed Angelo's wrist as he stood. "You and I have some business to discuss yet. An opportunity. For you."

Angelo glanced down at the hand on his arm.

His father released him. "Barbarasso and I are founding our own electrical company with some members from the consortium."

"I thought you were going to be a board member of a private company," Angelo said. "That's what Minister d'Oro told me."

The Colonel smirked. "That was the plan. But now it will be mine. Grimani Electrical."

"Congratulations," Angelo muttered. This would give his father all the leverage he would ever need to take control of projects. The money that he must have backing him! And if the Reschen Valley were ever to go to private...

"I would like you to run it with me."

"I'm happy where I am."

"I accept, only because I realise that a government position has its benefits, and I can also imagine working closely with the ministry—with you—but..." He glanced at Barbarasso. "Pietro d'Oro is holding up any decisions to move forward in privatising the Gleno Dam. He has the ear of several key decision-makers in legislature."

Angelo's pulse quickened, but he stopped himself from explaining that there were still laws that protected the Tyroleans' water rights.

"We want the Reschen Valley too, Angelo," his father continued. "I want it to be Grimani Electrical's second project. If my estimates are correct, that dam could be powerful enough to supply electricity to most of Italy's new industry. The Gleno and the Reschen: these two dams will start a dynasty for the Grimanis. They must take priority."

Angelo stepped back from the table. "Even if you were able to convince the state to sell out, reviews of the Reschen Valley project are slated only after the annexation has been signed into law. Maybe at the beginning of next year."

The Colonel looked thoughtful. "That's a very minor delay. Luigi? Who do we know up there? We could use this time to leverage support for us."

"I will make enquiries."

Angelo shook his head. "You can't—"

"Go back to your wife and your paperwork, Captain," the

Colonel said. "You handle this the way you must, and we'll see to making things easier for you."

"But I—"

The lumber baron lifted his hand. "Your wife seems to be rather anxious."

Angelo turned. Michael and Peter were leaving through the hotel, and Chiara was coming to the Colonel's table. When she reached them, the Colonel and Barbarasso stood up and took her hand in turn.

Angelo offered her his arm. He paid no attention to their goodbyes and led his wife out to the street afterwards, his head reeling with the news.

Grimani Electrical! His father's power would be incredible, and what the Colonel was suggesting was terrifying. He had to find a way to keep his father away from the Reschen Valley. And it was not only about the exceptional plans the man had for the lakes. It was his idea of getting personal up there, poking around for potential puppets.

He laughed angrily.

"I suppose they are just pleased with themselves about the renamed streets," Chiara said. "Slow down, Angelo. Please. What's wrong?"

"Just business."

"Business?"

"The Colonel just informed me of something, but it's nothing."

"Your father and the word 'nothing' in one sentence is an oxymoron."

He turned sharply to her. "Chiara, I want you to know that I do take the Fascists very seriously. However, the governor-general will prevail because it is what most of us here want in the end."

His wife gave him a look as if she had caught him lying. "If you're wondering how the Blackshirts are going to gain power, it begins with the newspapers. That's all they need to get the leverage they require. That is why they are putting the Tyrolean papers out of business."

He thought of what Barbarasso had said, but he did not know how to continue this conversation. What his father was planning... He'd have to convince Pietro to bait the Colonel with the Gleno project.

His wife was still talking. "These people are my friends, after all. I grew up with them, and I intend to help them. The king himself promised self-government after the war."

"Chiara, you are an Italian woman married to a captain of the Royal Italian Army. I'm asking you to remember your place. Stop parroting the locals. People are beginning to wonder whose side you're on. We fought a war against these people, and we won."

Her face flushed to a bright pink. "I suppose you would be much happier if I were one of those quiet, obedient wives?"

"Don't misunderstand—"

"No, Captain Grimani, I haven't misunderstood. It is obviously better that I have no clear idea or opinion of my own. Beyond my understanding indeed."

"Stop overreacting." He was angry, and not with her, but rather with the circumstances.

Chiara pulled away from him and halted before a store window. She stared at the porcelain as if she had never seen any before, her hat keeping her face in shadow. Angelo stepped behind her.

"The nationalists are calling the effort to Italianise the new territories *Italia irredenta*," she said. "I translated it for Michael. Unredeemed Italy. Explained to him what it means. He understood the word 'unfulfilled' and said he is certain that Italy's voracious appetite will never be satisfied." She spoke over her shoulder. "This is not who we are, Angelo. This is not who I am. I have never judged a single person based on their nationality or even their beliefs but on their acts of kindnesses, their character. I cannot help but feel we are creating monsters of ourselves. I am not bringing a child into this world that will be forced to become a monster."

She faced the shop window again, and in the reflection, Angelo saw her swipe her cheek with a handkerchief. "You men always believe you are the only ones who have something worth fighting for," she whispered. "Men underestimate the ferocity of a woman. They always have."

Angelo shifted behind her, frustration growing. His wife was changing, and the more she did, the more he regretted having ever encouraged her activities. Yet he was far from the perfect husband himself. A twinge of guilt spasmed through him, and he studied Chiara's image in the window.

He may have betrayed her. He may have slept with another woman, but Chiara was being seduced by politics before his very eyes, seduced by the idea that she could rescue the world. If this continued, he was going to lose her, and to hell if he was going to let that happen.

13

JUNE 1920, ARLUND

The cows were lowing. Katharina hurried out of the privy, whipping a shawl over her shoulders. The morning sickness had made her late for the milking, again. When she stepped into the warm animal-and-hay smell of the barn, Resi's adoring eyes followed her as she organised the milk jugs. She reached over the stall to stroke Alma's calf, who nudged her wet black nose up against Katharina's hand, blowing soft puffs of air, then curled her rough tongue around Katharina's finger. Whenever she tussled the calf's blond fringe, Resi's ears wiggled happily.

Another cow bellowed and kicked the stall, so Katharina gave the calf one last pat and set to work. Resi was a strong, good calf and one that would help boost the numbers of the herd. She'd have to talk Opa into keeping her, but Katharina's heart lurched at the idea.

Farm decisions would no longer be hers to make. As soon as Opa found out she was pregnant, she would lose all this. The ideas she had, the plans she'd made just a little over a week ago… Opa would hate her for what she had done, and the Thalerhof would never go to her.

"Herd's going up," Opa said from where he was milking.

His voice made her jump.

"Two weeks. We need one more hand for the alp or to stay here and help with the mowing."

She nodded, the lump in her throat there again, and ignored his quizzical look. She was pregnant, and he was talking about taking the herd up. Her concerns were about bringing a child into this world, into this valley, with no father to help raise it. Some six or seven weeks along, and for the time being, she did not have to explain anything to Opa except for the occasional delay in getting to the barn, but when she started to show, what would happen then? She pictured Opa casting her out, having to live at the inn, next to the Widow Winkler. Being laughed at behind her back. Being shunned by the community that was already careful with her because she was only half them.

Tears pricked Katharina's eyes, hot and stinging. It was best to stay silent, do her chores, and focus on the animals for as long as possible. She shoved her thoughts of the baby—and Angelo —away.

When she finished milking, Katharina led the two goats and their horse, Pfeffer, out to pasture with the cows before seeing to the chickens. Hund started barking in the yard, and she came out to see what the fuss was about and was taken aback by the sight of a strange man standing at the edge of their property. He wore a foreign black costume and a black hat, and only then did Katharina recall the Nuremberger. He'd led Alois away after the fight under the apple tree and had even made the boy laugh after being beaten up. What was he doing here?

"*Grüß Gott*," Katharina said, cautious.

Opa came out of the barn, wiping his hands on a rag.

"Good morning," answered the stranger. He took a few uncertain steps past Hund, who was still barking, and offered his hand to both of them.

"I don't believe we've been officially introduced. I'm Florian Steinhauser."

"What can we do for you, Mr Steinhauser?" Opa asked.

"Florian, please."

"Florian then," Opa said. "I'm Johannes. This is my granddaughter, Katharina."

"Hans Glockner said I should come by. He said you're looking for a hand to take the cattle up to pasture."

Opa grunted. "We need a herdsman. Someone to keep the animals away from the cliffs. Of course, you'll have to milk the cows, help the *Senner* process the milk for cheese."

"I don't know enough about being a dairyman," Florian said. "I'm a carpenter, you see. A journeyman. Jutta Hanny sent me to make some repairs on Hans Glockner's place and he said you need some help with taking the herds up to the alp. He sent me here to get acquainted with your cattle."

"You any good with animals?" Opa looked the German up and down. "Got any experience with Braunvieh?"

"Braunvieh?"

"That's the breed you see all 'round here. Best cattle you can find. Dairy and meat," Opa said.

Florian's face lit up, just as open as his manner. "Somehow I ended up with the cavalry in the war. I didn't have any experience riding into battle either, but I managed pretty well. I mean, I learn quickly. I can walk forever. I know a herdsman's on his feet up and down these mountains what, seven, eight hours a day?"

"Twelve to fourteen," Katharina said.

The news didn't seem to dispel his eagerness. He just grinned at her, and it touched a nerve.

"The war, you say." Opa scratched his head. "Where were you then?"

"In France. The Emperor's First Royal Bavarian Uhlans. Light cavalry." His smile turned apologetic. "My mother's originally

146

from Bozen, and I wanted to fight here, in Tyrol, but you can't choose your family, and you can't choose where you'll be stationed when you've enlisted."

"You're young," Opa said. "And strong. I can see that. And if you're from Bozner stock, well, you'll pick up quick enough. Besides, we need a hand with the mowing too." He seemed to make up his mind. "We were just about to have our breakfast. You'll join us. I'll be in when I'm done."

Opa indicated Katharina to take over and turned around to go back into the barn. She headed for the house and checked to see if Mr Steinhauser was following her. He was on her heels, like a puppy dog. As eager as this newcomer was, teaching him about cows would take precious time from her, and they had a hundred other things to do already. Yet if Hans felt this was a good man, they could not really send him back.

She set another place for Florian, who hovered behind her. She turned into him, and his cheeks turned pink. He sat down on the bench, and Hund sniffed his lap.

"You want me to send her outside?" Katharina asked.

"She's fine here, if it's all right with you." He scratched the dog's head.

Katharina watched him from the stove. She guessed he couldn't be two years older than her, twenty-three or so. He was tall. Tall and wiry, not skinny as if he hadn't eaten. Just wiry and strong. His hair was a wild mane of brown curls, much too long. He also wore no beard, another sign of his foreignness. His eyes tilted downwards at their ends, and when he smiled, she found him sympathetic.

"So Braunvieh, huh?" he said.

She turned her attention to the whey. "That's right."

She caught him licking the tip of his finger. She eyed the block of butter, then him, and he slipped his hand under the table.

"Your grandfather? He said it's the best breed for dairy."

"And meat. We have a very good butcher in Graun. Klaus Blech."

"I've met him." His grin came and went quickly. "So all those jugs of milk outside, that's going to the Dairy Association?"

"Uh-huh. For yogurt and cream. In the summer, we make cheese."

Her grandfather walked in, and she removed their breakfast off the stove, spooning the whey into bowls, then sliced the bread and put a wedge of cheese on the board next to the butter. This time, the visitor waited until after the prayer.

Opa made his usual noises at the breakfast table: his knife scraped butter onto the bread; he sniffed, then sipped his tea; and he made one-word comments. Finally, he pushed himself from the table and tapped out his pipe, filled it with new tobacco, and turned to Florian.

"Come back at sundown. Katharina will teach you to milk the cows. What are you doing for Hans Glockner?"

"He needs to secure his roof. He said the winter was hard this past year."

Katharina detected just a little bit of the Tyrolean accent, but mostly Florian spoke with a crystal-clear German that sounded strange to her ears.

"After we take the livestock up," Opa said, "he'll need you back down here to finish that. I'll stay up at the alp first. I'd be obliged if you would help with the mowing and check on my granddaughter here."

"I don't need any checking on."

Opa gave her a hard look.

"Thank you," she whispered.

"Sundown then. My granddaughter will show you what those cows need." He looked Florian up and down. "You'll need some new clothes too. Hans's won't do. You're about my son Josef's size. Katharina, get him your father's standard issues."

"But I was going to—"

"And the boots. They belong to a dead man, Mr Steinhauser, but—"

"What about Uncle Johi's? Or Uncle Jonas's?"

Opa frowned at her. "He's your father's size."

What ought she to wear, then, for the long hike up to the *Vorsäß*?

As if reading her mind, Opa said, "You'll wear the clothes meant for womenfolk. None of the other women ever complained about it before—no sense in you starting."

Two days later Katharina was getting the animals organised. Hans Glockner, Martin Noggler, and Toni and Kaspar Ritsch were also on hand with their livestock, with the Ritsch and Noggler herds being taken to the meadows around the other side of Graun's Head. David Roeschen, Lisl's and Georg's youngest, was in charge of organising Hans Glockner's sheep and lambs. He smiled shyly when he saw Katharina.

"They keeping you busy, David?"

"Yes, miss."

"It's good to have you back with us this season. You'll be helping Opa the first week."

David nodded and went back to fastening the sides of the lamb cart.

Katharina turned her attention to the cattle herd and called to her cows. She watched Florian from the corner of her eye. In the last couple of days, he had indeed picked up many things, but not enough to convince the farmers he could assuredly keep their animals safe for the summer. Graun's Head was steep, and it was a matter of Arlund pride that they had not lost an animal in over three years. Men, maybe, but none of the livestock. Each year, their animals were crowned in floral wreaths to symbolize that they were returning with a complete herd. Thus, Florian was to come back down with her and help with the mowing.

She was up front, glad to be alone, surrounded by the clanging of cowbells, sheep bells, and goats, the animals calling over the jolly raucous. It normally lifted her spirits, but the way to Graun's Head was mucked up from the rains, and it made the hiking all that more cumbersome. The hem of her dress was already weighted down with mud, and she envied Florian for the good boots and britches.

When she had taught Florian to milk the cows properly, his looks had not been lost on her, and they'd done nothing but irritate her. The city-boy-turned-gypsy might have been amusing if she weren't deeply troubled by her uncertain future. So she'd been short with him, often impatient, and risked a tongue lashing from her grandfather each time he overheard her. In fact, it still stung when she thought of how Opa had spoken to her in front of Mr Steinhauser. He'd never said anything before about her having to wear dresses, or ever made it a point to put her in her place, in the class of womenfolk. He'd taught her to hunt. She'd done as much work on the farm as any man. Since she'd become his last living relative and helping hand, not once did he treat her as if she were less worthy than his sons, so why now?

She put a hand on her belly. Maybe Opa suspected her pregnancy and now was humiliating her to punish her. How much longer before she would have to own up to it? She considered Jutta's offer to bring Katharina to Hannelore, but fear squeezed her middle, and Katharina shivered. Surely there was another choice.

What if she had misunderstood Angelo Grimani's information? Maybe if she found him in Bozen, she would discover that he wasn't married. Or that, maybe, just maybe, his wife was dying of a horrible illness and he would soon need another to take care of any children they had. That he was an honourable man was her greatest hope.

She recalled the night she had lain with Angelo. She could see the lamplight reflecting off their contrasting skins and remembered how they had moved together. He had called her *mia cara*, my love. It made her heart skip even now. But no matter how much she tried, she could not remember how he had looked at her.

It was unreasonable, impossible, she argued with herself.

Before her, a cow needed prodding, and Katharina tapped its hindquarters impatiently.

"He's Italian. I'm Tyrolean," she muttered to the heifer. "We barely spoke to one another. Have quite possibly nothing in common!" Except this child, she thought silently. And if it looked like him? Olive skin? Dark hair? How would the community react to that? She had, at the very least, a home to offer her child. Or had.

She stopped and turned to face the valley below. The farms of Arlund were a dot. Beyond that, the lakes and the church towers of Graun and Reschen. This was her valley, her home. It should be her farm.

Turning back to the livestock, she made her decision. As soon as they were back from Graun's Head, Katharina would go to Jutta, swallow whatever bitter pills she had to, and compound the immoral damages to her soul. She would ask for Hannelore.

Florian was suddenly at her elbow, and she jumped. "There are no sins when on the meadow," he said jovially. He touched her arm lightly. "Sorry. I didn't mean to frighten you. Isn't that what they say up here?"

"I have no idea what you mean."

"I meant if you'd wanted to wear britches, I don't see the problem with that. I'm just sorry about your father, first of all, and your grandfather's insistence that I wear his clothes when obviously they mean much to you."

When she said nothing, he added, a bit too jauntily, "You've got quite the fast tempo there, Miss Thaler."

Katharina looked over her shoulder and frowned. "Who's taking care of those cows back there if you're up here?"

He looked chastised. "Martin Noggler sent me. He said you might need some help." He pointed to the side of the path.

She had not seen that one of the cows was tangled within a low thicket.

"I've really lost my head now." Katharina jogged towards the animal, Florian right behind her. Hund barked and worked the cow out as best she could. It did not take a minute and the beast was back on the trail.

The way grew steep and slippery, and even Florian struggled, especially when they entered the woods, where roots and branches could even trip up the beasts. They had to be pushed forward, and soon enough Katharina was damp from the work. When she looked over at Florian working on the other side of the forest, she realised she had mistaken his patience for hesitation. He was calculating and could anticipate where the animals might have the most problems, diverting them in time. She worked with him through the forest until the path opened up to meadows again and the last bit of rock outcropping on Graun's Head appeared above.

"We still have a long way to go," Katharina said, wiping her brow.

"Your Opa said that we're taking them to the *Vorsäß* first."

"That's right. They stay in the lower meadows for a few weeks until the melt is over. Then we move them to the high pastures till the end of summer. Then it's back down to the *Vorsäß* for a couple of weeks more. The hut's at the *Vorsäß*. It's the last place for shelter. When you're on the high alp, you'll be victim to the elements." She looked at him in her father's things. "You think you can manage?"

Florian smiled, but there was an edge to it. "I handled a lot in the Great War. Victim to the elements and all."

She bit her lip. "Yes, well…"

"Besides," he added more lightly, "you have another saying, don't you? There's no such thing as bad weather, just bad gear. And I've got good gear." He marched past her, leaving her to glare after him.

They were far ahead of the rest of the group when David Roeschen caught up and told them the others had stopped to take a break. Katharina sent David on up ahead with Hund, happy to have someone who respected her authority. She instructed him to let the cows graze, then turned to see Florian standing near a boulder, his hand shielding his eyes from the sun. When she looked up, a falcon was rising with the warm current. Irritated again, she turned away to unpack her lunch from the leather satchel. She pulled out the pieces of Tyrolean bread—hard as crackers—a couple of chicken legs, a hard-boiled egg, and some cheese. The air carried the scent of sun-bathed meadow.

Florian flopped down next to her, unpacking his own lunch. The falcon called, and they both looked up. The bird hovered, but farther above now.

"I love it here," Florian said. "It's so peaceful."

She turned from him to watch the cows. "It used to be a lot more peaceful before everything broke apart."

He ate, obviously hungry. When he seemed to have satiated his first pangs, he waved an arm over the picnic. "I know there's a lot we're all worried about, but look at us. We're outside on a beautiful day, and we have something to eat. We've got healthy animals, an open sky, and this beautiful meadow. It's a good life, this. All of this."

He was already laying claim to her animals. He had no idea what it was like to live here, this practical tourist. Even his Tyrolean mother came from a large town.

"It must be nice to feel life can be so simple, Mr Steinhauser.

You can just go from one nice place to the next. There's nothing that ties you down."

"That's right: life is simple." He crunched on a piece of the cracker bread. His face read amusement and interest. "From what I've gathered, you don't strike me as someone who doesn't appreciate this yourself."

"I don't really have a lot of choices, do I?" She stood up and brushed off the crumbs, then quickly packed away the rest of her food. She could only keep bread down anyway. She packed up her chicken, but Florian had eaten his and was now sucking the marrow out of the bone.

"I'm moving on," she said. "You can pick up from here when the others come."

He scrambled to his feet, the chicken leg dangling in his hand. "Don't you want my help?"

She was already hiking up the path and whistled to Hund, who immediately broke into rounding up cows. She waved to David, and he helped Hund to the left of the path while she veered to the right where a dozen or so cows grazed. When she turned back to look down at the meadow, Florian was packing up his satchel as fast as he could.

"The men will need you," she called down. "David and I will take the front. Just wait for the others."

She returned to work, taking comfort in knowing that Florian's muscles would ache right painfully tomorrow. Tomorrow, he would not be so cocky.

Katharina pulled out her needlework to put the final stitches to the new curtains she was making. The dinner dishes were drying, and Hund was lying near her feet. They both raised their heads at the sound of someone approaching the farm. Outside the window, the sky was grey, and a light mist had rolled in with the dusk and the fog, but the source of those footsteps was unmistakable. Florian Steinhauser was back.

Hund was already at the door, whining and wagging her tail, then cocked her head to listen before wagging her tail again. Katharina sighed and put the needlework away. Florian came around every day while Opa and David Roeschen were at Graun's Head, and she'd only made peace with him when he'd returned her father's things, clean and in good shape. She'd told him to keep the boots. In return, she'd added the needed length and strengthened the stitching on two pairs of her uncles' britches. Florian had offered to pay for them, but they both knew he had almost nothing to his name, so she'd insisted they were a gift.

At the sound of the knock, Hund barked happily and Katharina opened the door.

He greeted them and patted Hund, who pranced around him, ears cocked forward. Florian pulled out a round stick from his bag and tossed it into the barnyard. The dog ran after it, scooped it into her mouth, and returned, tossing her head like a horse chomping at its bit.

Florian would likely be delighted if it were Katharina who danced around him like this. "Coffee?" she asked as they stepped into the house. "Did you eat?"

Florian always took coffee and anything she had left over from lunch, since Hans was not a cook. He always complimented her on her cooking and did not seem to care if the coffee was just roasted barley. He had once told her how he missed the dark and aromatic beans he'd drunk when he was in France. He would tell her such stories, never about the war or what he must have experienced on the battlefield. Instead, he told her about the French countryside or about the food, as if he had been on holiday there instead of fighting. Then he talked about Bavaria or about the peculiar personalities he had met on his travels.

When they were sitting at the table with steaming mugs, Katharina asked how he was getting on with Hans Glockner.

"Just fine. We're finished with the barn roof now. We've decided to help some of the other neighbours too. Martin Noggler's arranged for some cheaper materials, and as part of my journey, I'm not allowed to get paid, so free labour."

"That's really kind of you."

"And your grandfather? Is everything all right on the alp?"

Katharina shrugged. "I haven't heard anything."

"No news is good news, I guess."

They remained silent before Florian began digging around in his satchel. "I brought you something. I think you might like this."

He pulled out a thick tome and handed it to her, his face lit up with anticipated pleasure. It was a book about plants and herbs.

"Where did you get this?"

He grinned. "It's a gift. There was a *Kärner* peddling some old books and things. Hans and I had to pick up supplies at Jutta Hanny's, and we ran into him on the road. I fixed the wheel on his trap."

She smiled. "A *Kärner*? You're like a thirsty rag, picking up all our dialect." She flipped through the pages. There were watermarks on some of them, and the pages were brittle, but the illustrations were good, and she was pleased.

She put the book aside. "How is Jutta? I've been meaning to go visit her, but I've been so busy." In truth, after she finished her chores, she was too tired to walk to Graun. And there was the matter of having to decide for or against the old midwife. Katharina dreaded Jutta's solution for her. With the farm to herself, Katharina had almost convinced herself that everything would be all right.

"Jutta's just been asking about you," Florian said.

"Tomorrow I'll go to Mass at St. Katharina instead of the chapel."

"She'll like that, seems eager to see you."

156

Katharina sighed. It was time to face the inevitable.

There was a flash of light and a crack of thunder, and when Katharina looked towards the window, she saw dark storm clouds to the south. Lightning zigzagged across the sky, and the kitchen bulb flicked and faded before growing bright again.

She got up to secure the shutters, and Florian joined her. At the last window, he latched the shutters closed.

"That's going to be one messy storm. I suppose I ought to get going," he said.

She agreed, though she had to admit that she was always a little lonely just after he left. She moved towards the door, and Florian picked up his satchel under the flickering light bulb, but not before fat drops sounded on the roof. By the time he was at the door, the rain was pelting down as if someone had overturned a bucket of gravel. Hail.

In the doorway, she reached for Florian's elbow. He seemed as surprised by her impulse as she was. She let go, but he looked expectant when he stepped back under the overhang.

Over the hammering rain, she raised her voice. "You may as well wait out the worst of it, or you'll be pelted to death by the time you get to Hans's place." When he did not reply, she turned into the house. "I'll light the oil lamps. The electricity will likely go out soon."

She heard him close the door, the hail muffled behind it. As she reached for the lamps on top of the tiled oven, he moved around her and took them down.

"I'll do this," he offered. "Go finish your coffee before it gets cold."

Instead, she watched him as he lit the lamps, and when he'd placed two on the table, they both slid back into their seats, and Katharina busied herself by sipping her lukewarm coffee. Neither of them said a word, and then Florian searched his satchel again. This time he brought out a knife and piece of wood—cherry, she guessed, from the colour.

157

Hund was immediately at his side, and Florian patted her head, chuckling and holding it out for her to sniff it. "Not every piece of wood is for you to play with," he said to the dog. Then to Katharina, "I'm making a pipe for your grandfather, as a thank-you gift."

"He will like it very much."

As Florian examined what he had so far, Katharina realised she was just encouraging him like this. Reminded of the night she had been alone with Angelo in the storm—the night his fever had risen—she felt dizzy, as if she had stood up too quickly. She grasped the edge of the table to hang on.

Florian looked up. "Everything all right?"

Angelo's phantom faded.

Katharina steadied herself and stood. "Let's move into the sitting room. I'll get you a newspaper for the shavings."

Florian helped her carry the pair of lamps, and she took the plants and herbs book to her chair. When they had settled in, Hund lying on the floor between them, Katharina pretended to read. The rain hammered on, letting up for maybe a minute, at which time both she and Florian would look up, but then it would grow with intensity and continue. Katharina turned to the next page while Florian continued to scrape and whittle.

She became engrossed in the section about the healing effects of fennel before realising that some time had gone by and that things were quiet. When she looked up, the rain and Florian had both stopped and he was just watching her.

"What is it?"

Florian got his knife busy again.

"You were watching me."

He glanced up at her, then returned to the pipe. "You're beautiful."

"Oh."

"Yes." He continued to whittle the stick as if nothing had changed.

When she finally found her voice, even she was taken aback by the venom in it. "You don't want to have anything to do with me."

He looked up, a slow smile spreading on his face, as if she'd revealed something amusing. He said nothing.

"I'm difficult. I'm stubborn. I feel more comfortable in men's britches than in a dress. People in the village treat me like an outsider either way."

He lay the pipe in his lap, still watching her with that infuriating grin. The fire in the oven crackled.

"Besides," she said, unable to keep the exasperation from her tone, "you have your travelling to do. You can't possibly be happy in a place like this. You're not a country boy. You've grown up in a city. You'll quickly find out that these mountains close in on you."

"Do they close in on you or close people out?"

Katharina shrugged.

"All I said was that you're beautiful. I didn't ask you to marry me."

She looked down at her lap, her face hot.

"Although…"

Silence, save for the fire. A log popped and she jumped. "Although what?"

"Although, I do believe women should wear britches more often." He leaned forward, his mouth changing from a smile to a thin line. "Why do you assume to know what would make me happy and unhappy?"

"Experience."

Florian jerked back, his smile back again. "Experience? How many have you counselled before?"

She did not know how to answer the question, but he was talking again.

"I saw you for the first time at the Corpus Christi festival, and since then I've been looking for you. When I saw that this was

159

your farm two weeks ago, I thought I was going to die of happiness. There you were again." He paused, and Katharina's chest hurt. "If you're on the battlefield and watch as your friends drop dead around you and you're one of the few who manages to survive, well, you learn to believe in nothing but fate. And God's hand in those matters. I'm happy here. Just being here tonight, with you. This, here, makes me happier than I have ever been. Honest."

The cover of the book swam before her eyes, moving farther away. Just like the Thalerhof. It would never be hers.

"I know what I want, Katharina Thaler."

She finally released her breath, her lungs on fire. Only a whisper was what she could manage. "Don't say that. You know nothing, and I mean nothing, about me."

Florian leaned back into his chair and folded his arms. The pipe lay at his feet, and Hund nosed it. "As a matter of fact, I think I *do* know you."

"You *think*?" She remembered standing in that field as Angelo drove away. She remembered her shame. "You men don't think. You just do what you want. Then you lie about it." She stood but had nowhere to go.

Florian rose too, his voice urgent. "I don't know what to say. I suppose I do the things I want to do. That freedom is granted us men. I don't intend on wasting any of the life I have left." He took in a deep breath. "You're right, though. I did lie. I guess I *am* asking you to marry me."

He guessed? If she were a man, she would take a swinging punch at him. Instead she felt as if she would laugh out loud.

"I can't marry you," she finally managed. She stood up and went to the door. "Please leave, Mr Steinhauser. Now. Forget this conversation." She jerked the door open. "Please."

He stared at her before gathering his things. In the doorframe, he turned, and Katharina believed he intended to grab her. But he did not. Realising she wanted him to, she stepped away.

He pushed a curly strand of hair back with the palm of his hand. When he spoke, his voice sounded bitter. "I'm going now."

"Good."

"I'm not coming back. At least not until your grandfather's here again."

"It won't help."

Now she could swear smoke was streaming from his ears. "What on earth are you going to tell him? That I can't come back here because I'm in love with you? He knows anyway."

He might as well have slapped her.

"So you and my grandfather have conspired, is that it? You're going to make all the decisions for me, you two? Such as who gets my father's clothing, my father's knife, the shameful granddaughter?" She jerked her head towards the barnyard. Hail the size of pebbles lay about a finger-knuckle deep. "Please go."

He made to leave, but then he turned to her again. "What did I *do*? What did I *say* that's so bad?"

"Stop it."

He looked at his feet, then raised his head again, wearing a sad grin. "Am I that bad to look at?"

"Beauty fades."

"Yes," Florian whispered, "but love grows. Don't you believe that?"

"I'm afraid not." If he did not leave soon, she would get the rifle.

"What is it then? Why are you crying?"

"Is there someone else?" he asked.

"It's none of your business," she snapped.

"No, it's not. But I would understand if you told me there was someone else."

The touch on her arm was too much. She felt herself weaken.

"There was. All right?" She backed away.

"Was?" He leaned against the doorframe. "And where is he now?"

She flicked her wrist towards the road. "Gone."

"Did he die? In the war?"

She shook her head.

"So he's still around here? No? All right. He's not here. And?"

"And…" She choked back a sob, infuriated. "I loved him. Isn't that what you wanted to hear?"

"You *loved* him. But you don't anymore?"

"I don't know," Katharina whispered. It was an honest answer. "That's a complicated question."

Florian chuckled, and when she looked up, he stopped. "Go on."

"I don't want to tell you anything more."

"All right." He glanced up at the sky and stepped back into the house, though the rain had stopped. "I can see you need more time."

She followed him. "Nothing's all right! And no, I do not need any more time!"

He slid into his usual place at the table. "If you don't want to tell me, you don't have to. I respect your privacy. I think I may even understand how you feel."

"That's not possible." He was so sure of himself!

"I still would like to know whether I have a chance despite this…complication. I mean, if we take some more time to get to know one another, even though I know I won't change my mind about you."

"I don't think so."

"Ah."

She lingered at the edge of the table as he watched her. Her heart beat as if for the first time again, and her cheeks felt warm. Inside her, the baby made her stomach feel weak. How was she going to survive this? Surely Opa suspected and now was encouraging this stranger to pursue her, get her married, so he would not be shamed. Give the farm to a stranger! Or worse yet, have Florian take her away.

162

Never. She had to get to Jutta.

As steadily as she could with the threatening tears, she said, "You're a good man. I can see that."

"Why, thank you." His tone was sarcastic. "Look here, nothing is complicated. *We* make things complicated. When I first saw you, I knew that you're different. I just didn't realise how wonderfully so. You've got a way with animals, and you work as hard as any man I've seen. But there's something fragile about you too. What? I'm sorry, Katharina. I don't want you to cry. You're making my proposal into quite a miserable affair."

She wiped her tears away. "What else did you and my grandfather decide for me?"

He looked puzzled. "I asked for his permission to court you. That's all. What would we conspire—"

"So my grandfather wants to get rid of me. Send me off to Germany with you?"

"Why would you think that?"

"Because of the…" She threw a hand over her mouth.

Florian cocked his head, but then revelation slowly spread across his face. "Oh" was all he said.

"I thought you two had reached an agreement…" Panic pushed against her chest. When he shook his head, she dropped onto the bench, her face in her hands.

"Florian," she begged, "please don't tell my grandfather. If he doesn't know, then I don't want him to know. And if he does, he can't know that you do."

Ages passed. Not a sound. When Florian pried her hands open, his face was sombre.

"Is this man… Is he coming back?"

She wiped her face with the back of her hands. She'd done it now. There was no turning back. It was her bed—she would have to lie in it. "No."

"You must feel so alone in this."

His words brought a fresh stream of tears.

"How far along, Katharina?"

"Just over two months."

He sighed. "He may come back for you."

She shook her head, and something in his look told her he was convinced, perhaps even more than she was. She felt his gaze on her as he gently took her wrists.

"Katharina? If you will have me, I will raise your child as our child."

"I can't accept that," she said, miserable. She would never know whether she married him for love or out of sheer desperation. But the farm, the land…

He moved to her side of the table, then pulled her up before taking her hand and shifting it to her middle. Katharina tried to pull away, but he held her look, and there was no malice, no judgment. Fascinated by the intimacy he allowed himself, she let him guide both their hands onto where her child lay and understood what was happening. Whatever decision she made, it would be for the sake of this land. It belonged to her, and it belonged to the child she carried.

"Mr Steinhauser…" Her voice trembled. She swallowed and met his gaze. Hazel eyes. Not brown. Eyes that were on her, not flitting away. "You must promise me three things before I agree to anything."

He nodded slowly.

"We stay here, on the Thalerhof. No matter what. You will have to learn to become a farmer."

She could tell he wanted to smile but didn't dare.

"Yes." He nodded. "Absolutely. What else?"

"You will love this child?"

At first he shook his head, as if he could not believe she would even ask, then he kissed both of her hands. "Yes, Katharina Thaler. Yes. I will love our child."

He paused, clearly anticipating her third demand.

"And you are to never—" Her voice cracked, and she took a

deep breath before trying again. Her resolve returned. "I mean *never, ever* ask me about *him*. You are not to ask me for any details. Ever."

Florian remained silent, his eyes on hers as she held her breath. When he reached to touch her cheek, he was saddened.

"If that is what you want, I promise," he said and kissed her.

14

GRAUN/ARLUND

At St. Anna's chapel, Jutta put the finishing touches on the bellflowers and white daisies she'd affixed to the ends of the first four rows of pews, then walked to the back of the chapel and imagined how Katharina would react to the decorated altar. From Lisl's garden, she'd arranged a dozen red roses in a vase with three large white poppies for a little bit of the Austrian colour to go with the blue-and-white wedding bouquets. It was good. Everything was good. She had done the right thing bringing Florian and Katharina together.

She heard voices coming up the hill and went outside to watch the procession of people coming for the wedding. Father Wilhelm was in the sacristy with Florian. She hurried back to the altar. "They're here! They're here, Father!"

Florian peeked out.

"My, look at you!" She could hardly believe it. He had borrowed a traditional Tyrolean wedding suit: white shirt, black suit coat, and a wide black leather belt with an edelweiss tooled on the silver buckle. "You stay put," she said. "You're not to see the bride. It's bad luck."

With a good-natured salute, he backed up into the sacristy.

She liked him. She really did.

Father Wilhelm joined her at the front of the chapel, and they watched as Katharina approached with Johannes Thaler and Hans Glockner, followed by the other guests. She beamed at Katharina's *Tracht*: the blue-and-white smock, the red bodice, and the white satin scarf with gold fringe crossed over her chest. Her hair had been done up in a crown of braids topped with a white lace headband.

Jutta hugged her tightly. "You look beautiful. Listen to me— today is a happy day. A happy day, Katharina."

"Thank you, Jutta. I don't know what I would have done if you weren't here."

Katharina's voice was choked with emotion or fear, and Jutta pulled her away to take a good look. It was shame she saw.

"Remember, Jutta, he doesn't know that you're aware of, you know—"

"I'll tell you again," she whispered back, "you're not the first to commit adultery. And you won't be the last. The Ten Commandments weren't made because they'd be easy to follow. They're meant to control our weaknesses."

Tears shone in Katharina's eyes, and Jutta handed her a handkerchief. "Go on then. And smile. It's your wedding."

Before Father Wilhelm could call them in, Jutta greeted the other guests and observed Katharina out of the corner of her eye to see whether, despite her conflicted heart, she could cherish this day.

Jutta took her place near the altar, and Father Wilhelm began the marriage ceremony with the opening prayers. Florian reminded her of Johi Thaler sometimes. In just under a year, she could have been up here, Johi's bride. If Fritz really was dead, or would never return, she would be getting married to the only man she'd ever truly loved.

She caught Hans Glockner watching her, his face sombre, as if he knew her thoughts. Then Father Wilhelm started the marriage vows, and Jutta paid attention: Katharina's voice was barely audible, and Florian's was shaky. When Father Wilhelm pronounced them man and wife, the two kissed, tentative, shy. That would all change. Then Father Wilhelm indicated that Jutta and Hans should approach the altar, and next to Hans Glockner's signature, she added her own as witness to the marriage certificate.

She smiled a reassurance at Hans, but he looked away. "Hans?"

"It's time to congratulate the newlyweds," he said, leaving her to go outside where the others had already gathered.

In the churchyard, the Thalers' neighbours from Arlund were there, Georg and Lisl of course, and the regulars from Johannes Thaler's *Stammtisch.* The Planggers had come, and the Prieths.

Katharina's grandfather handed Georg the old camera that had once belonged to Johannes's youngest son, and Florian called to Jutta to join them for photographs. She lingered near the stone fence that enclosed the cemetery, waiting for Georg to tell her where to stand. All around her were their mountains, and below, the lakes' surfaces rippled on the afternoon wind. When Georg was ready for her, he had positioned them all with their backs to the lakes, the sun shining on their faces.

As Georg fumbled with the camera, Klaus Blech and his wife, their sons in tow, talked with Frederick and the teacher. From the bench where he sat with Sara, Alois waved at her.

"Alois should be in the photo," Katharina said.

Florian agreed and called Jutta's son over. Alois stood next to her, and she put her hand on his shoulder.

"Everyone look at the camera," Georg called. The bulb flashed followed by a pungent smell. Georg reset the bulb and prepared to take another photo.

As Lisl and Mrs Blech walked by, Jutta heard the butcher's wife say, "That was an awfully quick engagement."

Lisl shrugged. "But Jutta was right. Everyone will be up on the high alps in a week or two, and they'd have had to wait until October."

Mrs Blech clucked. "Couldn't wait that long, could they? The youngsters are so impatient these days."

Jutta shook her head. That woman!

A pop and hiss of the flash again and Jutta realised someone was missing. "Where's Frederick?"

"That's right," Florian said. "Where is Dr Hanny?"

"Jutta, hold still," Georg scolded.

"He told me he'd come later," Hans muttered beside her. "Some business or something."

Georg looked flabbergasted. "Jutta! Just a moment, everyone. We have to do that again."

Everyone groaned, and Jutta apologised under her breath. Someone poked her waist, and as Georg loaded the flash, she dared to take a quick look.

Florian grinned down at her. "Out of practise, are we?"

"Oh shush."

When the ordeal was over, Jutta took the reins again. She called to the lingering guests and announced that the newlyweds would lead them to Graun for the reception at the inn. She took Florian and Katharina to the wall of the cemetery where Hans had brought up his ox and cart, decorated with greenery and ribbons in blue, white, and gold. Florian helped Katharina onto the pile of hay in the back, then leapt in and tossed himself next to her, grinning. Hans flicked the reins to get the ox going and Jutta followed behind them.

When the other men pulled out flasks of schnapps and Toni Ritsch called for Florian to stop for a toast on the hillside, Florian shook his head.

"I'm a married man now," he called and raised his arm with Katharina's hand in his.

Toni Ritsch muttered next to Jutta, "He's a soft one, isn't he." He tipped the flask to his lips.

"Never been in love, Toni?" she said to Kaspar Ritsch's eldest. "I seem to recall when you and Patricia got married, you were all eyes on her." She left it at that and picked up her pace. No matter what the other folks might think of Florian, she'd done well by Katharina. She'd done well.

～

At the Post Inn, the *Stube* was decorated with a string of coloured lights and paper streamers, and the wedding table was spread from one end of the *Stube* to the next save for the round *Stammtisch*, which was already filling up with the regulars. The rest of the floor was left empty for dancing. Bouquets of poppies, hydrangeas, and freesia were in canning jars on the tables, and Lisl's middle son, Henri, was at the bar, already helping Sara with flasks of wine and mugs of beer. They were fine without Jutta. She was part of the wedding party, and she would enjoy herself.

She moved amongst the guests and found Florian with Georg. Nearby, Katharina was concentrating on something that Lisl and Frau Prieth were saying, and Jutta frowned. The girl still looked wholly uncertain and uncomfortable.

"Frau Prieth," Jutta called, "your strawberry cake is beautiful. Did you see it, Katharina? Go have a look." A gracious smile from the bride. Someone might have called it blushing.

When Katharina drifted off to the cake table, Jutta turned to Florian. "I wish you both all the happiness in the world."

He cocked his head, as if to examine her, then smiled. "I got very lucky, I would say."

"You both did." Jutta squeezed his arm.

He gave her that look again, as if waiting for her to say something more. Florian could only suspect her involvement in bringing the two of them together. Let him keep guessing.

"Florian, son," Johannes Thaler called from across the room.

He had a mug of beer raised above his head. "A toast! Drink with your Opa."

Everyone raised their glasses, and then Johannes, his eyes shining, made his way to where Jutta stood with the groom. "I have a son again. Someone who can help me with the farm. Florian, you and I will make the Thalerhof prosperous again."

Katharina whirled away from the cake table, her face crushed.

"Florian will have a lot to learn from his wife first," Jutta said. "Katharina's as capable of running that farm as any man."

Johannes's smile faded, and he turned to where Katharina stood. "Come to me," he beckoned.

She came, heavy footed, and Jutta wanted to wrap her arms around that broken-hearted girl.

Gently taking Katharina's hand, Johannes placed hers in Florian's. "This woman," he said to Florian, his voice heavy with emotion, "will make you a great man. She will show you how to be tender to the animals, how to get the most from the cows and the mountains and from this valley. Listen to her. She has great plans."

Katharina's eyes shone, and she bit her lip, looking down at the ground.

"That's right, Florian," Jutta interjected. "She'll get the cows running to you, not from you."

The others laughed, and Florian raised Katharina's hand to his lips.

Johannes gave Jutta a grateful nod, and she smiled at the way Katharina gazed at Florian.

Someone whooped in the corner, and a number of men—all the volunteer firefighters—raised their schnapps in responding cheers. On the other end of the room, a group of women started to sing a ballad, and the firefighters migrated towards them, singing along. In the corner, Walter Plangger strapped on his accordion, tuned it, and then played the melody.

Jutta raised her glass to the group around her. "Here's to your future. May it be a wealthy one."

Just as she turned to clink glasses with Lisl, she saw Frederick standing at the edge of the group. Her brother-in-law was unusually red faced, and when he raised his drink, he swayed, as if on a boat.

He took a step closer to them and swung his look at Katharina. "You hear that? A wealthy future." He laughed abruptly, then looked deadly serious. "The Italians are taking over the banks now, but Katharina, well, she has a great talent for making friends out of newcomers, don't you? She could probably negotiate new terms for your mortgages."

Katharina blanched. "Dr Hanny? I—"

"Frederick," Jutta warned, "I don't know what's got into you, but you know I don't tolerate debauchery in my pub." Whatever he was insinuating, she wanted to know, but not now. Not on Katharina's wedding day.

"All of you here"—he swung his mug over his head—"will have nothing left to stand on. Not even you, Jutta. They won't pay any compensation to you if they build that reservoir, Jutta. You don't own the inn. The banks can just take it from you. You have to talk to Fritz."

"Fritz?" she choked. "What are you talking about?"

Looking alarmed, he twisted away from her and went to Georg. "We have to *do* something, Mayor," Frederick said. "We have to stop the building of the dam. Jutta's inn—"

"Let's go outside," Georg said, his hand on Frederick's shoulder. "Now is not the time or the place to talk about this."

Johannes and Florian followed them as Georg steered Frederick towards the door.

Jutta then remembered the Corpus Christi festival. Frederick, talking to the *carabinieri*. Was that what Rioba had come to see her about? Did he know where Fritz was?

172

"Stop," Jutta ordered the retreating men. "I want to know what he's talking about. What does he know about Fritz, Georg?"

Lisl had her by the elbow though. "Don't, Jutta. Not now. Let them take care of him."

"Lisl, what does he know about Fritz?"

"I haven't the faintest idea. Really, I don't." Lisl led her back to where they had been, then took Katharina's hand. "Let's go to the women, Katharina. Dr Hanny has no idea what he's talking about. You heard him. He wants Jutta to talk to Fritz."

Jutta was not ready to call this fool's talk, yet. She searched for Hans. From the corner of the *Stube*, Walter Plangger played a polka. Even the youngsters went onto the floor to dance. Sara held Alois by the hand and led him to the kitchen, but before Jutta could go and tell her to let him dance, Hans stepped in front of Jutta.

"What's wrong?" he asked.

"Did you hear what Frederick said?"

He shook his head. "Though he looked as if he's had too much."

"Yes, that's the first thing that's out of character," Jutta said. "He was talking about Fritz…as if he knew where he was."

He offered her his arm. "Let's dance."

"Maybe the next one."

"Come now. Jutta, forget the past. If there's anyone who can make this a festive occasion, it's you."

She put her hand on his arm and let him lead her, and though thoughts of Fritz still gnawed at her, she was happy Hans had sought her out. It had been decades since they had danced together, and she tried to remember when that was. A carnival dance, just before Lent. She had also danced with Hugo, Hans's twin brother. "You and your brother were the ones who always made a party lively," she said. "Not me."

He bent his head towards her.

"Hans, do you remember when we were still in school? All the girls wanted to dance with the Glockner boys."

He shook his head, and she looked at his chest. He wore a flaxen shirt and smelled of freshly mown hay. She tried to follow his step, but with his gimp leg, she really had to concentrate. A vibration from his chest made her realise he was speaking.

She looked up. "What's that you say?"

"You always danced with Hugo," Hans said loud enough for her to hear. "Not me. You never danced with me."

She started to protest, but he was right.

The music stopped, and she still held his arm. "My memories are such a blur, sometimes I think they belong to someone else."

His eyes were on her, gentle. "That's because the things we observe often have very little to do with the truth."

Noises from the party in the *Hof* reached Katharina in her parents' bedroom. Now her bedroom, and Florian's. Hans and Opa were building a bonfire outside for the lingering wedding guests from Arlund, but Florian had sent her upstairs with an "Aren't you tired? We should go to bed." Except that he had not followed her up, and now she sat alone, in anticipation of when he would come.

She shivered in the linen shift she had taken from her mother's pine chest. Mama had maybe worn it on her wedding night. Even though the linen was mildly yellowed, Katharina liked the embroidered pink roses on the bodice. They made her feel more maidenly.

Lisl and Jutta had told her to put Dr Hanny's comments out of her mind. He had no idea what he was saying, they'd said. She told herself it didn't matter what Dr Hanny had said. Yes, he'd been there when she'd chased after Angelo. Of course he'd have suspected something. But she had trusted Dr Hanny. He'd never said a cruel word to anyone, and if he was insinuating that the kindness she had shown Angelo... Or did he suspect more? She wanted to weep. The small-minded people in this valley would never give her a chance if they knew what she'd done. To make her child legitimate in the community, she'd had to marry Florian.

Yes, Florian. She had to forget her stupid actions, her ridiculous obsession with Angelo Grimani. The Thalerhof would never be in her name. But she had a father for her child. Her husband. And he would come to her soon...

What she understood from the village women at the reception was that the marriage bed was where obligatory duties were attended to, not enjoyed. More than that the women had not—or would not—tell her. If she enjoyed it, however—if she gave herself like she had to Angelo—Florian would certainly think poorly of her.

Footsteps in the stairwell. She held her breath. In such a short time, Florian's footfalls had become familiar. These were the steady, solid steps of a husband now. Her *husband*. In the only home she knew.

A shudder ran through her at the thought of possibly having to live in servitude to Florian for the rest of her life. What if, when the child came, he would not be able to love it as he'd promised? What if he renounced her and the child, or told her secret to others and took the Thalerhof as his own? He was at the door. It was too late to question his motives or his character now.

According to Frau Prieth, she must learn to obey her husband and make certain that he was pleased with her. Frau Prieth probably had had too much wine, but she'd put it to Katharina directly and simply: being married meant meeting a man's demands and expectations—the husband's dinner on the table when he came in stinking from work, a woman who knew her place, and relations when he wanted it.

"And they always want it," Lisl had added.

Florian opened the door, and Katharina drew the wool blanket over her shoulders. He leaned against the doorframe, arms crossed, but she could not read his face in the shadows. The blanket slipped, and she felt naked. He moved towards her.

"Let me."

He took the two ends and tied them just under her chin, as if putting a cape on a child. Katharina remained still. When he finished, he hadn't even touched her. Instead, he sat down next to her, his eyes on her.

"Like a princess." His laugh made her jump. "Which of course you're not. You're far from a princess if I ever knew one."

She looked up.

"I didn't mean it like that." His voice was softer. "I meant, you're no princess in that you don't need to be pampered. You're not a spoiled woman, Katharina. You're quite resourceful, and I can't imagine that you're the kind of woman who would hang a noose around my..." He swallowed, his smile unusually shy and uncertain.

She knew what was happening. She had lived amongst the folk here long enough to understand that these so-called advisors had planted fears and doubts and, well, yes, old wives' tales into their heads because they themselves could not break the pattern. She leaned back on her arms, the loose knot under her chin coming undone and the blanket sliding onto the mattress behind her. He put a hand on her right shoulder and gently pressed her down onto the bed. She closed her eyes. Florian and she had kissed before their wedding, always as if something might break. Now, she decided, they would kiss to hold. She would make her marriage as legitimate as Florian would make her child.

She waited for him, imagining his eyes roaming over her body. When he didn't move, she took a fleeting look at him and was surprised to see that he was watching her face.

"What do you want me to do?" she whispered.

Florian shook his head then gazed at her again. "Nothing."

Feeling relieved, she pulled her legs up and turned on her side, her back a wall between them. The mattress shifted beneath her, then his body came close to hers, fitting against her like the cogs on a milling wheel. She tensed.

Angelo. Angelo. Angelo. She squeezed her eyes tight. *The baby.*

Florian's arm came over her waist, and he placed his hand on her rib cage, just below her right breast. She held her breath. Ever so gently, he pulled her closer to him, and she focussed on his breathing, making herself aware of *this* man. *Florian.*

The lamp flickered. The electricity would go out soon. She closed her eyes again and moved her arm over his, then put her hand over his, then laced her fingers with his.

They lay still for a long time, and though Katharina could not remember falling asleep, she awoke and the lamp was still on. She felt aware of every millimetre of Florian's body against hers. Although their breathing had not changed, she was certain he was also awake.

He gently squeezed her hand and then slipped it out of hers, and his fingertips reached for her breast. She shivered, but this time not from cold. She arched her back against him just a little and felt his knees on the backs of her thighs slide away. She was falling and had stopped breathing, but now that he stroked her, she had to let go. When he turned her towards him and kissed her on the mouth, she willed herself to feel joy, not fear. He tasted of wine, and she smelled the apple wood smoke caught in his long curls. When he opened his mouth against hers, she felt as if feathers were falling all around her body. His kisses were slow, considerate, and she didn't know whether to bury herself in him or take him into her arms and hold him.

When he undid the top of her nightgown, it slipped over her bare shoulder, leaving one breast to hang over the gathering of pink roses. He took it into his mouth while his fingers sought to find the bottom of her shift. He was still in control, though she felt his desperation growing, as if she were being bathed in an electric glow. She raised her leg and pulled the nightgown's hem up to her waist. His hand easily found her, while the other was still at her breast. His finger slid into her. She sucked in her breath.

"Did I hurt you?"

"The midwife told me you can't hurt the—" If only she were not pregnant, he would know that her desire for him was genuine. She wanted this. She wanted this union. More than that, she wanted him to believe that she did not easily fall in love.

She reached for the waist of his trousers and drew him on top of her. Florian was now the one who seemed to be holding his breath, and Katharina gave him a determined look.

"It's all right," she whispered. "Everything is all right."

Jutta had once told her that men on top of women were the most horrible things to look at. This was why, she had said, they should always have their relationships in the dark. *They roll their eyes back into their skulls as if the devil were taking them over. Or they grunt and snort like beasts in the brush.* Mere nonsense.

Just before the light went out, Katharina saw her reflection in Florian's eyes. She said to herself, *I am his wife. This is my husband.*

15

The newspaper rustled, and Angelo looked up from his breakfast to watch his wife snap back the pages of the *Bozner Nachrichten*. She wore a cream-coloured lounge suit that no longer hid the bulge in her middle. In just three months, she would give birth to their first child.

Thoughts of the baby made him happy, but when he saw Chiara's face, his sentiments were quashed. She was ready for another fight, and he did not feel like discussing the contents of the paper with his wife today. He finished his egg and pushed away his plate, stood up, and kissed her forehead. "I'm off to the ministry."

Her tight smile seemed accusing. Angelo sighed and put a hand on her shoulder. "I'll be back this evening."

"I may be out." She pointed to the paper. "There's a meeting tonight I'd like to attend. This manufactory has made over thirty women redundant, women who've had jobs there four or five years. This was their livelihood. Those jobs are how they support their fatherless children, their crippled husbands and sons—"

"Chiara, maybe the company's not doing well. We have a poor economy."

179

"No, Angelo. They're being replaced by men."

"Whose jobs the women had taken over when those men went to war. Chiara, the Fascists are just as concerned about unemployment and welfare. They will take care of these women."

She rolled her eyes, and he tried to remain patient. "My darling, there will come a time when your political friends will have to work without you."

"The cook will have your dinner ready for you. Don't wait up."

"Don't dismiss me like this. In your condition, you really must let up."

"Women have babies all the time. I haven't spent any of my pregnancy in solitary confinement, and I don't plan on starting now. Besides," she added, looking weary, "I'm bored. I'm going to the meeting."

Angelo sighed. "Don't tell your mother. She already worries you'll be arrested for starting riots."

Chiara patted her middle. "Nobody would accost a pregnant lady." Her eyes flashed, her smile sly. "Angelo, be happy that I'm open with you. Many a wife would say she has engagements with her ladies' circle, and instead she's meeting her lover. You can be assured that I'm true to two things: to my family and to fighting for the underdogs."

"I'm late." He kissed the top of her head and left.

Pietro was waiting in the hallway when he came down, and they walked to the ministry together.

"Did you hear about the rally?" his father-in-law asked.

"Chiara's going to it."

"No, there was one yesterday, at the textile firm."

"I'm afraid I didn't get a chance at the paper this morning. Chiara was faster than me."

Pietro smiled, but he still looked worried. "You've got your hands full with that daughter of mine."

"What happened at this rally then?"

"Two were beaten up quite badly. Each party blames the other for starting it. The workers want to strike, and they have the full support of the Socialists."

Angelo wished he'd been more adamant about Chiara staying home. "We're not making any progress in this country, are we?"

"I would not go so far as that," Pietro said. "Sometimes, it seems just a lot of noise when you're in the middle of it, and you don't notice the changes."

"Noise. That's interesting that you use that word. Chiara called it a 'cacophony of accusations, a symphony of complaints.'"

Pietro chuckled, and they crossed the street before Angelo continued. "The only thing that seems to be happening is that all the parties are throwing accusations and using misconstrued information. As soon as you disagree with one side—whether it's the Socialists, the Fascists, even the king, for heaven's sake…" Angelo halted. His father-in-law stopped too. "As soon as you say, 'Reason with me,' they accuse you of being misinformed and whisper of secrets and conspiracies. Even the newspapers have become a weapon."

"They always were," Pietro said. "They have the most power to manipulate."

"Aggression is being fought with more violence, and the disparity is polarising us. Where are people's scruples? Simply look at the job we do. Certainly some of these dams, the roads, the bridges, they can be considered progress, and yes, even necessary, but at what cost? If all of these parties are fighting for the greater good of Italy, who is taking the time to make the calculations? I am, but who else?"

Pietro stepped aside to let a woman with a shopping basket pass, but Angelo touched his elbow to keep his attention. "You told me my role as chief engineer is to reduce the risks to the people, their properties, and our infrastructures. I'm in charge of all the permits and inspections and for deeming a project viable in the first place. Yet I have people like the Colonel breathing down my neck to give his consortium leeway, and I cannot do the work when I know he's pushing for projects like, well, like the Reschen Lake, for example."

Pietro's eyebrow arched. "Angelo, it seems that you have worked in the ministry long enough to go into politics."

He shook his head. "I'm too simple for politics, Pietro. If anyone should, it should be my wife."

"*Mon dieu!*" Pietro smiled and clapped him on the shoulder. "I'm serious."

Angelo looked up at the building that housed most of the municipal and province offices. It was neo-Baroque, finished just a year before the war. It had a hipped roof, a stone facade in cream, and rounded corners with windows on each floor to create a turret-like feel. In the middle of the building were extra-tall arched French doors with a balcony each. Pietro's office faced the piazza and the cathedral on the backside of the city hall, and his office had such a window.

A policeman held the door open for them. Angelo nodded at him as Pietro kept talking.

"If you want to continue working for the ministry, you cannot remain neutral. You will be forced to pick a side."

Picking a side would be like trying to choose between the Colonel and Chiara. Pietro most likely meant exactly that.

They took the stairs to the second floor. Two men Angelo did not know were waiting outside Pietro's office.

They stood, bowed stiffly, and introduced themselves as members of the Consortium for the South Tyrolean Waterworks. "We represent the Committee for the Promotion of Electricity in South Tyrol," one said.

Pietro shook hands with them and invited the gentlemen into his office. He glanced to Angelo. "I'll see you when I'm finished here then."

Angelo went to tackle the stack of permit applications for

streets, roadworks, canals, and dams. With all the development now, he was always swimming in paperwork.

Shortly after he began reading a report, Pietro's secretary popped her head in.

"The minister has asked to see you."

"Thank you, Mrs Sala. I'll be there right away."

"Now."

Alert, he looked up from his papers.

"He's asked that you bring the files on Glurns and Kastelbell."

He now knew what the two men from the consortium were here about. This was his chance to divert attention away from the Reschen Valley.

He grabbed the documents, checked for the neatly stamped approvals at their tops, and followed Mrs Sala to Pietro's office.

Inside, the two men sat across from Pietro's desk. An extra chair had been brought in for Angelo. He nodded to the two men, eager to jump in with the plans in his hands for the other two electrical dams, but the visitors were deep in discussion with Pietro. Angelo sat down in the least comfortable seat and slid the files onto the corner of Pietro's desk, then shifted out of the sunlight streaming through the window.

Pietro acknowledged him, glanced at the labels, and nodded.

"The problem with Glurns," one gentlemen said, "is that we'll have to build a series of pipes *in* the mountain itself. Your budgets are terribly constraining. I cannot imagine how we can bid on projects where we are certain to lose money."

"I understand your concern with the costs," Pietro said, "but the locals have all agreed to withdraw their claims. That is more than half the battle won, and that's why I feel these two projects here are ripe for the picking." He indicated the files.

"The land owners are pacified—that's true," the man said. "But the costs our partners will incur for blasting into the mountain..." He glanced at his companion. "What I am trying to say is that if we're to compete in price..."

Angelo knew what was coming. They wanted information. They wanted to make sure a Tyrolean company could not underbid them.

Pietro stood and came around the desk, putting a hand on Angelo's shoulder. "If you need an idea about costs, this is your man. Captain Grimani here is the chief engineer on the projects and will have your best interests at heart. That is, if you win the bid. He'll help keep the costs down, guaranteed."

"Grimani?" the second man asked.

"Yes, sir." He stood and shook the two men's hands. "Captain Angelo Grimani."

"You're Colonel Grimani's relation," the first one said.

"His son."

The two representatives smiled at one another.

The second man said, "Where did you fight?"

"Marmolada Battalion."

"Good God, man. That whole scare about blowing up the Dolomites to beat those Austro-Hungarian scoundrels, that was something, wasn't it?"

"I was there, sir. I was involved in scouting out the mountains to tunnel under their fortresses."

The first man piped in, "I see what the minister means. Yes, then the captain here is the best man for the job."

Angelo opened the two files. "Kastelbell and Glurns. They are the best alternatives to the Reschen Valley project."

The first man frowned, and Angelo hurried to explain.

"There are quite some hurdles to overcome in that valley, including the water rights bills, and no real solution on how to divert the river and streams for the cofferdams. The permanent loss to agricultural land will cost us a great deal in recompense."

The second man cleared his throat. "Yes, but we are still up against your strict budgets, and for that matter, the consortium would like to propose a plan that might loosen the purse strings.

We wanted to run it by you first, that is, before we ask the state for a decision."

Angelo shared a look with Pietro. His father-in-law indicated that the representative continue.

"Well, Captain Grimani must know that the Colonel has founded his own private enterprise, Grimani Electrical. Colonel Grimani has approached the consortium about buying off the Gleno Dam and has canvassed for investors. There is great interest to privatise that project, and the sale of it would maybe loosen those tight strings you've got on Glurns and Kastelbell."

"Yes, I've been made aware of the Colonel's interests," Pietro said. "I believe we'll want to talk to the Colonel ourselves first. Make certain that our strategies correspond, so to speak. We'll be in a better position when selling the idea to the politicians if that is the case."

He rose and the two committee members followed, each offering their hands again. Angelo smiled to himself as Pietro saw them out. This was going better than planned. If his father had investors now and the state funds allocated to the Gleno were diverted to Glurns and Kastelbell, the Colonel would be so busy he'd have to leave the Reschen Valley idea in peace.

Pietro closed the door behind him and faced Angelo. "This is the kind of work I like. It benefits everyone. The people in Glurns and Kastelbell know they need the electrical power. And the Colonel can put the Reschen Lake plans on hold for the time being."

"For the time being? How long?"

"I never thought I'd have to say this, but your father is right. We're going to need a lot more energy. Much more. I happen to know that there are two or three automobile manufacturers looking to build factories here. And that's just the start."

Well, that was certainly a short-lived victory. "How long are we talking about though?"

Pietro shrugged. "As soon as South Tyrol secedes to Italy this

November, we have to put in a new proposal for the Reschen, then handle the appeals. Don't look so upset, Angelo. I know that this is a matter you would like to go away, but it won't. We will have to proceed with caution and with sensitivity. For the time being, you have these two other projects to worry about. Glurns and Kastelbell are going to require years before they're completed."

Pietro was right. Perhaps by the time the two dams were finished, he could be as far away from the Reschen Valley project as possible. He could finally forget about the attack on him, and the Thaler girl, who also still haunted him. And he could stop worrying about the devastation the Colonel's plans would bring on those farmers. He could not say why exactly, but everything in him resisted the idea of that reservoir.

"I'd better prepare to meet the Colonel tonight," Angelo said.

Pietro smiled. "Now that will be time well spent."

The Laurin Hotel was noisy with diners, but the Colonel had arranged for a quiet table in the back, a palm tree serving as a barrier between them and the next table.

"How is Mama?" Angelo asked his father before taking his seat.

The Colonel already had a Scotch and soda in front of him. "She sends her love."

"This must be pretty serious if we're meeting like this," Angelo said. "No family members, no party members, no consortium members, and no Luigi Barbarasso."

"Tonight you are meeting with Nicolo Grimani. Not the Colonel. Not your father. Just the owner of Grimani Electrical, prepared to make a lucrative offer."

When the waiter came, Angelo ordered an aperitif. His father ordered the wine and meal: a bottle of Lagrein and an antipasti platter, followed by ragu with mussels and finishing with the bistecca alla Fiorentina.

"Do you remember our conversation about the Gleno Dam?" he asked Angelo as soon as they were alone again.

"How the ministry has problems and you have solutions?"

"Grimani Electrical has the funds." The Colonel pushed a folded piece of paper at him. "This is our offer to buy it off the state."

Angelo thought the paper looked familiar. He unfolded the note and masked his astonishment. The figure was generous.

"I cannot imagine they will be able to refuse," he said.

"This is the future, Angelo. We're in the market, and the Gleno needs the help. If the state cannot afford the projects, then its best that they offload them to the private enterprises. You'll see that we have covered the money spent on its development so far, and a little bit of a profit for the ministry. We simply expect some subsidies later. In return."

The waiter brought Angelo his Martini Bianco, and he waited until the man had gone again. "We met some of your men from the committee," he said. "They wanted to talk about the budget constraints on the Glurns and Kastelbell dams."

"I'll get to those projects later. First, *salute*." The Colonel raised his Scotch and soda, drank, and smacked his lips before setting the glass down again. "That's good. Your mother has nothing to say about what I drink outside the house, and that, Angelo, is why she rarely finds me there anymore."

The antipasti also arrived, the portion smaller than Angelo remembered the hotel serving, and his father indicated that Angelo should start.

"Listen, Angelo, supposing that this sale goes through, I want you to know that Grimani Electrical has found ways to save money on the Gleno construction. We'll need your department to approve the new permits. You should keep your eye on things, of course, the inspections and so on. There's just someone else paying the bill."

"Yes, and that someone else will be making a lot of money when it begins producing electricity."

"The Gleno Dam will be better off in our hands." His father eyed him, then picked a slice of salami off the platter with his fork. It vanished in an instant. "Besides, business is business, and the state needs to start doing the business that makes money. Immediately. The Reschen will be the next one we will want." He wrapped two more slices of meat around his fork, stabbed a caper, and slid them between his lips.

"I don't believe it's a viable project." Angelo gazed at him. "Nicolo."

His father smirked. "You've been against this project since you returned from there. I would even say your heart is bleeding over it. What are you not telling me?"

"With your ideas, it's a lot of people to relocate. If it were my business that would have to pay all that money, I'd be against it. Seven villages, hundreds of families." Angelo shrugged and unrolled his napkin before placing it in his lap. "Besides, I still haven't got an answer about the soil conditions, nor do I have a solution for the—"

"The waterways, I know. All right, Angelo. Strategically, we'll move one step at a time. First things first: I want the ministry to vocally support the Gleno being sold to me."

"That's why I'm here. In peace. Pietro wants you to know you have our blessing."

"Good. That's very good news. Then I want you to go back up to the Reschen Valley and finish the job you were supposed to do this spring." His father unfolded his hands and reached for another slice of salami and an olive. He poured olive oil onto his plate and dipped a piece of bread into it.

The nightmare, the feeling of dread, washed over Angelo. Someone needed him in that dream. Katharina? Angelo tapped the edge of his dinner plate with a fingernail. There was a line before him, and he was not sure if he could cross it, but—

"Angelo, eat. Why aren't you eating?"

"Put the Reschen project on hold and I'll make certain that the consortium gets a, let's say, better opportunity on the bids for Glurns and Kastelbell."

His father paused long enough in his eating to look up. He nodded, solemn, as if Angelo had just given him a sage answer.

"You're beginning to see how this is all done. You will do that for us, Angelo, and much more."

The spaghetti arrived.

"Now, let's just eat," the Colonel said. "Your mother would never forgive me if you left this table hungry."

16

SEPTEMBER 1920, GRAUN'S HEAD

The alpine hut was cold. After putting the last slabs of wood into the oven, Katharina held her hands to the heat before closing the grate on the crackling fire. She picked up the basket and opened the door to the *Stadl*. Compared to the warmth inside, the cold here nearly took her breath away. She refilled the basket with kindling and then stepped outside into the crisp dawn.

Cowbells chimed from high and low. As the sun rose behind her, the hoar on the meadow glinted and shimmered. The fog had not made it this high but instead encircled the lower edges of the meadow so that the *Vorsäß* was a fairy-tale island floating above a sea of dense cotton.

David Roeschen came out from the stalls, carrying a tin jug of milk. He muttered a sleepy good morning and looked out onto the herds.

"Another week," she said to him. "Two at most, then we all come down to the valley again. You miss your family?"

"Yes, ma'am."

"Where are the others?"

"Already gone to the high plateau. Fetching the sheep."

Katharina nodded and took the milk jug to the stove inside. Ravenous, she started breakfast, one hand on her middle. At five months along, it was becoming more difficult to pretend that she was only three months with child. She often dreamt of a girl and imagined making wreaths of alpine flowers with her. They would drape them over the cows before coming back down to the valley. She and Florian might even let the girl ride on one of them, holding her up between them. And they would never hit her. Never. They would raise her child with love, for Florian had proven to be a good man.

Four weeks after their wedding, they agreed he would announce that they were expecting. He'd strutted about then, doted on her a little in public and in private. It made her smile now. Even in their marriage bed, though sometimes quick and urgent, he'd exhibited exceptional tenderness.

When the milk was warm enough, Katharina mixed it into the frying wheat, added more butter, and then removed it from the stove. She stepped outside to see if the men were back and ready to eat. On the horizon, Opa and her husband appeared side by side, their feathered hats bobbing as they discussed something in earnest. Hund was also with them, and tongue lolling, she sprinted towards Katharina.

"We've lost one of the spring lambs," her husband said when they reached her.

Opa indicated the ridge. "Hans is already out looking for it. Breakfast will have to wait."

"I'll help you search for it," Katharina said.

Florian eyed her middle. "Then take the woods. The ground is level there. We'll go towards Graun's Head."

Katharina fetched a halter from the wall of the *Stadl*. With Hund at her side, she walked west of the pastures. To her left were the steep slopes of the woods leading up to the end of the tree line, and then the high meadows of Graun's Head. Here came the din from the Karlinbach's waterfall, and the breeze carried the scent of summer's end.

She'd walked for some time and was about to call the search futile, when she heard bleating. Hund also stopped.

"That's our lamb," she said to the dog. "Go find her."

Hund cocked her ears forward, then jogged up the path, Katharina behind her. The lamb's call was more distressed now. Up ahead, the woods opened onto a clearing. Before she and the dog reached it, Katharina whistled softly. It would do them no good to surprise the lamb and scare it off. Hund stopped, and Katharina took the dog by the scruff of the neck to lead her to the edge of the path. Across from them, in an almost perfectly circular meadow, she saw a man struggling with the missing lamb, as if he were trying to wrestle it to the ground. He wore dirty rags, and his hair was long and matted. Grunting from the strain, he managed to take the heavy spring lamb down, and Katharina saw him raise his hand. Something flashed in the sunlight.

"No! Stop!"

Hund barked and dashed out of the underbrush, straight for the lamb's attacker. Katharina shouted after her, but Hund was already near him, her hackles raised, and when the man twisted to face the dog, he leered, as if he were not only prepared to kill her but relished the idea. Katharina saw the gaps in his teeth, but it was his face, his eyes that made her freeze. The lamb cried again, struggling under the weight of its attacker. Hund snarled, just far enough away from the knife. The man looked at Katharina, sneered, and raised his knife again, thrusting it straight into the animal's eye. Its cry was cut short, but after he jerked the handle out, he brought the knife down again. Blood erupted from the wound as if he'd just hit an underground spring.

Hund's barking turned frantic. The man stabbed the lamb once more and then a fourth time, the animal long still. When the killer stood up, Katharina imagined that knife being driven into her unborn child.

Her initial screams were soundless. She gasped, trying to force the air out of her lungs, and finally one howl after another tore through her. The madman made jabbing motions in their direction. As he moved towards them, the dog backed away to where Katharina still stood. Hund's throat rattled with the sound of wet fury and terror.

Katharina tore into the underbrush and called for the dog to follow. She had almost reached the path, when she felt her foot catch. Hands out, she tumbled to the ground, and her head hit something hard. Hund's barking dulled as a high-pitched buzzing pierced through her head. She gave in to the darkness.

"Katharina?"

Faces hovered over her. Florian. Opa.

Katharina blinked and tried to raise herself, but one of them had a hand on her shoulder.

"Don't move," her grandfather said. His face was grave. "You've had a bad fall." He wiped something away from the left side of her brow and came away with a bloodied handkerchief.

Her head hurt, but the buzzing in her ears was receding. She touched her middle, but there was no pain, nothing that made her think she had injured the baby.

Opa lifted her to a sitting position. "It's a good thing we heard you screaming. What in God's name happened?"

"Where's Hund?" she asked.

"She's not here," Florian said.

"You have to find her. He'll kill her."

"Kill her? Who?" Opa asked.

"The man."

"Katharina, what happened?" Florian helped her to her feet.

Opa put an arm around her waist, and she felt him shaking.

"The lamb is dead," she said, pointing in the direction of the clearing. "He stabbed the lamb over there."

Florian shook his head. "Who around here would slaughter someone's livestock?"

Someone hungry.

"I'll look," Opa said.

"Don't go alone, Opa. He has a knife. He was ready to use it on me. I ran."

"Who is *he*?" Florian demanded. "Johannes, who is she talking about?"

Opa looked at her questioningly, and Katharina closed her eyes. She saw him again, the hanging, greasy hair, the grizzled beard, the missing teeth. The madman leer.

"It was Fritz," she said. "It was Fritz Hanny who killed the lamb."

She felt Opa pull back. "Fritz. You sure?"

"You would hardly recognise him, but it was him. Jutta was right. He's out here."

Florian sounded impatient. "Who is this Fritz?"

"Jutta's missing husband. Abandoned her and Alois almost five years ago," Opa said.

"Dr Hanny's brother then?" Florian asked.

"And Lisl Roeschen's," Opa said.

Katharina's head swam a little, and she took slow breaths to stop the dizziness. "I'm afraid for Hund."

"We'll take Katharina back to the hut," Florian said. "Then I'll go after this Fritz."

"No, Florian," Katharina pleaded. "He's dangerous. He's already left a man for dead…"

Her husband frowned. "What? Who?"

"Last spring," Opa said. "We never found out who the attacker was, but a man was stabbed near here."

"I know it was Fritz who did it." Katharina looked hard at Opa.

He took her around the waist again. "Let's get you back to the hut. Florian, we'll come back for the lamb. Katharina's right. Fritz —if that's who it is—is dangerous, and we're not armed."

"Shouldn't we alert the authorities?" Florian asked.

"Alert the Italians?" Opa said. "Our men get a chance at him first."

Katharina only wanted to know where Hund was.

The men left the hut again with Opa's rifle and instructions to David Roeschen to go fetch Dr Hanny for Katharina's head, and Hannelore if possible, for the baby. Katharina waited with the *Senner* at the hut.

The sun had almost set before David returned from his nine-hour trip. It was Hannelore, the midwife, he'd brought back. "Dr Hanny was nowhere to be found," he explained, looking worse for wear. "Jutta said to bring Hannelore and she'll bring Dr Hanny herself tomorrow."

"Get yourselves something to eat and some water."

She was relieved to see the midwife. Hannelore gulped down a cup of water, then set to work on pressing around Katharina's middle. She was thin as a reed, and her long dark hair had not seen a brush in probably weeks. She had a thin face, smooth despite her age save for the spiderweb-like wrinkles around her eyes. She smelled of sweat and herbs, and she moved around Katharina with a calming assurance.

After a few moments, Hannelore looked over her shoulder at David and the *Senner*. "You two, go on out and give us some privacy."

As if they had been waiting for their release, the menfolk left in a hurry.

Hannelore pressed a bit more, then checked Katharina's head. She raised a finger and asked Katharina to follow it. "Dr Hanny really should see about that."

"What about the baby?"

The midwife narrowed her eyes before turning to a bag she'd left on the bench. She withdrew a packet. "In truth, chances are great that—after this—the baby will come awfully early."

She opened the packet, and Katharina smelled a mixture of pungent herbs.

Hannelore put them into a cup, poured something from a bottle she had with her, and kept talking as she worked. "The first ones usually come late. This one, though, will come early." With a grimy finger, she stirred the contents, then handed the cup to Katharina. "This tea will keep everything in order."

Katharina sniffed the cup, then drank, the taste bitter but not wholly unpleasant. She took the midwife's hand and looked her in the eye. "My husband knows."

Hannelore pressed her lips together and raised both eyebrows. "Then you keep them both. Him and the baby. Now, lay down. I'm worried about that head of yours."

Katharina released the midwife's hand and did as she was told.

The room was warm from the fire in the tiled oven, and Hannelore was asleep on the bench, her head back, mouth slightly open. The hike had done the poor woman in. She was something like out of old folklore, a character pulled from the past. Katharina listened to Hannelore's soft snoring, feeling a kinship to the woman.

The door opened, followed by the sound of boots stomping on the mat. Had they found Fritz? Had they captured or shot him?

Florian came in first, and Katharina raised a finger to her lips, pointing to the midwife. He nodded. Woozily, Katharina went to the stove where Opa and Hans were warming their hands. They still had their boots on.

"How are you?" Florian asked.

"The baby is fine. I'm fine. David could not find Dr Hanny. And you? Did you find Fritz?"

"He's disappeared," Opa said.

"And Hund?" Katharina's voice cracked. "Did you find any sign of her?"

"I'm afraid not," Florian said. "We called for her over and over. Which is probably why we never found Fritz. We weren't quiet about our search."

"If you didn't find her," Katharina said, "then she's likely to still be alive."

"We've got what's left of the lamb," Hans said. "I'll need to butcher her."

No wreaths for Hans this year. "I'll help you in the morning," she said.

"Let the midwife take you down to the *Hof* tomorrow," Florian said. "Let us do the work, and we'll bring the herds down in a week or two."

"Then let me make a bed for her," she said.

She went to the room containing the bunk beds, and the men convened by the stove. The sound of barking made Katharina run to the door, and she yanked it open.

"Hund!"

The dog barrelled down on her and danced around her. Katharina squatted down to wrap her arms around the dog, but Hund could not keep still. She ran to the men standing in the doorway, then back to Katharina, licking her face, then back to the men.

Katharina felt someone's hands on her shoulders and turned to see Hannelore standing over her.

"Get up slowly," she said.

Katharina did so, but the blood rushed to her head anyway, and she felt queasy. She leaned into the woman and made her way back into the hut. Florian brushed a hand over her cheek as she passed by him.

"Hund's all right," she said before going in. "Everyone's all right."

But where was Fritz?

17

FEBRUARY 1921, BOZEN

T he city hall conference room was crammed with bodies. It was hot as Hades. Angelo placed his hands on the table, eager for a glass of water and the close of the meeting. Pietro gave him the nod.

"Gentlemen." Angelo raised his voice over the din. He waited until the room grew quiet. "I'd like to finish with the announcement that the call for bids for Glurns and Kastelbell will be published tomorrow. It is a sealed bid procedure. We wish you all good luck."

"Captain Grimani," someone called with a German accent, "what about the Gleno Dam in Bergamo? That was not on today's agenda." It was Ernst Schneider, of the Tyrolean Schneider Electric.

"I beg you to defer that question to the owner of the dam," Angelo said and indicated the back of the room, where his father stood. "Colonel Grimani?"

"It's on schedule," the Colonel said.

Someone else piped in from the back. "We've heard that the current design for the gravity construction will bring the project far over your budget, Colonel Grimani."

199

Angelo threw the Colonel a warning look. He'd answer this one himself. "That is correct. We've received an application for a new design that could fit with the current masonry basement and reduce costs. The ministry is currently reviewing it. We'll table that discussion until our next meeting. If that's all, gentlemen?"

The meeting was adjourned, and Angelo shuffled through his file on the Gleno. He sought Pietro across the table and mouthed, *Permit application.*

Pietro shrugged, then turned to Schneider, who had tapped him on his shoulder.

The Gleno was a headache, and the department in Rome was not listening to the ministry's reports and concerns—concerns Angelo had taken up with Pietro since September last year—mainly about the inspectors reporting on inadequate materials the Colonel's company was using. The cement mortar, for one, had been found to be of the cheapest materials and wholly inappropriate. Though his father's company repaired the issues required by the ministry's inspectors, the delays were costing Grimani Electrical too much money.

It was also causing rifts between the Colonel and the ministry. His father accused Pietro and Angelo of blocking his way with "unnecessary" bureaucratic red tape, and Pietro even fired one of the inspectors when Angelo discovered the man was accepting bribes from Grimani Electrical. It was embarrassing, really, though he personally could have little influence over it, and that frustrated Angelo even more. Pietro said little, never suggested Angelo do more to interfere, to make the matter a personal one. It actually made things even worse, this silence. So bad, in fact, Angelo had stopped talking to Chiara about anything that had to do with work.

He found the Colonel on the other side of the room, scratching something into a small leather notebook. He knew those notebooks. His father had dozens of them locked up in a safe behind his desk. Once when Angelo was a boy, the safe had been left propped open and Angelo had gone in to see what was in one of the journals. They were all the same on the outside: black gleaming leather books, the size of a bank note and bound by a matching leather band. Checking over his shoulder first, Angelo had opened one and saw that, on each page, either a word or a name or a figure had been written in. Sometimes the words or numbers or names were crossed out and initials or acronyms written in the corner of the page. He'd reached for a second one to see if it contained the same thing, and it had. Assuming they all served the same function, Angelo figured the Colonel collected lists and reminders, but Angelo never understood why his father felt it necessary to keep them locked up.

He got his father's attention, and the Colonel strode over and clapped him on the shoulder.

"Well done, Angelo," he said. "The consortium is anxious for the published call. They're not earning a living sitting and waiting for the signals to go ahead."

Oh, they would earn plenty, thanks to his help, Angelo thought. If anyone found out, he'd share the same fate as that inspector.

"Where's the application for the new design?" he said instead.

The Colonel looked over Angelo's head, as if searching the room. Another diversion tactic. "There's been a delay," he said nonchalantly. "The designer of the multiple-arch construction is holding me hostage for payment. You will get it soon."

Angelo started to reprimand him, but his father interrupted, finally looking him in the eye. "I want to take you somewhere before you go home. It will be worth your time. Besides, I want to speak with you."

What Angelo wanted was to spend the evening with Chiara and his son. He'd not seen enough of Marco in the weeks before tonight's meeting. His father must have sensed his hesitation, because he put a hand on Angelo's shoulder and steered him towards the door.

Luigi Barbarasso was waiting for them.

Angelo shook hands with the lumber baron from Piedmont, though he'd have preferred to just walk on. The Glurns and Kastelbell dams would require an extraordinary amount of lumber, and Angelo had heard that Barbarasso was already felling trees in the forests of Italy's new northeastern provinces.

"I expect yours will be the first bid we'll receive," Angelo said to Barbarasso.

"A bid I am certain your ministry will be unable to turn down," Barbarasso said.

A look passed between him and the Colonel.

Angelo's pulse quickened, and he stepped in close. "You will do better to hold your tongue," he hissed at the fat man. "The minister and I have promised a sealed bid, and a sealed bidding process is what we will have."

Barbarasso looked amused. "But of course." He winked. "I quite like this game."

Angelo itched to put his hands around that greasy neck and strangle him. The lumber baron was provoking him on purpose, he reminded himself. It was a test. A test to see how coolly Angelo could deal with the pressure. Nevertheless, the pinpricks of anxiety began at his back and moved all the way up his arms, and a cold sweat with it.

The Colonel was gazing at him, then as if decided, turned Angelo towards the door. "You're coming with us."

Angelo pushed past Barbarasso, too angry to ask where exactly his father planned to take them, so he had to let the two men lead the way. Almost immediately they rounded the corner and stopped before the neighbourhood gymnasium.

Inside, the hall was crammed with what must have been hundreds of men, mostly wearing black shirts, though there were a few women amongst them, dressed mainly in sombre colours, not the flashy, modern fashion that had begun filling the streets recently. The gymnastics rings were pulled up to the ceiling.

Ahead on the low stage, the black gymnastics mats were piled up onto the back end, and someone had set up a podium and microphone.

Above the stage hung a black banner with white lettering: *Above all else, remain Italian!*

This was crossing the line. "You've brought me to a Fascist rally?" Angelo exclaimed.

The Colonel put a finger to his lips and nodded towards the podium. A small woman was approaching it, and as she did, the people around him quieted down.

She was attractive with dark, wavy hair that fell just above her shoulders. On someone with Chiara's build, the white blouse and black skirt this woman was wearing would look straight and shapeless, but on her, the outfit accented an hourglass figure. It was both a tremendously feminine and powerful effect. That she was amongst this crowd of men—men who had earned their reputation for being bullies—further confounded Angelo.

"Ladies and gentlemen," the woman called, her voice tinny, unnatural through the microphone. She scanned the faces in the room and leaned in closer. When she spoke again, Angelo had to admire her steady, strong voice, confident and authoritative.

"I call upon you tonight," she said, "to help reconstruct our Italian army. A citizen's army. An army to rebuild our nation, and it requires, first, a reformation of our troops."

There were murmurs in the crowd. Angelo heard some agreement, but mostly surprised chuckles.

The woman stood up straight and gave the audience an ingratiating, patient smile. "I hear some of you laughing. Perhaps you deem me to be one of those loudmouthed, outspoken women you have seen on our streets, demanding equal pay for equal work, demanding voter's rights for women, and meddling in the politics of men."

Angelo stiffened.

"Do not fear," she continued. "Unlike the disrespect you have been shown by those women, I am here to recognize you men as the honoured warriors of our nation."

Now all eyes were on the speaker, and Angelo could feel the growing interest in the room as the muttering began to cease.

"Who the hell is that?" he asked his father.

The Colonel narrowed his eyes, still focussed on the woman. "Signora Gina Conti."

Barbarasso leaned in and gave Angelo one of his wolfish smiles. "Your wife should know her. They are rivals."

"That is a little exaggerated," the Colonel muttered. "What he means is that Signora Conti is on the other end of your wife's political interests. She too has a family. Four children, if you can believe it. The aura of motherhood enhances a woman's beauty. But you know that, don't you, Angelo?"

"Yes, Father, I read Mussolini's article as well."

The Colonel turned his attention to the podium again. "Signora Conti is the kind of woman who makes men."

Barbarasso chuckled. "Not the kind that makes a man question himself."

Angelo looked at him with contempt before concentrating on the smallish woman once more.

"You have lost your brothers in arms," she was saying. "Who sacrificed their lives for Italy's bright future, and now we are reigned by chaos and confusion. You fought for a strong nation, a proud nation. You fought in hope of unifying our states and regaining—as we have here in the Alto Adige—land that has always been rightfully Italian. We are no longer guest workers in this territory. This is our home!"

The crowd broke out into enthusiastic applause, upper arm muscles flexing beneath the black shirts and shabby jacket sleeves, elbows jutting and hitting those directly next to them. The loud shouts of approval grew, but Gina Conti went on as if she had not heard, earnest and urgent.

Over the din, she shouted, "We face our toughest battle in

saving and restoring our proud Italian legacy. We require progress, but not the kind that the Socialists are fighting for. They cause delays in our factories when demanding equal wages and better working hours. We must work harder than ever now, not call for strikes! We need new machines, new innovation! The front line of our citizen's army must unite against those who would otherwise halt any progress in the Alto Adige.

"You men with your technical expertise, your skills, your cleverness, and your muscle, you are the ones who must—who will—move Italy to the forefront." She paused dramatically, her heart-shaped face level over the heads of the crowd before looking down and suddenly casting a warm smile on a group of women nearby.

"Please do not misunderstand me. We women have done the best job possible when we had to take over in the factories. We supported our husbands, our brothers, our sons and helped while they were fighting for our great nation. The reformation of this citizen's army I refer to includes the women because there are roles that they can, and must, fill.

"We are indispensable."

She smiled slyly and got an appreciative laugh from the men standing shoulder to shoulder at the front. Someone else whistled from the back of the room.

Angelo let out a low whistle himself, but only in admiration. This woman knew how to make a crowd dance to her tune.

She raised a hand, and as soon as the audience had quieted down, she became no-nonsense again. "It is time to delegate. The women and men of our citizen's army must be given the tasks that support their strengths. Only in this way will we become the strong nation we are meant to be. Women, you are skilled at nourishing our families. Women, you maintain the inventories of your households and your pantries. Women, you maintain order and cleanliness. You are the ones who tend to your families' needs with ease and efficiency."

Again Gina Conti gazed at the crowd before raising her voice. "Let us put our muscle onto the front lines. For who is the breadwinner? The man!"

There was some clapping and shouting again, but Signora Conti stayed above them.

"Who is the first to protect his family and his country? The man! Who is in charge of building foundations? The man!"

The crowd was wild with agreement, feeding off the energy, whistling and cheering.

Gina Conti waited, and when the room was sufficiently calm, she continued. "Our country needs its men back. Those with the skills and the strength to work in our factories and bring us forward." She shook her fist towards the banner above her head. "Instead, our politicians have taken away the materials we need to rebuild. They throw our veterans scraps, mock them, and smear their reputations. How?" She pointed at the door. "By keeping the women in men's jobs, stealing from our men the means of a decent income. By threatening to ruin our proud heritage in the name of Socialism! In the name of liberalism! In the name of some unachievable equality!"

Gina Conti leaned away from the podium as the hall erupted into outraged cries. She looked pleased with her audience. Her eyes rested on someone, and Angelo saw a tall, gaunt man, dressed in a military uniform and bearing a general's insignia.

"Is that General Conti? That's his wife?" Angelo asked the Colonel.

His father nodded. "She made him, but the war destroyed him. He was at Caporetto, in the worst days. Real shame."

The slight frown, the upturned mouth. It was an insincere sentiment. His father seemed to be gloating.

Angelo remembered hearing about the general. Some said he no longer spoke to anyone, that he was insane. As Angelo observed the man, he noticed the pockmarked face, the sunken cheeks. Just then the general turned his head in Angelo's direction, and he saw something flash in the man's steel-grey eyes. Just as quickly, the light went out again and his stare was blank. General Conti was a spectre, hollowed out by something that had crawled under his skin.

Gina Conti was still on stage, and when she spoke again, her voice was so soft that everyone had to quiet down. "If we strip ourselves of all that we are, of all that we know, what will remain of the Italy we have *all* fought so hard for? Our only hope is to reestablish order. Reassign the tasks within our companies, within our chain of command. We must do this within this very army, in this very room." She opened her arms, as if to give a final benediction. "Go home to your women tonight, and you, this handful of courageous women who came to hear me tonight, you too go home to your mothers, to your sisters, to your daughters. Remind them that *their* front is the home front. Remind them what it means to be an *Italian* woman."

She steepled her hands and bowed her head, and the room erupted into cheers and applause once more.

Angelo clapped this time too, though he did not agree with everything she'd said. It had been a fine performance; she deserved the encore. Chiara would have laughed. Bitterly.

Once more, Angelo glanced to where Signora Conti's husband stood. Some men encircled the general and were congratulating him with vigorous handshakes and slaps on the back. His body flexed, as if he were being whipped by a mob.

The Colonel leaned in and said something in Angelo's ear, but Angelo shook his head. He could not hear him. His father then shouted, "Pietro d'Oro will be ousted from the ministry."

Angelo faced his father. "But why?"

The Colonel indicated the podium, where Signora Conti was descending into the crowd. Angelo felt something pressed into his hand. It was a folded piece of newspaper. He opened it to a cartoon of a mob in front of a landscape of factories. In the middle of the crowd was a caricature very similar to Chiara. She was holding a sign, the colours and crest of the Austro-Hungarian flag flying above her, held in the hands of other caricatures. But Chiara's placard read, *Kaiser lovers unite!*

"Did you listen to Signora Conti?" the Colonel said when Angelo looked up. "If your wife had chosen which side to fight on correctly, her father would not be in this predicament, Angelo. We all know what a weak heart he has for the Tyroleans. The seed does not fall far from the tree. Unfortunately, the minister's daughter—your wife—has made it public knowledge."

Stunned, Angelo folded the cartoon and put it into his pocket. The noise in the hall was decreasing to excited murmurs, and the Colonel lowered his voice.

"The ministry will need you," he said.

"You can't mean to just hand me the position."

"Don't worry. You will be legitimately placed. You can still use Pietro as your advisor, Angelo."

"I'm not a pawn in this game of yours."

"You mean I'm not your commanding officer any longer." His father swept his right arm around the room before leaning into him again. "Angelo, if not you, then one of these other men. I promise you that. What would you prefer?"

Angelo lowered his voice as the volume in the room also fell. "I'm not even a member of the party."

The Colonel scratched his neck and glanced at the podium. "All it takes is your pledge."

Angelo stared at Gina Conti, who was being congratulated or adored, he could not tell. His father moved some feet away to shake hands with men Angelo wanted nothing to do with. The Colonel waved him over, but he pretended not to notice and left the hall.

Outside, he exhaled and watched as his breath floated up into the cold air, finally dissipating under the light of the streetlamp. He heard someone come out and braced himself. When he turned, the Colonel's eyes were on him.

"You're out of line," Angelo said. "You are accusing my wife of being responsible for putting Pietro's job in jeopardy. My wife has been at home with our son since his birth. She's as model an Italian wife as you will ever know."

"There's no reason to get defensive, Angelo. You may consider me a scoundrel, but I'm not your enemy. There are far greater obstacles you'll have to overcome than me—some of them are right under your roof."

"How dare you? This, coming from the man who moves outside the law whenever it suits him? You believe that nothing could possibly stand in your way. Make me minister, Colonel. I'll be only too pleased to put you and Barbarasso into your rightful places."

The Colonel stepped back. "I'm disappointed in you."

"Yes. Well. I was stupid to believe that we could actually be…" Angelo took in a deep breath. It was no use. "Your views and mine have never been the same. From where you stand, you see Italy as something that needs to be restored back to the glory days of the Roman Empire. But I, Father, I see us as key figures in a world that must become more tolerant, more respectful. Peace is what we fought for."

The Colonel flipped his hand at Angelo. "You and Woodrow Wilson."

"Wilson? And Mussolini is preferred? The Fascists think that the answer is to conquer people. The same elitist class you want to destroy is being rebuilt under a new name and new leadership. My wife supports those who want to live with one another without the fear of that very elitist class crushing them under the heels of their boots." Angelo paused to get his trembling voice under control. "Or cutting someone's tongue out, Colonel, because he offends you."

The Colonel jerked his head. "It was insubordination, Captain, and required disciplinary action. It is a tragedy that the little episode in the war is what you use to measure and judge all my actions."

Angelo said nothing.

The Colonel sighed. "Someone once told me that there are only two types of sons: those you can be proud of, and those who will always go against you, no matter how good of a father you try to be. I fought my father, and he cursed his sons, saying we should have children just as we were."

Angelo glared at him in the darkness.

"You see? I do understand you, Angelo. You may want nothing to do with Grimani Electrical directly, but as long as you and I are building this country's energy sources, we'll be working closely together. Especially when you are installed as the new minister."

"By whom, Colonel? Who will install me? The powers that you and your cronies plan to build up?"

"The powers that be, Captain," his father said.

The doors swung open again, and men from the rally spilled out onto the streets, dark shadows against the snowy night.

"You see, Angelo?" his father said quietly. "We are already here."

The lights in the sitting room on Beatrice and Pietro's floor were still burning when Angelo arrived at the Villa Adige. The windows to his apartment were, however, dark. Chiara must be downstairs with her parents, he thought, and was surprised to hear raised voices when he came into the house. He opened the doors to the sitting room.

His wife was lifting Marco out of the bassinet she kept downstairs for these occasions, and straightened with the baby in her arms. Pietro was on the divan, Beatrice standing behind him, one hand on her husband's shoulder.

Two other people Angelo did not know were also there: on the divan, opposite Pietro, sat an elegant woman, her dark-blond hair cut short, the ends plastered to her cheeks. The hairstyle was kept in place by a jewelled headband. Angelo thought, *la maschietta,* the tomboy. It was a fashion that he frowned upon, but he had to admit that he could not picture this woman in any other style. She was smoking from an enamel cigarette holder and wearing an expensive and daring blue gown.

The other person, a man with dark hair slicked back and dressed in an evening dinner jacket, stopped pacing the room to face him. Both strangers looked as if they had rushed away from a formal dinner party, and though something about them was familiar, Angelo could not place them.

Pietro indicated Angelo. "My son-in-law, Captain Angelo Grimani."

The man in the dinner jacket extended his hand to Angelo first. "Count Edmond Rath. A pleasure." The count indicated the woman. "And this is my wife, the countess."

"Nonsense, Edmond," she said, her German accent unmistakable. "Just call me Susi. Everyone does." She faced the count with a playful frown. "These titles, darling, they're out of fashion. It's so *bourgeois.*"

Angelo bowed over the woman's proffered hand and kissed it. "Countess, I am a man of formalities."

"Susi. I insist." She smiled. "And I'll call you 'Oh Captain! My Captain!' I am certain Walt Whitman was thinking of you when he wrote that." She turned to Chiara. "Darling, he's delicious, this husband of yours. Why didn't you tell me he was so divine? I would have forgiven you immediately for not marrying a Tyrolean."

Her familiar manner was startling, and Angelo looked to his wife.

"Susi and I know one another from the old days," Chiara said.

The countess chuckled and tilted her head back to exhale.

"Oh, darling, the old days. You make it seem like ages. Why, it wasn't that long ago that Edmond was pursuing me all over the place in that uniform of his."

"You can be so very primitive," the count muttered. He turned back to Pietro.

Susi waved a hand and winked at Angelo. "Like you, my husband prefers formalities."

There was more to her than her lightness, something that made Angelo decide to be careful with her. He turned away to listen to the conversation the count had started up with Pietro again. He did not like what he heard.

"When the German League gains those seats in the house in May," the count said, "the first thing we will do is contact the Austrian and German heads of state. We must find a way to regain self-determination. Our borders may have been cut off by the treaty, but I've been assured that we have Austria's and Germany's support in helping us to protect our language and culture."

Chiara shifted Marco to her other hip. "No, Edmond, the first thing the German League should do is to assure that positions like my father's are not threatened by the Fascists. You need Italians like him for leverage against the nationalists, someone who can buffer the conflicts and see to the interests of all parties."

Angelo waited, head cocked. The Colonel's words earlier this evening echoed in his head.

"I'm afraid that will be more difficult," the count said. "The Tyroleans are keen on taking back the positions where they will have power and control. They want all the Italians removed from these positions. It doesn't matter if they are old settlers or new authorities. I'm sorry, Minister, but that will mean you as well."

Chiara put Marco down in the bassinet and stood before the count. "Edmond, the League must remain patient. For now, we have to fight fire with fire. There are plenty of us with national leverage and interests who will help the Tyroleans fight against Tolomei and the Fascists."

"I don't understand why Pietro will lose his position," Beatrice said, her brow furrowed. "The Tyroleans were the ones who voted him in in the first place."

Pietro patted her arm, "It's nothing to worry about, my dear."

"It is something to worry about, Minister," the count said. "That's why I've come here. Your situation is very grave indeed."

The countess pointed her cigarette holder at her husband. "You said it in Vienna, darling. This is not a battle of equals. A quarter of a million Germans against forty million Italians, remember that. When you are president of the German League, take the help you can get, especially if it's Italian. We need people like the d'Oros to tip the scales."

She glanced in Angelo's direction, and now he knew where he'd seen her before. He turned his back on the party and took the newspaper cartoon out of his pocket. There they were, the count and countess in front of Chiara in the caricatured mob.

Chiara surprised him when she appeared next to him and took his arm. "Darling, you must talk with the Colonel. You must try to rally your father's support for the German League."

The count's eyes widened, "The Colonel? Oh, good God. Chiara, are you talking about *Nicolo* Grimani? Why did I never put the two together? You're married to the—"

Susi let out a low whistle and grinned at Angelo wickedly. "You're his son?"

Angelo bristled, and Chiara sounded annoyed. "Of course he is. Why wouldn't you know that?"

"Pietro," the count said, sinking next to Pietro as a doctor would to a sick patient. "You have been too vocal in your support of the Tyroleans. This will not help you with the Fascists in any way." He cast Angelo a distasteful look. "Even if you are related to one of Mussolini's biggest supporters."

"And what about you?" Angelo challenged Chiara.

"Me?" Chiara asked, obviously stunned. "What about me?"

"Are these really your friends, the count and countess?" he asked. "The modern, bourgeois, Communist, Socialist Tyrolean party, set to free the enslaved Germans?"

"What in God's name are you talking about, man?" the count exclaimed. "That's an awful lot of terminology—"

"I'm talking to my wife," Angelo snapped.

He saw Susi reach out a hand to Chiara, as if to stop her.

Angelo continued, "You are the real reason that your father is going to lose his position."

Chiara looked as if he'd slapped her.

He turned on Susi. Who was she anyway? "I suppose my wife is the one who's been supporting the count's campaign while I believed she was taking care of my son."

"*Your* son?" Chiara said.

"Yes, my son. Woman, I was defending you to my father tonight, bragging about what a model wife you are."

"I don't need you, Angelo Grimani, to defend me, and especially...especially!...not to your father."

Pietro stood up. "Now, Chiara—"

"No, Father, I've heard enough."

"You remember where your place is," Beatrice said shakily. It was an uncommon show of bravado.

Chiara's face crumpled. "My place? I *do* remember it. I was raised here, Mother. I cannot simply stand by and watch this systematic oppression of..." She glared at Angelo. "*My* people."

He itched to strike something, anything, even Chiara. "You are an Italian woman. My wife," he said through gritted teeth. "The wife of possibly the new Minister of Civil Engineering, and that, my darling, will mean you have to play and accept certain roles you may not be comfortable with."

Chiara stared at him. "You? The new minister? You know all about this? Of my father's position being threatened?"

Suddenly clearheaded, Angelo looked around the room.

Pietro's expression was unreadable. The count looked smug, and the countess leaned back on the divan, one hand resting on the back and the other with her cigarette holder poised before her lips.

"My, my," she said softly and inhaled.

Angelo reached into his breast pocket once more, removed the newspaper cartoon, and jabbed at the drawing of Chiara. "Madam, you have crossed the line. *You* chose these people over us. *You've* done this to us. And now you leave me no other choice."

He left her standing there, all of them, and took the stairs to his apartments. Even if he had to do it just for show, to maintain order in his house and to maintain his standing in Bolzano, he would have to join the Blackshirts. The Tyroleans—this German League, whoever and whatever they were—were in no position to win a scrabble in a pub fight, much less the war the Blackshirts were about to wage. His father had been right. The Fascist tide was here; Mussolini would rule Italy sooner or later.

And Angelo had to be in a position where he could win what he was fighting for, which was—first and foremost—his family.

18

MARCH 1921, ARLUND/GRAUN

The scratching sound of boots on the mat reached Katharina where she was elbow deep in the potato dough for *Schupfnudeln*. She glanced up long enough to notice that her grandfather looked tired. When had he aged so much? His brown work boots, splattered with mud, were old as well. She could remember them from as far back as to when her father had moved her and her mother from Innsbruck to Arlund.

"Don't bring that cow dung in here," she scolded.

"It's not cow manure."

"Were you out in the fields?"

"*Humph.*"

"Then it's cow dung."

"It's mud, Katharina, and I'm wiping it off. Your grandmother, God rest her soul, got me properly housebroken long before you were even being considered."

Katharina smiled. "Sit on the stool over there."

"The stool's inside."

"Just get on in here and sit."

Opa stepped into the house and landed on the stool nearest

the door. She watched him ply off the shoes, then put one over his hand, like a mitten.

"Did you forget to buy new laces again?" She rolled pieces of dough out from between her fingers.

"You've become a meddling old wife. Don't forget how you were raised."

"Yes, yes, Opa," she teased. "Don't speak unless you're spoken to."

"There is real wisdom in that."

She laughed. "With Florian that might work, but with you, well, we'd never do any talking around here if I followed such rules."

Opa had pulled out the shoe-cleaning kit and was laying the paste and the brush out. "I like it quiet."

As if to provoke him, Annamarie burst out crying above them, and Katharina started up to her daughter's room, but when she heard footsteps, she paused.

"Florian up there?" Opa asked.

Annamarie's screams were defiant above Katharina's head. She nodded, fighting the urge to go upstairs and take over.

"She's so colicky," she said before going back to the table. "It's a wonder she hasn't sent Florian running all the way back to Germany."

"You may have rights to that kitchen floor, but you've no right to complain about your family. Except, that is, that Annamarie's got Florian wrapped around her little finger."

"She does," Katharina said, smiling wistfully. She rolled the dough out.

Fact was, her husband really should go to Germany. His mother was in bad health, but Florian felt he could not leave them right now, not with spring just arrived and all the work they had to get done. And that was another thing, the way the men had fussed over her as soon as she was pregnant. Katharina had ceased reminding both Opa and her husband how much work she'd done before Annamarie had come into the world, but she was outnumbered by men—all around her—who seemed determined to keep things in order, the way things were supposed to be, at a time when nothing seemed right anymore.

She blamed the new Italian laws hanging over their heads, which brought uncertainty and a fear of losing all that they knew. So, quietly, she'd retreated, deciding to keep the peace.

Her pregnancy had also forced her to stop wearing Papa's breeches. Instead, she'd slipped into the more traditional roles like one would slip into a pair of house slippers that were just a bit too tight. And with that, everyone seemed to simply forget all that she was capable of.

There would be a time, she assured herself, when she would be able to convince Florian of her earlier ideas for the Thalerhof. She just needed time and to let things settle. It was the least she could do for a man who'd, so far, kept his word to her.

She heard a newspaper rustle, then slide to the floor, followed by the whisper of the brush on her grandfather's old boot. Above them, Annamarie's crying had quieted down to hiccupping sobs.

After a moment, Opa said, "You can steal horses with a man like Florian."

"Yet you all still tease him and remind him how different he is from the rest of us."

She dropped dumplings into the boiling water, then looked up to see if Opa had heard.

"You're not listening," he said, still working on his boots. "That's because we like him."

Like her, Florian would never be considered anything other than an outsider, never really be "one of the fold." He would carry his *Außenseiter* on him for the rest of his life in this valley, just like she did.

There was something else. Something that had cropped up more often in her conversations with Florian, in their brief talks about the annexation looming ahead of them, about his mother's health. About Germany. He spoke with such wistfulness that she knew he was homesick, but more so, her bones were telling her that Florian was disappointed, unhappy even. About what, she could not be certain. Their marriage? Their life in the valley? Annamarie?

"It's difficult being an outsider here," she finally said, more to herself than to her grandfather.

Opa was still busy with his boots, and she paused, deciding to change the subject. The backs of her wrists rested on her hips so as not to get flour on her dress.

"Tell me, Opa. When are you going to buy new boots? We have a little money to spare."

"And leave old Jakob with nothing to do? Twenty years he's been coming here to repair our shoes, and he's never said a word about new ones needed. Fixes them up just fine."

"You only like Jakob's stories, and a reason to pull out your schnapps."

"He plays the harmonica like nobody I know. Besides, we need a new wheel for the wagon, and there're tools to be sharpened. Need money for that too."

Katharina lifted the lid off the pot of boiling water and dipped the slotted spoon in, quickly fishing the finger-length pieces of *Schupfnudeln* out.

A knock at the door made them both pause. Though it was a long time before Jakob would be in the valley peddling his services, Katharina thought their conversation had conjured him up. But when Opa opened the door, it was Hans Glockner who filled the doorframe.

"They've found Fritz," Hans said without greeting. "They've taken him to the police barracks."

"Fritz?" Katharina said. The pot's lid slipped out of her hand and clattered to the floor. She scrambled to pick it up and replace it, then stared at Hans. "But...dear God. Jutta? Does she know?"

Hans nodded solemnly.

"Jutta's been on pins and needles the whole winter," Opa said, "hoping Fritz wouldn't suddenly return."

Poor Jutta! The inn would have been hers in just a matter of weeks. Katharina shook her head, unable to believe it.

She heard movement above, and when Katharina looked up, Florian stood at the top of the stairs. He cradled Annamarie in his arms, the baby girl's face streaked red from crying.

"No more break-ins," Hans said, shaking his head. "No sign of him. Not after that incident on Graun's Head."

Katharina sighed. "Jutta guessed he'd either moved on or that he had, well…"

"I think," Florian said, "we all figured Fritz for dead after that winter we had."

"They caught him," Hans said, "in the church sacristy in the middle of the night. Fritz broke the lock, and Father Wilhelm walked in on him. Fritz must have panicked, because he started waving his knife. Father Wilhelm ran straight to the *carabinieri*, but the church was empty when they returned. They went searching for him and found him hiding in the baker's cellar this morning. He tried to make a run for it. Prieth heard shots—"

Katharina made the sign of the cross.

Florian came downstairs and handed Annamarie to Katharina. The baby stared at Hans with wide eyes and hiccupped, as if she were considering starting up again.

"Martin Noggler said the *carabinieri* are asking questions about all the theft. And then there's…" Hans's eyes skirted over Florian and rested on her. "That incident up at Karl Spinner's hut."

"From the spring, you mean?" Florian asked. "Some man, you said, was stabbed."

Katharina's head reeled. Of course Angelo Grimani would have filed a report with the police. He'd certainly described an attacker with a knife. The *carabinieri* would have put the two stories together.

"I'm going down to be with Jutta," Opa said. He pulled on his boots faster than Katharina had seen in months, stood up, and grabbed his hat off the hook.

"You'll get Dr Hanny to translate," Florian said.

Hans turned from the door and sighed, as if he carried the weight of the world. "He's already down there."

"Of course he is," Katharina said. "He's Fritz's brother." She badly wanted to go with them, but what if something about Angelo came up and she would have to answer questions, and Dr Hanny would be interpreting…

She hugged her baby to her tight and went to Florian, her heart hammering against her chest. She couldn't go.

Hans had pulled his hat off again and was studying it, looking sheepish. "It seems," he said slowly, "that Dr Hanny knew where Fritz was all along."

"Frederick," Opa said from the door, as if to give Hans the opportunity to correct himself. "Our Frederick?"

"But, Jutta," Katharina breathed. "The inn. How could he?" Against her, Annamarie was fussing and pushing herself away. Katharina shushed her, struggling to hear Florian, who was talking slowly, as if putting together the pieces.

"If Dr Hanny's known about Fritz…," he started. "Well. Well, then he's led Jutta to believe she had hope of inheriting the Post Inn."

"I can't make heads or tails of it either," Hans said. "But if I were to guess, he was doing it for Jutta's good. She won't see it that way though."

He put his hat back on and went out the door, Opa holding it open for him.

When they were gone, Florian turned to her. "Give me the girl. She doesn't want to be held that tight."

Katharina obliged him, and when Annamarie immediately calmed down, she felt as if everything was out of balance. She leaned against the table and wiped at her brow.

"Poor Jutta." Florian echoed her earlier sentiment.

Annamarie was grasping at a lock of his hair, almost smiling.

"I know," Katharina said. She gathered another plateful of *Schupfnudeln* to boil. "Jutta's wanted nothing more than to own that inn, to have it be hers."

"Like you'd once wanted the Thalerhof," Florian said matter of factly.

She shot him a look, stunned. "How did you know that?"

Florian shrugged a little. "Opa told me."

"He did?" She felt faint and turned to the stove so as to avoid looking at him. She dropped the balls into the pot, hot water splashing onto her hands, her wrists, her upper arms, and sealed the lid back on the pot before answering, softly to herself more than to him. "It was a short-lived dream."

She felt his hand on her shoulder, and she went stiff beneath the touch.

"Would you have preferred things to be different?" Florian said.

She turned her profile to him, but her eyes were on the floor. "Do you?"

He took in a breath. The hesitation sent a chill through her, and she felt anger rising. He'd wanted this. That's what he'd told her. To live on this farm, to be a farmer, to marry her, to be a father to her child. To be Tyrolean. It was too late to realise he'd just been a romantic tourist.

"Sometimes," he said, "I wish I knew…" But his voice trailed off as Annamarie began fussing again.

Katharina whirled on him, but he was focussed on the baby, trying to pacify her.

How dare he? Had he any idea how much Annamarie and she now depended on him? How much it cost her to forgive herself for her mistakes? How she had just begun to feel as if she might be safe, and this with a man who was more than generous with her? How dare he?

"Give her to me," Katharina commanded.

"I'm fine," he cooed to Annamarie, still bouncing her and turning in half circles. "We're fine, aren't we?"

Katharina clenched her teeth. "Give me my daughter."

Florian's smile faded, and when their eyes met, she saw the hurt in his. How often had she done this to him?

Wordlessly, he lifted Annamarie and held her in the space between them, but Katharina could not say she was sorry. She took the baby and pressed Annamarie against her.

"What happened at Karl Spinner's?" Florian asked, his voice stone cold. "You told me that Fritz almost killed a man. Who was that man, Katharina?"

She stared at her daughter for a moment, willing Annamarie to stop Florian from going down this path. Behind her, the water boiled up and over the lid.

She was not going to do this with him right now. He'd promised never to ask her about it, and she wasn't about to volunteer anything regarding Angelo Grimani, about any of the decisions she'd made. She'd thought she'd been in love. She thought she would own land. None of that had been true. And if Florian made her talk about any of it, only God knew what might still keep them together. She needed something to be true, steady, hers.

"It's just what I've heard," she said as lightly as she could. "You know Opa and Hans don't tell me anything. What good does it do to share anything with the womenfolk?" The bitterness had seeped out anyway.

Her timing perfect as always, Annamarie burst into screams again, and Katharina gratefully hurried upstairs, abandoning Florian and the hissing pot of hot water.

When Jutta stepped out of her apartment into the unlit hallway, she could barely make out the faces of those who had come to escort her to the police. Lisl. Georg. Johannes. Their silence was telling. They too had to be shocked by the news. And Hans. Hans hung back at the registration desk, solitary, but when she met his look, he took a step forward—just one—before stopping again.

Yes, Jutta thought, her husband was back. Where did Hans have left to go?

To all of them, she said, "I filed his death certificate last week. Five years. It was five years last week since he abandoned us." The inn would have been hers within a week or two. And then Hans and she...

Georg said, "I have the deed. We will make Fritz sign it."

Jutta wanted to laugh, but her throat turned watery, and tears pricked her eyes. *You do that, Georg. Make him. You Hannys owe me that much now.*

She turned her back on the party and walked out of the inn, the sound of them following her a cautious comfort.

On the way to the barracks, she led them past the oak tree next to the church, and when she saw Frederick sitting on the fountain's edge, she marched up to him, flung herself on him, and pummelled his chest.

"You knew where he was all along! You knew! And you didn't tell me?"

Someone pinned her arms down. Georg was behind her.

"He's my brother, Jutta," Frederick said, rising from the bench. He'd not even defended himself against her punches. "I tried to help him. I told him to stay away. He's ill, Jutta, and no matter how much I gave him, he wanted more."

"I never asked for your help with this," she snapped. "Never. Hell, you never even told me, so how could I have asked?" She glared at him. His face was pale, his mouth drawn. "I want nothing," she said, annunciating each word, "from you ever again."

When she stepped away from him, Lisl grabbed for her hand, but Jutta turned away and marched to the barracks. God knew what the Hannys had conspired; they had all probably worked together to keep Fritz's whereabouts a secret from her.

Hans caught up to her first.

"The police should find out about your lamb," she said without looking at him.

He said nothing.

"You should tell them about the lamb, Hans, and they should know about that Italian man, the one that got stabbed." She turned to Johannes on her other side, but his face was expressionless. These men never had anything to say when she needed them to. She faced the road and hurried on, just noticing her mud-splattered shoes from the slush.

They walked the rest of the way in silence, past the Blechs' butcher shop and the sundry goods store, then the bank, but the villagers along the way said everything loudly and clearly with their glances and averted looks, with their wan smiles and their shaking heads. When Lisl reached for her hand again, this time Jutta let her take it.

"Don't look back, Jutta," Lisl whispered. "Frederick is with us." She squeezed Jutta's hand so fiercely, Jutta cried out.

"He's with us because he can help," Lisl said. "He wants to help."

Jutta gritted her teeth until her jaw hurt. Let him come then.

At the *carabinieri's* barracks, she saw Vincenzo first, but then Captain Rioba stepped out from the main building and waved them over. Frederick shook hands with him, and she kept her eyes glued on the two men.

When Frederick returned, he asked, "Do you want to see him first? Before we go to the captain's office?"

She pointed at Georg. "You will do everything to make sure Fritz signs the deed over to me. I don't know what this family has been up to, but—"

"Neither Georg nor Lisl knew anything about this," Frederick said.

"And you," she growled at Frederick. "You are to tell me everything, and I mean everything"—she pointed at the *carabinieri* gathered there—"that these people say to you, or I swear to God you will regret the day you were born."

Frederick was grave. "I never meant to betray your trust, Jutta."

"But you did." She stepped past him. He would not see her tears.

Captain Rioba indicated the hallway, his manner sincere and even sympathetic. The sound of chains and violent coughing echoed down the corridor, and he showed Jutta and Georg to a dim room with a single table and two chairs. When the door opened again, it was Vincenzo and Ghirardelli, the two *carabinieri* who seemed to be welded to the hip, bringing Fritz in.

Except for his eyes, Jutta did not recognise the man who was her husband. His face was slick with greasy sweat. He was emaciated, and there was a sweet, fermented smell coming from him. His clothes were rags, patched with sweat and dirt. Beneath the tatters were festering sores.

Fritz kept his eyes on her as he moved to the chair and was pushed down by the two *carabinieri* onto it. His wore an ugly, stinking smile. Most frightening was that, despite his madman look, Fritz seemed perfectly lucid.

"Hello, wife. It's been a long time." He coughed a deep, rattling, and phlegmy cough, and she had to cover her nose and mouth.

Georg pulled out a sheaf of paper. "Fritz, we only came here to have you sign the inn over to Jutta."

Fritz leered at Georg. "Is this your last act of duty as mayor?" He pointed at Jutta, his hand shaking. "That bitch tried to lock me out when I needed food. She's the reason I'm like this." He swung his look at her and wiped spittle from his chin. "Want me dead, don't you, so you can take what's mine? Well, woman, I'm back. The Post Inn is mine, and you, you're mine too."

"You're in jail," Jutta said.

"What're they going to do for breaking into a church?" Fritz rasped. "That's nothing. I'll do my time, and then I'm coming back." The phlegmy cough erupted again. He bent as low as the chains behind his back would allow him and wheezed.

Georg glanced at her, his face reading the same question she had: How sick was her husband? She rubbed her fingers deep into her neck, glad for the pain that shot into her shoulder and up her left jaw. Anything to keep her from breaking Fritz's neck.

Georg pulled the chair opposite Fritz and sat. Jutta stayed standing.

"Fritz, I think we all know it's over," he said. "It's been five years since you left her. Since you left all of us here. Jutta's even filed…"

Thankfully, Georg stopped.

Fritz looked at her, then at Georg, then at her again. "Filed what? What did you file, woman?" He sneered. "You're not getting anything. And that boy you squeezed out of you? He's going to an institution—"

"You devil's spawn!" Jutta's spit landed on his cheek.

Ghirardelli sprang onto her and pulled Jutta away from the table. Fritz wiped his face on his shoulder, giggling. It was not just his stink that made Jutta's stomach churn—it was the sight of him. When she turned away, Ghirardelli's eyes held hers, and he gently released her pinned arms.

"The Italians want that inn, Jutta," Fritz taunted.

She whirled to face him.

"They want to buy it, so I'm going to sell it."

Yes, it was she who would do time for murder.

She lunged for him, felt the edge of the table bruise her pelvis and had her hands on Fritz's neck before she was yanked back once more.

She struggled under Ghirardelli's hold as he swore to himself, and when the squat, brute one threatened to put his hands on her too, she turned on her husband again.

"You will do nothing more, Fritz Hanny. On my mother's grave, you will never see the light of day, again." She wrenched herself away from the two policemen, her voice high pitched. "Get Dr Hanny. There are other charges to be brought against this man. Like Hans Glockner's lamb, which Fritz killed."

The policemen looked uncertainly at her. She poked a finger into Ghirardelli's chest and spoke each successive word loudly. "Get the *Dottore*."

Ghirardelli jerked his head to Vincenzo and moved himself between Jutta and Fritz.

When Vincenzo left, Jutta stood on tiptoes to see Fritz over Ghirardelli's shoulder. "You will hang, Fritz Hanny. By the love of God, when we're done with you, you will hang."

In Captain Rioba's office, Frederick played the translator again and turned to Jutta when he finished.

"With no court seat in this part of the country now, they will have to try him in Bozen. Fritz has pneumonia, Jutta. I sincerely doubt my brother will survive the dungeon in Bozen."

Jutta smoothed her skirt and then looked down at her hands as Captain Rioba continued speaking with Frederick. She considered her situation: if Fritz died, the inn would go automatically to Alois. If they hung him, Georg had told her, the Italian state would most likely just seize the property. Pressing further charges was not going to help her situation. She made the sign of the cross in response to the evil thoughts in her head.

Captain Rioba was still speaking in low tones, and Jutta heard the name Grimani. Frederick nodded, glanced sideways at her, and leaned closer to the desk before practically whispering a response back. She watched as Rioba took notes. When he was finished, the captain looked at all of them with calm eyes.

"*Finito.* Finished."

Jutta and Frederick stood and went into the corridor, and though she was far from forgiving him, she put a hand onto his arm.

"What was that about Grimani?"

His hesitation made her narrow her eyes, and he looked down before answering. "Grimani's the Italian man Katharina found last spring. Based on Captain Grimani's report, it had to have been Fritz who attacked him and left him for dead. Captain Rioba will have to go down to Bozen and get his testimony."

Jutta looked over her shoulder where the others were waiting outside. "Sweet Virgin Mary," she breathed, thinking of Katharina. "Will we ever be left in peace?" The last thing anyone needed was to bring up yet another ghost.

"I'm going back to Fritz. He needs my medical attention."

"How bad is he?"

Frederick's mouth was a taut line. "His condition is quite serious."

"Is there anything you can do for him?"

He held her look. Slowly, he said, "I thought you never wanted my help again." He touched his hat.

When Jutta returned to the others who were waiting for her, Hans fell in line at her side. They returned the way they had come, in silence, but Jutta could not stop imagining what might happen if Angelo Grimani were resurrected.

19

APRIL 1921, BOZEN

Compared to the bright, spring day outside, the cathedral was cold and damp, and Angelo could hear the songbirds, which were more pleasant than the monotone drone of the priest. The colours from the stained glass windows were making a pattern on Chiara's lap and onto Marco's dark hair. His son was sleeping with one tiny fist jammed into his mouth. Angelo reached for it with his little finger, but Chiara—with a scolding glance—shifted the boy out of reach.

These days the only thing that brought him and his wife together was Marco, depending on which way they used him. Their son was like a magnet: turned one way, Marco could repel the parents. Turned another, like when he was ill or when they had baptised him, and Angelo felt close to Chiara again, even agonizing affection and love. Otherwise, Chiara and he moved in their own orbits, though Angelo's new political environment was still an unfamiliar one. His membership with the Fascists was passive. He made his appearances but kept the peace at home by not sharing his comings and goings with anyone on the d'Oro side of the family. Certainly not with Chiara championing the German League.

Pietro and he also cautiously moved around one another. The discussion about his father-in-law being removed as minister came up again two days after the count's visit. Even then Pietro had said he might be getting too old for modern Italy. Angelo had automatically—even sincerely—insisted that the ministry needed Pietro d'Oro. Still his father-in-law had dismissed the idea. "It's time for you to lead, Angelo. This old horse wants to rest."

If Pietro was going to bow out of the ministry, then Angelo's only recourse was to support his father-in-law in doing so with dignity. Yet Pietro still hadn't written his resignation, and in the last month, he'd also done nothing differently to help Angelo get a foothold on his eventual new role. As the German League grew in strength, Angelo suspected that Pietro would change his mind and put up a fight. That was to be avoided at all costs. He did not need to clash with another d'Oro.

In the pew in front of him were his parents with his sisters. Sitting directly before him, his mother was stiff as a polished cane, the only gaiety around her an uncommon hat—a russet wide-brimmed cloche decorated with a weave of burgundy, pink, and yellow flowers. Even his mother was victim to the latest Paris fashion, and her tightly pulled-back black-and-grey hair did not match it.

Next to her, the Colonel had his head down, as if in prayer, or perhaps in sleep. Cristina and Francesca nudged each other and whispered about something they had between their laps. Their mother raised a finger, her neck arched like that of a snake prepared to bite, and both girls froze.

When Angelo looked to his left, past Chiara and across the aisle, he was surprised to see that Signora Gina Conti and the general were right across from them. His eyes rested on the gaunt figure of Gina's husband. One side of his pockmarked face was visible and appeared to have succumbed to the pummelling of age. Between Gina and the general, Angelo could see their brood of children sitting in various stages of impatience.

The noise of the parishioners standing up made Angelo return his attention to the altar. The priest was giving the final blessing. As everyone filed out of their pews, Angelo almost bumped straight into Gina Conti, who was shovelling her four children before her. The eldest, a sullen boy, was maybe twelve or thirteen, and the youngest, a pretty, wide-eyed girl, a toddler.

Angelo lifted his hat and saw that Gina's eyes were also wide and grey, and they smouldered as she brought her irritated children back into order. When she saw him, they sharpened with interest, as a cat's would at the sight of something moving in the grass.

It stirred something in him.

He murmured a slightly flustered apology, then searched for his in-laws and Chiara, who were just stepping out of the church and into the sunshine. When he joined them, the street was crowded with people, and he watched Gina and her family descend into that crowd.

"It's the opening of the Bolzano Fair today," Beatrice said.

From around the corner of Via Alto Adige, a parade of Tyroleans, in traditional dress, marched towards the piazza. The men wore feathered caps, breeches, wool socks with tassels; the women were in traditional *Tracht*. They were lined up along the street leading to Walther Square, where the statue of the medieval German poet stared stonily back at them.

Angelo's parents and sisters crowded around him.

Pietro said, "The parade's just starting."

There were carts loaded with hay and children, and the Tyroleans broke into a song, something suspiciously battle-like and jaunty.

"A little eerie without their instruments," Angelo said.

Cristina tapped him on the arm. "Why aren't there any brass bands? Last year they had the bands."

"They're illegal now."

"But why?"

He ignored her question.

"I'm interested in how the plebiscite will turn out, today," Pietro said.

"What's a plebiscite?" Cristina asked.

"It's a special vote," Chiara answered. "The Tyroleans are voting whether Austria should join the German Reich."

Angelo's mother scowled. "What have these people got left to say about that?"

"It does concern them, Signora Grimani." Chiara's voice was terse. "They still have a lot of ties in the north, and they still have a right to their say. At least until they have officially been annexed."

Angelo's mother snorted at that. "The German League is just encouraging them. It's treasonous."

Francesca was already halfway down the church steps when she turned back to them. "Mama, may we go and watch the parade?"

Both girls looked ready to run at their mother's signal.

"You can see it just fine from here," Angelo's mother said.

"Come now, Mama," Angelo said. "Let them have their fun." He scanned the crowd again, but the Contis had vanished.

Cristina and Francesca ran towards the kerb, but the Colonel scowled. "What about our luncheon?"

"We'll be late," Angelo's mother added. "Beatrice and Pietro won't want to hold up the Sunday meal just for the girls."

"Chiara and I can wait here for them," Angelo suggested. "Why don't all of you go back to the villa and take Marco with you?"

The Colonel continued to look reluctant, but at the insistence of the others, he finally agreed to leave with them. Chiara passed Beatrice the pram and, when they'd left, returned to Angelo on the church steps.

Angelo searched the crowds for his sisters, looking for their lace-fringed dresses—Francesca in a pale blue, Cristina in a pale green—and the straw boaters. He had just spotted them when Chiara grabbed his arm and pointed towards the square.

"What in heaven's name is that?"

At the far end, men in black were pouring into the square from the alleyways, a renegade of army ants. They surrounded the parade-watching crowd from behind. One small group broke off, something in their hands. Angelo heard the smashing of glass before he saw a shop window explode into shards. By then the other men had spread out amongst the parade goers.

Most onlookers were facing the parade and would not have recognised what was happening, even when roughly pushed about from behind. An explosion made Angelo jump, though he could not see where it had taken place. Smoke rose into the air to the left of city hall.

Surprise and panic rippled through the crowd. Chiara opened her mouth but made no noise. More explosions, this time at the Tyrolean Farmer's bank.

He could finally move. Running down the steps, Angelo shouted for his sisters. People fled in every direction.

When he could not find them in the scattering crowd, he turned to see his wife being accosted by two black-clothed men on the church steps. Angelo charged back, and Chiara pushed one man away from her. The bullies laughed and backed away, and before Angelo could reach them, they disappeared into the mass of people.

He pulled Chiara into his arms. "Did they hurt you?"

"They realised I'm Italian. They said they knew you, Angelo. How do you know them?"

"I have to find the girls," he said.

At the end of the street, before an alley entrance, he saw a flash of blue and the boater. Francesca. Cristina was also with her, and someone was pushing his sisters along, but their backs were to Angelo. Cristina's arm went up, and he saw that a man had her by the hand.

"Chiara, there they are. Someone's with them."

"Is that Peter? My God, it is. It's Peter Innerhofer, my friend. The teacher, Angelo. Remember?"

Peter was guiding the girls, but whether into safety or into danger, Angelo could not say.

He ordered Chiara to wait in the church until he returned, then pushed towards the alley. Another explosion, this time from behind, followed by the crack of a baton hitting something. Another thud next to him sounded as if a baton had landed on a body. People screamed, from terror or pain or both. Glass shattered again, and Angelo smelled smoke. To his left, the German apothecary erupted in flames. He pushed on towards the alley but stopped when another familiar figure strode into the middle of the parade. Luigi Barbarasso, flanked by six young, strapping men, like sailors roughed by the sea.

Angelo's throat constricted.

The lumber baron was beating a club into his palm, as if keeping time to music only he could hear. Before him, a number of Tyrolean parade men were cut off and trapped in the middle of the street. People bumped into Angelo and pulled him away from the alley, closer to Barbarasso, who now sneered at the group. The Tyroleans were wide eyed, like cattle who'd caught the scent of slaughter.

A renegade on Barbarasso's left waved a grenade and laughed. "Here's your self-government! It'll blow you all the way back to Germany!"

Angelo had to stop this. No. He had to find his sisters. A high-pitched scream from the alley made him act, and he pushed mercilessly into the panicked crowd. A butcher was confronting three Fascists, shouting in German as one smeared something brown on the shop window. The smell of faeces hit Angelo's nostrils. He heard the girls' screams again, followed by a gunshot.

Angelo halted midstride. A man on horseback held the smoking pistol, his focus on the ground as his horse moved nervously in the narrow and crowded alley. Someone lay before the horse's hooves.

"What are you doing?" he shouted at the horseman.

The rider glared at him, got his horse under control, and steered it out of the alleyway. Angelo dropped next to the man on the ground, his ears roaring. Two sets of girlish legs and the fabric from a pale-blue and a pale-green dress were underneath the body of the man. Angelo rolled him off his sisters and now recognised Peter Innerhofer. Someone helped remove the girls from underneath Peter, and Angelo pulled each of his sobbing sisters to him, then checked them thoroughly. Neither had been hit by the bullet. Peter had. His upper arm and shoulder were soaked in blood.

"Help me get this man to a hospital," Angelo shouted to those around him.

Beneath his feet, the ground shook from yet another explosion.

The taxi was not far from the villa when Angelo glanced at his wife. Chiara had one arm around Cristina and the other over Francesca, and the three stared ahead in silence. Cristina looked destitute in the hospital gown the staff had provided her, but his sisters had come away unharmed. Peter, on the other hand, would probably never have the full use of his right arm and shoulder. The bullet had shattered his collarbone. The last thing Angelo had seen before rushing to the hospital with him was that the police had rounded up the Fascists into wagons and autos. But whether anyone would be brought to justice, that was the question.

The taxi rolled to a stop outside the villa, and Angelo helped the girls climb out, then paid the driver. Beatrice and his mother were already standing at the door when he reached the top of the stoop.

"Good Lord, what happened?" Beatrice cried. "We heard about the attack—"

"The girls are fine. Take them upstairs," he said. He looked hard at his father in the hallway. "They were shot at."

"Where did the Tyroleans get weapons?" the Colonel demanded.

"Not by Tyroleans, Father. By one of the Fascists."

"Maria, blessed Virgin." It was his mother.

Angelo touched her arm. "They're safe, Mama. They're shaken, but they are safe."

Cristina whimpered, and Francesca still leaned against Chiara, who now steered them towards the stairs. Beatrice and Angelo's mother followed them.

He went into the salon, gesturing for the Colonel to enter. "Where's Pietro?" he asked.

"He's gone to city hall. There's been some damage, and he was to look for all of you."

Angelo glared at him. "Do you know what your associate, Luigi Barbarasso, was up to?"

"I was here, Angelo. Not at the parade. How should I know what Barbarasso was up to?"

"*Madre di Dio!* Stop assuming that I'm a fool, Father. I know damned well that the Fascists planned all of this. That's why you didn't want the girls to go down into the parade."

A servant entered the salon but backed up when she saw them. She scurried to a full tray of sweltering meats and cheeses and carried it out.

"Follow me," Angelo said, and led the Colonel to Pietro's study. Inside, he went to his father-in-law's credenza and pulled out a bottle of grappa, poured two glasses, and sank into the chair behind the desk. He downed the grappa in one gulp and then filled the glass again, his head already lighter. His father seemed to be waiting.

"Colonel, I'm leaving the party. You cannot expect me to have anything to do with a political group that goes about knocking heads, shooting people. Christ, shooting at young girls."

The Colonel raised a hand. "Our men were not responsible for today's events. These men were from Trentino."

"How do you know that?"

"I'm not going to lie to you, son—"

"Then don't."

His father's demeanour changed from fatherly to one of authority again, but Angelo refused to back down. Not this time. If his household ever discovered that he was a member of the Fascist party, especially now, he would most certainly lose whatever was salvageable between Chiara and himself. And Pietro.

"Go ahead. I'm waiting," he said.

"We knew that a group of Blackshirts was coming, but were ordered to do nothing about it."

"Even if you had wanted to, why couldn't you?"

The Colonel was earnest. "Because it was a staged practise. Mussolini has plans for something bigger. He wanted to see what our party members are capable of. Whether we're ready to take control. If we can manage the Tyroleans, then certainly we can manage our own countrymen."

All the rhetoric Angelo had heard in the last month now made sense. "Rome. Mussolini is going to march on Rome." And wrest away power for himself and the party.

The Colonel leaned back. He looked satisfied as he raised his glass and drank. "Party votes have been increasing, but we still require seats in the senate, and Mussolini is impatient. Nobody trusts the politicians. They go in, get thrown, and leave more to clean up. Mussolini is the most steadfast leader this nation has seen in a year. Even the king is beginning to recognise this. If everything goes according to plan, Giolitti will be removed from office, his worker parties will never form, and Mussolini will be the next prime minister. He will bring our country forward."

"Forward? With attacks like today?"

The Colonel cocked his head. "It's a drill, Angelo. To prove that we can subdue an entire race. It's that simple. And to flush out anyone who might come to the Tyroleans' aid. On this point, we have yet to wait and see who those traitors will be." He leaned back. "It's a good thing Chiara was with you."

Angelo tensed. "From now on I want you to tell me everything, Father. Everything that this party plans to do."

"The more ignorance you can plead, the better it is for you." His father was serious. "Remember your goal. You are to be the new Minister of Civil Engineering. You will not do so without the Blackshirts. You cannot afford to have both you and your father-in-law out of work." He spread his hands and scanned the study from ceiling to floor. "Before your family is out on the streets, you'd have to come work for me."

Before Angelo could react, there was a knock on the door, and the servant appeared again. "Captain Grimani, there is someone from the police here to see you."

Angelo rose from his seat. "Show him in. Father, please wait in the salon. He must want to question me about the shooting."

The Colonel stood. "I do know the policemen here quite well. I might be able to help."

"Thank you. I can manage this. I work at city hall, remember?"

Just as the Colonel was stepping out, the police official was at the door of the study. Angelo did not recognise him. He was short but carried himself straight, as if in a permanent state of military attention. Under his police cap, he had tight black-silver curls. In his late forties, maybe early fifties, he had a handsome face, with a straight nose and intelligent, dark eyes.

"Good afternoon," the man said to the Colonel. "I'm Captain Emilio Rioba."

"Colonel Nicolo Grimani," the Colonel said, his face reading the same confusion that Angelo was feeling. "Are you with the Bolzano police?"

Captain Rioba shook his head. "Although, I imagine there are a lot of them coming around right now. My apologies. My timing is not very appropriate after today's events. I'm the police captain in the Reschen Valley."

Angelo's back and underarms prickled. This was not the man he'd filed his report with. He'd spoken to someone named Ghirardelli.

"I'm here to see Captain Angelo Grimani about—"

"Captain Rioba, I'm he." Angelo shook hands with the man and pulled him deeper into the study.

"Reschen Valley?" the Colonel interrupted. "How are things up north?"

The police captain's smile was indulgent. "Fine. Just fine."

"Father, we can discuss the north another time with Captain Rioba. I lost some important equipment, as you know, when I was up there. I'm sure that is why the captain is here. Why don't you wait in the salon, and I will be with you as soon as I can."

The Colonel eyed Angelo with interest. "As you wish. Captain Rioba, I look forward to meeting you again."

Before Angelo could shut the door behind his father, he saw the Colonel withdraw his black notebook from his breast pocket.

Angelo turned to the police captain, his pulse racing. The scar on his head tingled, as if it sensed the onslaught of the memories to come.

"Captain Rioba, it's been a very hard day. May I offer you a drink?"

"Thank you," Rioba said. "I'm fine."

Angelo gestured to the chair his father had just occupied. "So what can I do for you?"

"I travelled here because I have to report to headquarters tomorrow. I've just come to tell you that we found the man who attacked you."

Angelo pictured the snow. The blood. How he had run and crawled to the hut. He pictured the girl. He rubbed a hand over his hair, applying pressure to the pins-and-needles feeling around his scar.

"We caught him stealing from St. Katharina's."

"I beg your pardon?"

"The church. In Graun. He had broken into the sacristy to steal valuable items, and we caught him. Apparently he'd been stealing from a number of homes, but the locals, you know, they don't trust us, and they don't report everything. It's quite a problem there, actually. I can't say I blame them entirely, but taking the law into their own hands is also not the right thing to do. I'm going to have to find a way to work with them, but with the ordinances I get, it does not make my job easy."

Angelo raised a hand. "This man…"

"Yes, sorry. This man." Rioba crossed his leg over his knee and rested his black cap on his thigh. "We caught him in the act. Afterwards some of the villagers came forward and filed charges against him for theft and other crimes. Fritz Hanny was his name."

The name meant nothing to Angelo. He signalled Rioba to continue.

"He had stolen and slain a lamb from the Steinhauser family, or was it Glockner? I think it was Glockner."

Angelo dropped his hands to his side. *Get on with it, man.*

"The Thalerhof? You know the Thalers, don't you?" The captain's face was friendly, even curious.

"Perhaps." Angelo shrugged.

The bell buzzed at the front door again. Who was here now?

The captain placed his cap on the desk and leaned forward. "Certainly you remember the Thalers. The girl, Katharina—

although she's not a girl anymore. She's a married woman with a child now, a pretty little thing, the first generation of Italy's new Alto Adigeans...the baby girl, I mean, not Frau Thaler. I mean, Steinhauser. She's Frau Steinhauser now. She was called Thaler before she found you." He smiled apologetically. "All these name changes. It's hard to keep them straight."

"Thaler. Yes, of course." Angelo let out a breath he didn't know he was still holding. He suddenly remembered the doctor.

"Wait a moment. What is the name of my attacker?"

The captain smiled again, as if delighted. "Fritz Hanny. He's the brother of the doctor, whom you must also know. It's a small valley. Unfortunately, they're almost all related. Seems Fritz Hanny disappeared and abandoned his family several years ago. In the meantime, he'd joined up with the smugglers and was hiding out in the wilderness. He was a real mess when we got to him. Terribly ill too. Anyway, he never confessed to attacking you, but from the reports we got from those people up there, we're pretty certain that was the man."

"Was," Angelo said. "You keep using the past tense."

The captain rubbed his forehead. "I'm afraid he died while we were holding him. He was to come to Bolzano to be tried, but he had pneumonia. Died coughing up his lungs."

Angelo felt numb.

"Nevertheless, I have a photograph of him here."

Rioba reached into his coat pocket. He placed two images on the desk and turned them to Angelo. One showed someone who was much older than the other. The first one was of a man who certainly drank a lot but was otherwise not bad looking. He had the longish beard typical of the Tyroleans and wore a feathered cap. The second photo could not have been the same person, but Angelo knew it was. The man in this photo was thin and bedraggled. His eyes were half-closed, but there was a slight grin on the ends of his lips. In his mind, Angelo saw flashes of details: the man who spoke to him, the rags, the matted hair, the knife. And that laugh. That horrible, mad laugh.

"That's him."

The captain made a clicking sound. "Was." He took the photos back and put them carefully into his coat. "So I guess it's case closed. I just need your signature here. I'll file the report tomorrow."

Angelo signed quickly, and Rioba stood. They moved to the door.

"And when do you return to the valley?" Angelo asked. He really did not care.

"I'll be here for a little while," Captain Rioba said. "End of the week. Shall I pass on a message to the Thalers, perhaps? Say hello for you?"

God help him! "Certainly. Yes. Please. And my appreciation again for their help."

Rioba smiled and placed his cap on his head. "I'll be happy to do so, Captain Grimani."

At the door, the police captain paused. "Awkward, isn't it?"

"What is?"

"Owing your life to a Tyrolean." He shook his head as if he couldn't believe it, turned, and finally left the room.

Angelo moved to the veranda outside the study and let the breeze cool him off. He gazed at the grapevines, still stubs from last fall's cutting, and thought about the Reschen Valley. Was it over? Could it finally be over? He would have to make sure that his father's curiosity was pacified. That was priority number one. But the rest of his family knew nothing of the attack nor how Katharina had nursed him back to health.

Captain Rioba had said she was married. And had a child. Maybe Angelo had been wrong about her. Maybe she had been waiting for someone all that time, had even been engaged to her husband when he'd been there. If that was the case, then she was a loose woman for coming into his bed. He should have known. The Tyroleans were always so loud about their piety. Maybe he had also been wrong about her being a virgin. Then again, he'd enjoyed her; she'd been surprisingly sensual.

He forced himself to shut down his thoughts. It was time to face his father.

He walked down the veranda towards the salon but stopped when he heard men's voices, his father's the loudest. Angelo paused at the door, which had been left slightly ajar. He peered through the muslin curtains and saw the Colonel's profile. Luigi Barbarasso and one of the policemen—Angelo recognised him from the Bolzano headquarters—were with him.

The Colonel was saying, "Everything according to plan? They almost killed my daughters."

The pleased looks of the other two men vanished. Barbarasso cleared his throat. "What happened?"

"I'll tell you what happened. One of your men used his revolver. The only thing that saved those girls was a Tyrolean. I have to be grateful to a *cretino*."

The policeman stepped forward as if testing a pool of water, and Angelo's father swung his glare at him.

"Colonel, are the girls safe?"

"Fortunately for you, yes. They weren't hurt, but they've been scared out of their wits. The Tyrolean was shot in the back or something and taken to a doctor...by my son. *My* son, who will probably now become a German sympathizer just like his wife."

The two men remained silent, and his father said, "I want to know what the damages are. On both sides."

The policeman recovered, obviously pleased by what he was about to report. "We escorted the men from Trentino back to the train station. We made it appear as if they were being chased out of town, but we managed to get them safely back on the train. As you know, we had expected around two hundred men, but nearly three hundred came."

For the first time, the Colonel looked pleased. He moved towards the veranda doors, and Angelo stepped back.

Barbarasso took over. "We had the voting boxes seized. They're on the train to Trentino as well. The men have assured me they will be publicly burned. The city hall will be burned down, and all the Austrian colours as well."

When Angelo crept back to where he could see, the Colonel had his back to him.

"Fine," Angelo's father said. "And the Tyroleans?"

The policeman sounded nervous. "Approximately fifty injured."

"What is it?" the Colonel asked.

"We had one death," he said.

"Who?"

"A butcher. He got into an argument about his shop, and one of the men shot him."

Angelo recalled the scene in the alley.

"Who shot him?"

"One of ours," Barbarasso answered quickly. "He was provoked."

The Colonel turned towards the veranda again, his face alight. "Splendid. Have the man arrested." He took a glass from the side table and faced the men, raising his drink.

They looked confused, and when the Colonel began explaining, Angelo recognised his father's voice being the one he used when faced with detested incompetence.

"We have to make this look good to the Tyroleans. We arrest someone. We look as if we're doing our duty in protecting the community. That's what we want in the end, *capisce*?"

The policeman brightened but was still cautious. "Of course, Colonel. We put on a show for the Tyroleans, gain their trust, show them that we're fighting for them, and the Fascists are viewed as the evildoers. Not the police."

The Colonel nodded slightly.

"We'll have the papers make a big fuss about it," Barbarasso added. "When interest has died down, we'll release our man."

"And relocate him to Trentino," the Colonel added. His father waved a dismissing hand. Lesson finished. "Go to the festivities. We'll talk more about this later. Luigi, you stay."

The policeman thanked them, and when he had left, Barbarasso moved nearer to the Colonel. They were close to the veranda door.

"What is it?" Barbarasso asked.

"I've heard from Rome."

Angelo's heart beat faster.

"Did they make it? Are they in?" Barbarasso almost purred.

"Deep in."

"Good. Then we should be able to handle the issue with Minister d'Oro."

"Indeed," the Colonel said. He reached into his breast pocket and pulled out that black notebook. He licked a finger and turned to a page. "I've met someone very interesting this evening. He's next door with my son. Do you know Captain Emilio Rioba in the Reschen Valley? He's heading the *carabinieri* up there."

Barbarasso frowned at the same time Angelo did.

"Emilio Rioba? No. But I can find someone who does."

The Colonel closed the notebook and twisted the glass in his hand. He turned towards the window again. "Good. Do that. Find out who this Rioba is. See if he is the right man to be their prefect, and if so, make it happen. If we're to get the Reschen Valley project, I need the right people in the right places. Someone who can keep tabs on all the landowners."

Barbarasso nodded, and the Colonel remained thoughtful.

"We need land. Lots of it. Find out which farmers are most vulnerable. The more we buy out now, the less we'll have to worry about compensating later. Rioba may know the weak links, who we might most easily drive out."

The Colonel paused, as if assessing what he'd just said, and absentmindedly tapped the notebook on the edge of the side table. *Tap. Tap. Tap.*

Angelo watched his father lift his head, chest expanding, as if the Colonel now grasped something that had earlier eluded him. "This Rioba. He seems to know something about Angelo that I don't." He held the notebook close to the side of his face. "And I want to know what that is."

EXTRACT FROM THE BREACH

CHAPTER 1
Arlund, November 1922

At the cemetery on St. Anna's hill, Katharina stood with Annamarie's hand in hers. She pointed out her two great-uncles and Annamarie's great-grandmother.

At the engraved photo of her parents, Katharina said, "Annamarie, that was your Opa, Josef Thaler. And this was your Oma, Marianna Thaler. They were my mother and father, just like I am your mama and Papa is—"

Katharina could try all she wanted, but Annamarie was Angelo Grimani's. Her daughter had his long fingers, his eyes, his slight dimple on her chin, and even a shade of his Italian colouring. Everyone in the valley would say that Annamarie looked like Katharina. Even Jutta and Florian, the only two who knew Annamarie was Angelo's, said with careful diplomacy that Annamarie would be tall like her mama, and a beauty like her too.

Maybe. But Katharina saw her daughter's other half just as prominently.

Annamarie slipped to the ground and grabbed at the black-eyed Susans on the graves, and Katharina bent to rescue the flowers, but a sharp pain in her back halted her, and Annamarie had the first daisy's head off in no time. Katharina stretched, one hand on her rounded belly: her next child, Florian's. Before her daughter could get hold of another flower, Katharina scooped her up and winced at the strain of it. Annamarie was what weighed on her most. It would be the father's side of the child's story Katharina would never be able to properly share.

She remembered how, when Florian received news of his mother's death the month before, he'd slowly folded the telegram and said, "I'm sorry my mother never got to meet her granddaughter." His voice had faltered at the end, and he looked at Katharina's belly. "Or maybe it will be a boy."

When she had Annamarie wrapped and tied to her back again, Katharina called for the dog. Hund loped up the path back to Arlund, turning sideways to stop and check on their progress. Before entering the woods, Katharina looked down into the valley at the skeletons of new barracks between Reschen and Graun. The area for the Italian officials was growing, the buildings becoming sturdier, more permanent. In the last two years, the wives and children of the border guards and police had joined their husbands. There was a new schoolteacher from farther down in Italy. And Captain Rioba was now prefect, which meant Georg Roeschen was no longer mayor of Graun. Jutta had complained, with a sour face, about how the landscape was changing, and Kaspar Ritsch had said that if the Italians were building so much, then chances were that the Etsch River wouldn't be diverted to where the *Walscher*—the Italians—were living.

"Then we should all relocate to the Italian quarter," Opa had retorted.

Katharina reached the wayward cross and put a few daisies into the vase at Christ's feet. Above them, she heard the cry of a goshawk. It grasped something in its claws, but she could not make out what. It was a fine day for the first of November, warm and sunny, and the mountain peaks were not even covered in snow yet. She crossed the bridge at the Karlinbach and came to the clearing leading to Arlund. In the distance, smoke curled from the chimney of the Thalerhof. She smiled at the thought of surprising Florian with the hare she'd caught in one of their traps. She would bake it in the Roman clay pot with cabbage and a thick sauce, the way he liked it.

At the sound of running water in the *Hof*, Hund dashed for the fountain set just before the house on the garden side. That summer, Florian and Opa had carved out a fresh log, hollowing it out first, then tapping into the spring below with a wooden spigot where the water ran through the small plug at the bottom of the log, nonstop. When it was very hot, the dog would jump in and crouch to her midriff, lapping up the water as if she'd just crossed a desert. But now Hund just stood on her hind legs to drink, and Katharina untied Annamarie from her.

The girl awoke and began fussing, then grabbed the crucifix hanging around Katharina's neck. After she set the child down, Katharina went to the fountain and splashed cool water on her face. At the sight of the window boxes, she realised she'd forgotten to water the geraniums, which were wilting in the unseasonable heat.

With a bucket in hand and a blanket in the other, Opa came out of the workshop. His cough had returned, rattling within him like loosened gravel rolling down a slope.

"I've pulled some of the softer apples out," he said when he caught his breath again. "They won't make the winter. Thought you'd make a cake tonight."

"That, and something for your chest." She pulled the pouch away from her side and held up the hare. "I've got something too."

He glanced at her middle. "Your husband should be doing that kind of work, not you. Gives him a feeling of self-worth, a tie to the land."

"Now, Opa," she started, but he walked away, muttering that he was going to Graun.

"Been two weeks since anyone's picked up the post," he tossed over his shoulder.

She would go, she wanted to say, but voices from behind the house stopped her from calling after him. Florian appeared with Toni Ritsch. She hung up the hare before greeting Toni and asking about Patricia.

"She's fine," Toni said. "The baby is keeping her busy. Spirited boy. We've named him Andreas."

"A fine name. Tell her I'll stop in tomorrow and help her."

"We're negotiating the bull," Florian said. Though he smiled, he gave her a look that signalled he was not pleased about the business.

Toni rubbed his beard and nodded at the hare. "Looks like dinner. I should make my way home."

"Nonsense. It's early," Florian said. "Come in and have some refreshment."

"I won't change the conditions," Toni said. He turned to Katharina. "Florian's showing me new ways to earn money. Told me about his mother's house in Nuremberg and the rent he's earning from it. It's a good idea. Think I'll do something similar. We Ritsches have lots of property, and we could build something to lease out. Maybe even to some Italians. It's time I got something back from them. I'll show them what *bauernschlau* means."

Katharina glanced at Annamarie. Nobody—not even Florian—knew her daughter's real ethnic background, and the way people talked about the Italians, she would do anything to keep it that way.

"And the terms of your bull have now changed?" she said. "Is that why you two are still negotiating?"

Toni at least had the decency to look sheepish. "It's the economy—"

"Indeed, Toni. Just that. And loyalty. My grandfather and your father go a long way back. There are certainly some things that have not been squared away over the years." She knew about how Opa had lent the Ritsches money when Kaspar had fallen on bad times, and Opa had never asked for a single *Heller* back. "We're not Italians either, Toni. We're your neighbours. Remember that as you negotiate."

Florian clapped Toni on the shoulder. "Let's go in and have a glass. We'll just talk, and then you can think about it."

Katharina watched the men go into the house, remembering how Toni and his friends had once forced her and the other schoolgirls to climb the Planggers' tree so that they could look up their dresses. Patricia had refused to do it, and Toni had pinned her down on the ground. Their saving grace had been the call of a farmer looking for one of his sons.

"Florian," she called after them, "where's my father's knife? I need to dress the hare."

Her husband returned to her and lowered his voice. "You want to tell me about those dues owed now?"

"I'll tell you what kind of a neighbour you're dealing with," she whispered. Just the least of the worst. "A few years before my mother passed away, we used to have hares in the hutches out back. My mother went to feed them one day and found one that had died, of old age, we supposed. She buried it out in the meadow somewhere.

"Toni's dog dug it up and left it on the Ritsches' front stoop as a gift. When Toni found that hare, he brushed it off, got it as clean as he could, and went and put that dead animal back into the hutch, like nothing happened."

"No," Florian said, eyes wide, clearly stifling a laugh out of respect. "Tell me he didn't."

Katharina nodded. "My mother, bless her soul, went out to

feed those hares the next morning. When she saw the one that had returned from the grave, her heart dropped into her pants. We all came running at her screams."

Florian coughed into his collar, his shoulders shaking, and Katharina felt a laugh rising in her as well.

"Did he ever admit it?" he asked.

"Kaspar had to."

He sucked in a deep breath, trying to put on a straight face. "I understand."

"Now you know what kind of people he is."

He held out her papa's knife to her. "You'll tell me the other things later."

"Oh, I certainly will."

She took the handle and started to dress the hare.

Toni and Florian were still discussing cattle and properties in the sitting room when Opa returned from Graun. Katharina folded the apples into the cake batter as he greeted Toni first, and then, as a way to apologise for his earlier brash comments, she supposed, Opa said something about the delicious smells from the baking hare before handing her a small package.

"This came for you."

It was the size of a book and posted from Bolzano. Katharina knew what it was but pretended to be surprised.

"Well, open it."

"When I'm done with the cake."

He cupped a fist to his mouth and coughed again. She touched his arm.

"Next time," she said, "you send Florian or me into town for your papers and post. With winter coming, you need to get that cough under control."

Opa patted Annamarie's head as she played amongst the

scattered pots and pans. Katharina watched him wander into the sitting room, organise the stacks of newspapers, clamp his empty pipe between his teeth, and unfold his first paper, the back page for the farmers' news first.

She poured the cake into the tin, popped it into the oven, and discreetly unwrapped her package.

It was her Italian primer. She leafed through the pages, holding the book close to her middle, and mouthed the conjugations for the verbs *read* and *write*.

She heard Toni say he had to leave, but when Florian came up behind her, Katharina nearly jumped out of her skin.

He reached for the book. "What's this?"

"Don't tell Opa," she whispered. "He won't have it." She showed him the primer.

Her husband looked unconvinced. "You had better put it where he won't find it."

Toni was at the door when Opa slammed his newspaper into his lap, face flushed.

"Look at this." He jabbed at the front page with his pipe. "The Fascists are positioned in the Po plains."

"When did this happen?" Toni strode over to Opa and stood over his shoulder.

Opa looked at the top of the newspaper. "October twenty-fourth."

Florian asked for the paper and read aloud. "At a Fascist Congress in Naples, Mussolini was quoted as saying, 'Our program is simple: we want to rule Italy.'"

"And this one," Opa complained, raising another issue, also on the front page. "The twenty-ninth."

Florian scanned the article, and Katharina placed the Italian primer on the corner of the counter, intending to go to him, but he lowered the paper before she reached him.

"Forget about the Po for a moment," her husband said to Opa and Toni. "There are twenty thousand Blackshirts marching in

Rome right now. The prime minister ordered a state of siege, but the king's refused to sign a military order."

"What does that mean?" Katharina asked.

Her husband faced Opa, as if he'd asked the question. "It means the king will give Mussolini whatever he wants."

Toni came around from Opa's chair and put his hands on his waist, his anger taking up the middle of the room. "To hell if I'm going to be called Antonio from now on. Should've stayed up on the alp, that's what. Crossed the border as soon as I could have."

"Good thing I'm still a German citizen," Florian scoffed.

Opa looked bewildered. "What good is that to you now? You going to pick up this house, the barn, and all the cattle and move them across the border, or what?"

Katharina groaned softly. *Don't give him any ideas.* Her husband had not been able to hide his growing admiration for the nationalists in Germany.

"If the Fascists take over Italy," Toni said, "the first thing they'll do is make that Ettore Tolomei head of something and make sure all of our rights are signed out of law."

"I won't have it," Opa yelled. "I won't have Tyrol taken over by thugs."

Florian turned to Toni. "What do we do then?"

"Fight." Toni wagged his hat at Opa. "Johannes, it's time we start that resistance."

Opa stood up. "I'll back you and anyone else who wants to take a stand."

Florian bit his bottom lip, a gesture Katharina recognised as her own when in duress.

"I'll talk to the boys." Toni nodded. "We'll get ourselves organised. Florian?"

Katharina turned away, closing her ears to the nonsense. There would be no resistance. Father Wilhelm or Jutta would talk them all out of it. Against the two of them, the "boys," as Toni had called them—she cringed when Opa coughed again—would get a scolding, that was all.

She picked up the cake bowl to wash it out and inadvertently knocked the primer she'd lain on the table. It fell to the ground, and before she could bend over to pick it up, Toni had already scooped it up and held it out to her, until his gaze fell on the cover. When he pulled the primer away from her reach, she noted the grim look on his face. Her blood froze, and as he leaned in, he was so close she could smell the wine on his breath.

"You remember whose land you're on?" he whispered.

Katharina's heart banged against her ribs. She recalled how he'd pinned Patricia to the ground. She stared at the book in his hand, and she could feel his breath on her neck.

"Hmmm? That you're not one of us has always been clear with your mother's mixed blood. Something Slavic, wasn't she? Polish? They ain't got a lick of loyalty to them. Shows in how they govern their country, foreign kings and all."

"I'm as Tyrolean as any of you," Katharina choked out.

"Yeah?" He tipped his head towards the book in his hand and pressed the upper corner into her waist. "Seems you've forgotten. Married an outsider. None of us were any good for ya?" He sniffed, checked over his shoulder.

Behind him, Opa and Florian were still arguing about what form a resistance could take.

Toni finally moved away from her, but he wasn't finished. He pretended to examine the empty cake bowl, and spoke softly.

"Shame on you, Katharina. Feel sorry for your Opa here. Only people he's got left is a strange tall girl and a German. Both half-Tyroleans and ain't got no respect for tradition and what this country's gone through to get the freedom it once had."

"I didn't forget any of that." Katharina found courage in her growing outrage.

He smirked and rubbed along the edge of the bowl, her sweet cake batter gathering on the rim of his index finger.

"Good thing you're not getting this farm, Katharina. What did you think you were going to do with it as a spinster? Huh? Just wouldn't have been right."

He licked his finger before turning his back on her.

If the Thalerhof were hers—like it should be—she'd march to the barn right now, fetch Opa's rifle out of its hiding place, and chase Toni all the way into the valley and across the border herself.

Toni was addressing the men again. "You throw your hat in with us, Johannes, and we'll get a resistance going, but you make good and sure you know who's in the fight with you."

At the door, he pressed his hat on his head, buzzard feather quivering, before facing Florian. "Many thanks for the wine, but my terms for the bull haven't changed. Take it or leave it."

A GUIDE TO THE RESCHEN VALLEY

You can learn about why I wrote this series, what got me started, and even some history around the Oberer Vinschgau Valley, the valley depicted in Reschen Valley.

For historical background pieces, a list of characters in the series, maps and a glossary, visit www.inktreks.com.

Please do consider leaving a book review on Goodreads, Amazon, Bookbub, or any of your other favorite platforms and share them with social media. Your opinion *does* count.

THE RESCHEN VALLEY SERIES

1 | NO MAN'S LAND

A plan to flood a valley. A means to destroy a culture.

It's 1920. The end of the Great War has taken more than Katharina Thaler's beloved family; it has robbed the Austrian Tyrol of its autonomy and severed it in half. As her grandfather's last living relative, Katharina also faces becoming the first woman to own a farm in the Reschen Valley. While her countrymen fight to prevent the annexation to Italy, Katharina stumbles on a wounded Italian engineer on her mountain. Her decision to save Angelo Grimani's life thrusts both into a labyrinth of corruption, prejudice, and greed. Trapped between a new world order and the man who threatens to seize her land, Katharina must decide what to protect: love or country? *No Man's Land* is the first book in the Reschen Valley series.

2 | THE BREACH

Burying the past comes at a high price...

It's 1922 and a year after the Italian Fascists marched on Bozen.
   Nationalism in the Tyrolean Reschen Valley creates enemies out of old friends and Katharina Steinhauser fiercely protects the identity of her daughter's father from both her family and her community. Meanwhile, the Fascists have wrested control from the monarchy and momentum behind the Reschen Lake reservoir increases with plans to wipe out the Reschen Valley's towns and hamlets. Katharina risks writing to Angelo Grimani,

the man in charge, and begs to have the project reassessed. But Angelo is hemmed in by a force that steers him far from his dealings with the Reschen Valley and that which binds him to Katharina. It's the opportunity the Fascists have been waiting for.

3 | BOLZANO

In the process of understanding who you are, more often you discover who you are not.

1937. Northern Italy. New international conflicts loom on the horizon, and Italy must feed its war machine. Angelo Grimani has a plan to keep the Reschen Valley reservoir out of his father's hands but he needs a local front to succeed. He faces his past and seeks an alliance with Katharina Steinhauser.

Meanwhile, Annamarie Steinhauser is convinced her future lies beyond the confines of the valley. When an Italian delegation arrives to assess the reservoir, Annamarie believes she has found her ticket out…in the form of Angelo's son and a Fascist uniform.

Love, betrayal, and deception explode in the third installment of the Reschen Valley.

4 | TWO FATHERLANDS

How do you take a stand when the enemies lurk within your own home?

1938. South Tyrol. Katharina, Angelo, and Annamarie are confronted by the oppressive force created by Mussolini's and Hitler's political union. Angelo puts aside his prejudices and seeks an alliance with old enemies; Katharina fights to keep her family together as the valley is forced to choose between Italian and German nationhood, and Annamarie finds herself in the thick of a fascist regime she thought she understood. All will be forced to choose sides and none will escape betrayal.

Releases April 13, 2021! Order now!

Early readers are calling this "...gripping, taut, packed with moral dilemmas, and nail-biting twists!"

5 | THE RISING

A homecoming like no other.

June 11 1961. Explosions rock South Tyrol as pylons and electric masts are toppled by members of the South Tyrolean Freedom party's underground. Annamarie Steinhauser-Greil's documentary and reports on the flooding of the Reschen Valley some twelve years earlier are used in the defense of her brother, Manuel, who is facing a death sentence if found guilty of taking part in the terrorist act. But when Annamarie returns to the valley to prepare for her testimony, she must wrestle with what has become of the family she left behind, and the past that lies beneath the Reschen Lake reservoir.

Coming in 2022!

0 | THE SMUGGLER OF RESCHEN PASS: THE PREQUEL

Pride comes before the fall.

1900s Austrian Tyrol. Fritz Hanny, confident and optimistic, enjoys the prestige of belonging to one of the most respected families in the Reschen Valley. When he falls in love with Cecilia, a young girl in a neighboring village, he is certain he has found his purpose in life. Already on his way to making his own fortune, Fritz pursues Cecilia only to be cut down by one external force after another. Disappointment, violence, and conflict turn Fritz into a desperate man.

"Lucyk-Berger has explored the darker side of human nature in this tale, and she has done so with great skill and splendour. This story appalled, impressed, and fascinated in equal measures. It is wonderfully told and impossible to put down." - Mary Anne Yarde, Coffee Pot Book Club blogger

For a guide to this series, including historical notes, maps, glossaries and articles, visit **www.inktreks.com**.

DEAREST READER

I'll get to the acknowledgements in just a minute. It is you I wish to thank first for choosing *this* book.

The first ideas for NO MAN'S LAND began in 2005 while I was travelling through Austria to northern Italy. I crossed the Reschen Pass and discovered one of the most amazing and—at the same time—disturbing sights (you can Google it, but it won't be me who gave you the spoiler). Because I did not understand what I was experiencing and faced mega language barriers (both German and Italian), it took me another five years before I wrote the first scene you find in Chapter 1.

Over the years, I got to know Katharina and Angelo as you would any person: gradually. Three years of sketching them out, fleshing them out, and researching is what it took to get the first *draft* done. Another three years is what it took to get the story to sing. That brings us to 2016. Add one more year of putting the last meat on the bones based on the fact that I was now working ahead on books 3 and 4, and even outlining 5, the story stretching all the way into 1950. That's 30 years of these characters' lives. I often went back to the beginning to make certain I had all the pieces in place.

We storytellers thrive on your word-of-mouth recommendations and critiques. We want to do the best job we can, and so your feedback is critical. Would you be so kind as to leave an honest review any platform you may have found this title? Feel free to reach out to me on any of my platforms and start a discussion.

Thank you and I hope to meet you again on the last page of THE BREACH. **For a complete guide to this series including maps, glossary, character list and background articles, please visit my website at www.inktreks.com.**

Servus!

Chrystyna Lucyk-Berger
Vorarlberg, Austria

ACKNOWLEDGMENTS

There is no end to the list of people I want to thank for helping this series come to fruition: from the first South Tyroleans I met in Graun and in Reschen, who spent time talking about their memories of the reservoir and the Italian occupation, to my writing colleagues and the professionals who, with great support and loads of encouragement, helped me hone my profession. Special recognition and thanks go to Ludwig Schöpf, Hansjörg Stecher, Theresa Theiner, the work of Briggite M Picher and most of all Pepe. The La Torre Writers, who were invaluable, especially Cathy Snarey and Ann Aylor—*gràcies*. To my Riding Circus group: Theresa König, Christine Schneider, and Susanne Gorbach—*vielen Dank!* To Ann Howard Creel, whose final nudge was absolutely necessary. To Dori Harrell for your superb work on this final version. Tom Bromley, thank you for your guidance. To my mother, for reading this however-many times: You can stop now. To Angelina Berger, Magdalena Schertler, Ursula Hechenberger, and Kathrin Meier, for your feedbacks, as well as the artistic and dedicated support you offered to help make this happen, thank you a million times over.

And most of all, to my husband, Fred-with-a-y, for your unwavering belief in me and the freedom you give me to get things done. *Schatzi*, you are my dream come true and I will call you whatever you want me to.

ABOUT THE AUTHOR

CHRYSTYNA LUCYK-BERGER is an award-winning American author. She travels for inspiration and is inspired by what she encounters. She lives in Austria in her "Grizzly Adams" mountain hut with her hero-husband, hilarious dog, and cantankerous cat.

Her Reschen Valley series, which takes readers to the interwar period of northern Italy's Tyrolean province, has been hailed as "wonderful historical fiction," and "a must read." Her World War 2 novels have garnered awards and recognition. You can find all her works on her website, Goodreads, Bookbub, Facebook, Instagram and Twitter.

~

Author Homepage
www.inktreks.com

Subscribe to get news from behind-the-scenes, historical backgrounds from upcoming projects and inspiring author interviews from the historical fiction genre.

~

Dear Reader, your reviews matter.
Please be so kind to consider sharing your impressions with other potential fans. Or if you were not thrilled with this book— if it did not broaden horizons, surprise you with new insights, or

move you—feel free to reach out and let me know how I might do better.

Yours,
  Chrystyna

ALSO BY CHRYSTYNA LUCYK-BERGER

The Smuggler of Reschen Pass: A Reschen Valley Novella

Prequel to the series and a stand-alone psychological thriller

Reschen Valley 1: No Man's Land

A plan to flood her valley. A means to destroy their culture.

The first book in the award-winning series about a woman who fights for her homeland when an oppressive Italian government moves to eradicate her valley's Tyrolean identity and wipe it off the map.

Reschen Valley 2: The Breach

Burying the past comes at a high price.

Reschen Valley Box Set: Season 1 – 1920-1924

She wants her home. He wants control. The Fascists want both. Contains books 1 and 2 and *The Smuggler of Reschen Pass.*

Reschen Valley 3: Bolzano

On the journey to figuring out who you are, most often you discover who you are not.

Reschen Valley 4: Two Fatherlands

How do you take a stand when the enemy lurks where you thought was safest?

Reschen Valley Box Set: Season 2 – 1937-1949

Sometimes, when you're trying to determine who you are, what you discover is who you are not. Contains books 3 and 4.

Reschen Valley 5: The Rising (2024)

A homecoming like no other.

～

Souvenirs from Kyiv

Unforgettable stories based on the heartbreaking experiences of
Ukrainian families during WW2

～

The Girl from the Mountains

Not all battles are fought by soldiers.

The Woman at the Gates

They took her country. But they will never take her courage.

And stay tuned for more books published by Bookouture, Hachette UK

Printed in Great Britain
by Amazon

25059753R00158